Leona Deakin started her career as a psychologist with the West Yorkshire Police. She is now an occupational psychologist and lives with her family in Leeds. She has written three novels in the acclaimed Dr Augusta Bloom series: *Gone*, *Lost* and *Hunt*.

www.penguin.co.uk

The Imposter

LEONA DEAKIN

PENGUIN BOOKS

TRANSWORLD PUBLISHERS
Penguin Random House, One Embassy Gardens,
8 Viaduct Gardens, London SW11 7BW
www.penguin.co.uk

Transworld is part of the Penguin Random House group of companies
whose addresses can be found at global.penguinrandomhouse.com

First published in Great Britain in 2022 by Penguin Books
an imprint of Transworld Publishers

A CIP catalogue record for this book is available from the British Library.

ISBN 9781529176971

Typeset in 12.5/14.75 pt Garamond MT Std by Jouve (UK), Milton Keynes.
Printed and bound in Great Britain by Clays Ltd, Elcograf S.p.A.

The authorized representative in the EEA is Penguin Random House Ireland,
Morrison Chambers, 32 Nassau Street, Dublin D02 YH68.

Penguin Random House is committed to a sustainable
future for our business, our readers and our planet. This book
is made from Forest Stewardship Council® certified paper.

For Jamie.
Thank you for being the best partner in crime
I could ever wish for.

Reason has always existed, but not
always in a reasonable form.

Karl Marx

Life isn't about finding yourself.
Life is about creating yourself.

George Bernard Shaw

Zander checked his reflection. The custom-made suit made him feel taller and slimmer. He squared his shoulders and brushed the jacket flat over his stomach before smoothing his hair down with both hands. The glass inside his thick-rimmed spectacles was clear. He didn't wear them to aid his vision.

'You look good.'

Lexi's voice sounded distant; he was consumed with what he was about to do: if he was up to it; if he could get away with it.

'I need to go alone,' he said.

She didn't reply, but he knew she understood. They had learned to respect each other's need for space over the years. The walk to the lift was short and the trip to the 36th floor swift, with just enough time to put on his gloves. He stepped out and checked his watch: 4 p.m. Philip had said he liked to sit in the bar in the early evenings on weekends because it was always empty then.

Zander moved to the entrance. The door glass was smoked but the window next to it had a small border of clear glazing. He angled his head so he could see the black-and-white room within; there was no sign of anyone there.

Perhaps Philip was late today.

Before he could type in the six-digit code that Philip had used a few days earlier, a figure opened the door from within. Zander quickly stepped away and moved towards the lift. He couldn't risk being seen.

The suit felt heavy and hot on his body and the shirt underneath was sticking to his skin. He risked a glance back and saw a barman walking in the opposite direction. He hadn't anticipated that the bar would be staffed. That was stupid. The risks were too high. He had Lexi and AJ to think about. He reached out to the lift call button.

Then again, the barman leaving might be a sign.

He turned to watch the young man reach the end of the corridor and disappear around the corner. He felt it in every muscle and sinew: he wasn't the prey racing for cover. He was the panther.

Zander checked his watch; then he strode back to the door and typed in the code. If the bar was empty, he would return to his room and rethink. But if Philip was here, alone, then game on.

The door felt heavy as he pushed it wide and stepped inside the room. The interior smelled of freshly cut lilies and espresso. There were plush black and white chairs in pairs around glass tables, each set positioned far enough away from the others to afford residents the privacy they expected. Floor-to-ceiling glass ran the length of the right-hand wall, looking out over the Thames to the city beyond: a city still drenched in afternoon sun.

Zander placed both gloved hands into the pockets of

his trousers. At a table tucked into the corner, out of sight of the door, a lone figure sat sipping whisky.

Zander was unlikely to afford his target any mercy, and all hope was lost when Philip Berringer looked his way. His eyes widened in surprise and then narrowed as he said, 'You came back.'

'I moved in.'

'Congratulations.' The words were contradicted by the man's body language. Philip was evidently irritated that someone like Zander would live in the same building as someone like him: someone so important and sickeningly rich.

Zander's eyes scanned the room, taking in every last detail. He was hyper-alert, his breath steady. He felt calm, in control, powerful. The room was empty other than the two of them but the barman could come back at any moment.

'Have you seen what's going on down there?' Zander walked to the glass door and slid it open. The breeze felt cool on his face. He stepped out on to the balcony and looked back at Philip. 'Come see.'

Zander rested his arms on the balustrade, taking care to cover his gloved hands with his elbows. He glanced down at the grass, thirty-six floors below.

For a moment, it seemed that Philip might not move. Zander had spent hours – days even – fantasizing about ways to show the smug bastard that he wasn't someone to cast aside. And, in his mind, this scenario had run without a hitch.

Make it happen, said the voice in his head.

'You'll never believe it,' Zander said.

Philip remained in his seat.

Hold your nerve.

'Seriously, man. You will not believe your eyes.'

Finally, he heard the tinkling of glass as Philip lowered his drink to the table and slid back in his chair.

Zander smiled. No one could resist a mystery.

'I don't see anything.' Philip sounded bored as he reached the balcony.

'No,' Zander said. 'Down there.' He leaned forward as far as he could so that his torso was folded over the glass and his head hung low.

As anticipated, Philip copied him. 'I still—'

Zander stepped back, bent low and – with both hands – lifted the man so that his feet came up from the floor. Philip's body pivoted forwards. He grabbed at the glass. He tried to push backwards, but Zander kept lifting his legs higher and higher. Philip kicked and wriggled and banged but didn't scream or cry out.

Well, not until he fell.

Afterwards Zander walked back into the bar and collected one of the white chairs. He carried it on to the balcony and placed it where Philip had been standing. This had been Lexi's idea, as had the latex gloves.

'If you insist on doing it, do it right,' she had said.

Then he removed the matchbox from his pocket. He'd bought it on a whim in the market. Bulls Eye Matches. It felt fitting. He took a single match, struck it,

4

and watched it burn. The whole thing had taken less than four minutes. He looked towards the balcony and listened to the distant sound of a woman screaming.

Smiling, he placed the matchbox on the table opposite his victim's drink and then carefully laid the extinguished match on top.

'One down,' he said to the empty room.

Bloom arrived at the custody suite five minutes earlier than she had been requested. The call had come from an officer working for Detective Chief Inspector Nadia Mirza. Bloom had been surprised. She had first met Mirza a few months earlier. The DCI had been holding the then Foreign Secretary Gerald Porter in custody while investigating claims that he had sold British secrets to an unknown foreign power. Porter had told Mirza he would only cooperate if Bloom handled a personal matter for him first. He wanted his estranged niece Scarlett found and reunited with the family. But his motives were not pure. He had used Bloom to unwittingly pass coded details of his location to his associates, who had then liberated him, much to Mirza's fury.

Bloom had called Mirza to apologize for her part in the whole mess and reassure the DCI that she had not been complicit in Porter's escape. They had ended the call on good terms, but Bloom knew her card had been marked, so she was surprised to be asked to provide a consultation today.

The custody sergeant checked her identification and then made a call to say she had arrived. A few moments later DCI Mirza entered the room with a fair-haired young man in a shirt and tie. The fact that Mirza was working out of a police station meant she had been removed from her post heading up a specialist police unit within the Ministry of Defence.

'Dr Bloom, thank you for coming in.' Mirza did not meet Bloom's eye. She was either embarrassed by her change of professional fortunes or still seething over Bloom's part in it. 'This is Tyler Rowe, our behavioural investigative advisor.'

'Nice to finally meet you, Dr Bloom. I've read a lot of the case notes from your time with the police,' said Rowe.

Behavioural investigative advisors were the National Crime Agency's new term for offender profilers. Bloom had spent the first decade of her career as a police psychologist, producing suspect profiles and assisting with interview techniques. In those days the field had been new and most officers were highly sceptical of it, but she had been employed by a forward-thinking assistant chief constable who had put together a small team of specialist advisors to assist major crime inquiries. It had been a fascinating time and she had earned a great deal of respect from officers, becoming one of the most well-known and consulted of her profession. But there was never sufficient access to either witnesses or perpetrators. She was always questioning them via others, a reality that she found increasingly untenable. She needed to be in the room to really find out what made a person tick, and so she'd taken up the challenge set by a sparky, ex-secret service agent she'd met at a conference where she had been speaking on the Psychology of Crime. The man in question was now her professional partner, Marcus Jameson, and the challenge he'd set was to prove no one is better placed to solve a mystery than a psychologist and a spy. Nearly six years later they had a strong track record investigating cases that were too tenuous for the justice system to take on, such as locating some of the UK's hundreds of thousands of missing people.

'Please call me Augusta,' Bloom said to Rowe, wondering if she'd ever looked so young when she'd been starting out in a similar role. 'I'm not sure why you need me when they have you on staff.'

'We've brought someone in for questioning and would like you to observe the interview,' Mirza said.

Bloom followed DCI Mirza and Rowe into a small office. She wouldn't be allowed in the interview room – that was reserved for investigating officers and legal advisors – but she would be able to watch it all live on a TV screen in an adjacent room.

DCI Mirza took a seat in front of the screen. 'A body was found decomposing in the passenger seat of a Lamborghini outside the St Pancras Renaissance Hotel on Thursday last week. The gentleman in question, Sheikh Nawaf al Saud, had checked in the previous Friday and checked out again on the Monday but his car was left covered on their forecourt.'

'I take it he didn't die from natural causes if the car was covered?'

'That's the crazy part,' said Rowe. 'The pathologist found the body's organs had begun to accumulate gas, which suggests he had been dead going on for a week.'

'Which is impossible if he checked out on Monday,' said Mirza, finally looking Bloom in the eye. 'We believe from his previous movements on Friday that the deceased hired the car himself and drove it to the hotel where he was seen checking in with a Caucasian female. Then at some point over the next twelve hours he was murdered and left under the cover of the car outside. After which point the murderer stayed on for the rest of the weekend living his victim's life before checking out on Monday.'

'That's fairly brazen. Did CCTV not see who covered the car?'

'Whoever did this is smart. There are very few blind spots in the CCTV coverage, but the Lamborghini was parked in one.'

'So, how—?' Bloom was about to ask how she could help when she saw on screen the person they were about to interview.

Seraphine Walker was immaculately dressed as always with her long blonde hair fastened at the nape of her neck; her legs were crossed and her hands rested casually on her lap. She looked as if she were sitting in a waiting room, rather than one designed for interrogation. Her gaze momentarily moved to the camera and for a beat or two Bloom looked into her eyes.

Despite looking like a woman of wealth and re-spectability, 29-year-old Seraphine Walker was a high-functioning psychopath. Twelve months earlier Bloom had revealed her to be the mastermind of an elaborate game designed to tempt other psychopaths to compete for a position in her organization: an organization set up to manipulate and control global events from the shadows. Bloom and Jameson had managed to expose the game, but Seraphine had walked free thanks to her network of allies within the justice system. But this was only part of the story. Bloom and Seraphine's history ran much deeper. Their mothers had been best friends at school. Bloom was twelve years older, so they'd had little contact as children, but when fourteen-year-old Seraphine had stabbed her school caretaker with a pencil, Bloom had offered to help. She had been a freshly qualified psychologist keen to practise her new skills and it hadn't taken her long to realize Seraphine was different. Suspecting the young girl was showing early signs of psychopathy, she had tried her best to help and guide her. But it had all gone horribly wrong.

'Does she know I'm here?' Bloom sat heavily in the chair with her coat still buttoned. She and Seraphine could not be more different in their appearance. Where Seraphine opted for glamour, using her outfits as a weapon of distraction, Bloom believed clothes were for comfort and, on occasion, blending in. Hence the plain grey coat and comfortable shoes.

'No.'

'You think Seraphine is involved in this murder? How?' Bloom said.

'I would prefer not to say at this stage, but I would like your professional eye on how she handles herself. After all, you were key to uncovering her activities over recent years. I've studied the case files for her Psychopath

Game and I know she is a tricky interviewee. The consensus from police and prosecutors alike is that she is highly intelligent, seemingly helpful but ultimately slippery.'

It was a fair description of a high-functioning psychopath's character. They often conducted themselves with a veneer of superficial charm but underneath were, almost without exception, focused on personal gain.

'I doubt she'll tell you anything useful.'

'We'll see.'

The door to the right of the screen opened and two plain-clothed officers entered. Seraphine remained perfectly still as the male officer explained that a voluntary interview is used to question a person about their possible involvement in an offence. He then asked if she was happy to proceed on that basis.

'That all depends on the offence you're referring to.' Seraphine's expression was serious for a moment and then she smiled widely. 'I'm messing with you, Detective Peters. Please carry on.'

The male officer twitched at the mention of his name. He and his colleague had yet to introduce themselves. Bloom suspected he was surprised their interviewee knew who he was, which showed just how out of their depth these people were. Seraphine Walker didn't go anywhere without fully researching whom she was meeting.

The officers continued with their formalities, explaining that Seraphine was free to leave at any point and also free to have a lawyer in attendance. Seraphine nodded and smiled and confirmed she was happy to carry on.

'Could you confirm your whereabouts on the evening of the twentieth of last month? That's Friday, the twentieth of April?'

'Where do you think I was?' She looked curious and just a touch amused, as if she were indulging youngsters who were playing pretend.

'Please answer the question,' said the female officer, who had introduced herself as DC Morgan.

'What offence are you questioning me in relation to?'

'There was an incident at the St Pancras Hotel where we have reason to believe you were attending a charity fundraiser for UNICEF.'

'What sort of incident?'

'At this stage we'd simply like to confirm what time you arrived and left the event, please?' DC Morgan spoke a little too quietly. It made her seem anxious: a factor that Seraphine would use to her advantage, given half a chance.

'Well, you've piqued my interest. I do like a good mystery. What was the incident?'

'Can you confirm that you were at the St Pancras Hotel on that evening?'

'If I had been, don't you think I'd already know about the incident of which you speak? I expect it was hotel gossip.'

'Are you saying you were not there?' said DS Peters. He had a no-nonsense confidence about him.

Seraphine smiled. 'What was the incident?'

'A gentleman died.'

'Oh dear. How sad.'

'Were you attending the fundraiser for work or pleasure? I understand you are a psychiatrist?' asked DS Peters.

'I'm no longer practising. You might say I'm in between careers, considering my options. Maybe I should consider police work.'

'You can't be an officer if you have any convictions,' said DC Morgan.

'It's fortunate I don't then, isn't it?' Seraphine held the young woman's gaze for a long moment.

The young detective constable dropped her eyes.

Next to Bloom, Mirza sat forward to look at the screen a little closer. 'Any thoughts so far?'

'Only that I hope your officers are good at their jobs,' said Bloom.

'I only hire the best.'

'Good,' said Bloom, 'because something tells me they are as much under interrogation as she is.'

DS Peters was asking Seraphine to tell him her movements before the event on Friday evening.

'Were you in the vicinity of the St Pancras Hotel between four p.m. and five p.m. on the twentieth?'

'Why do you ask?'

'Were you there?'

'This is a voluntary interview where I volunteer information. I will answer what I believe is relevant. So, to help me decide, tell me why you are asking.'

'We have reports that the deceased man arrived with a tall white woman with long blonde hair.'

Seraphine's eyebrows rose and she glanced up at the camera.

Bloom looked at DCI Mirza. 'You are kidding me. That's why you're questioning her?'

On the screen DS Peters said, 'Could this have been you?'

'Why would you think it was me?'

Peters took a photograph from the file in front of him and laid it on the table. 'Do you know this man?'

Seraphine sat up a little. 'Your deceased man is a member of the Saudi royal family?'

Bloom noticed Mirza straighten in her chair. 'So you do know him?'

'Is this your dead guy? If so, I can see why you're flapping around trying to find out what happened. How funny.'

'You think murder is funny?' said DC Morgan.

Bloom heard DCI Mirza sigh.

'Murder. Wow.' Seraphine spoke in a whispered voice.

Morgan rolled her shoulders a little. Peters didn't miss a beat.

'How do you know this man?'

'I don't.'

'So how do you know he's a member of the Saudi royal family?'

'I didn't, but I do now.' She winked at Peters.

DS Peters hesitated for a brief moment and then composed himself. 'Did you see this man at the fundraising event?'

'I wasn't aware I'd confirmed my attendance.'

Peters took another photograph from his file and presented it to Seraphine. 'I believe this is you arriving at the event.'

'Gosh, I do look fabulous, don't I?' Seraphine held eye contact with DS Peters. 'I knew that dress was a good choice. I look great in red.' This stare was entirely different to the one she had used on Morgan, but to his credit Peters didn't waver.

'Were you aware that someone had offered up the chance to drive a top-of-the-range Lamborghini as part of the charity auction?'

'Why do you ask?'

'Were you aware?'

'I can't say I paid much attention to the auction. People rarely offer up anything of interest.'

'Do you know who won that bid?'

Seraphine's smile was a touch impatient. 'Like I said, I didn't pay attention. Was the winner your victim or your killer?'

'So you can confirm that you attended the event. Did you have any contact with this man during the evening?' DS Peters pointed to the picture of Sheikh Nawaf.

'Not as I recall.'

'Have you or anyone you know had any previous dealings with this man?'

'Anyone I know?' A flash of something crossed Seraphine's face.

'I am trying to establish whether you have any connection to the deceased. Please answer the question. Do you know him or anyone who might have reason to harm him?'

'I have never met this man.'

'Never met,' repeated DCI Mirza under her breath.

'You say you've never met him but have you had any dealings of any nature with him?'

Seraphine began to drum her red-painted fingernails slowly on the table, making a clickety-clacking sound. After four rotations she stopped and relaxed back in her chair before looking up at the camera. 'To whichever genius is watching up there I am not playing games with people's lives. I have not done so in the past and I will not be doing so in the future.' She stood and held a hand out to Peters. 'You have an impressive interview technique, DS Peters.' She looked at Morgan. 'Pay attention, Fleur, you could learn a lot from this guy.'

In the room down the hall Bloom let out a long breath. 'You'd better fill me in on what you're thinking. You don't show a woman like her your hand unless you're happy stirring up trouble.'

3

Six months earlier

The cold November air penetrated Keith Runnesguard's polo shirt and raised the hairs on his chest as he stepped outside. He should have worn his overcoat, but it was packed in the suit carrier he held in his left hand. In his right hand he carried his sports bag and squash rackets. It was only a short walk back to his car. A familiar route he took every Tuesday and Thursday. He could see the Range Rover parked in its usual spot at the far edge of the car park, away from any other cars that might clip it. He picked up the pace, blowing warm air out of his mouth and up towards his nose to give some comfort against the wind. Only as he neared the vehicle did he see that a dark figure crouched by his front passenger wheel.

'Can I help you?'

'You've got a flat, Keith.'

Relieved that this person wasn't vandalizing his car, Keith felt irritated at the idea of calling out the break-down service. As CEO of a global pharmaceuticals giant, he wasn't the kind of man who changed his own tyres. And he had a 9 p.m. call with the US he needed to be home for.

'Do I know you?' Keith said as the figure stood up. Keith didn't recognize the man's face. He wore a black woollen hat pulled low over his ears and leather gloves. Was he another club member? Staff maybe? Without answering the man took two quick steps towards Keith and struck him hard in the chest.

The sensation of warm liquid soaking his shirt made Keith look down. Even in the dimly lit car park he could make out an expanding circle of red against the white material. Still holding his suit carrier in one hand and his sports bag in the other, Keith dropped to his knees as the world swam in front of his eyes. He would have toppled forward into the dark figure had the man not started to hit him over and over in the neck and face, causing Keith to rock backwards. His head hit the tarmac with a loud thud.

In his last moments Keith felt his attacker prise his left hand open and take the car keys he had been holding alongside his suit carrier. He heard his door unlock and had time to think, *Did he attack me to steal my car?* before he heard a sound he could not place until it was joined by a familiar smell.

He lit a match.

Oh God, he lit a match. What was he going to set alight?

4

By the time they had moved to a more spacious room to debrief Seraphine's interview, Bloom had been able to reflect on what she had heard and generate a theory for what DCI Mirza might be suspecting.

'You said the killer had lived the victim's life for the weekend – in what way?' said Bloom, pulling a chair up at the table.

'Room service and champagne were ordered each night as well as tickets to the opera on Saturday, and according to the concierge he entertained at least one young lady on Sunday evening,' said Rowe.

'So if Nawaf died within twelve hours of checking in on Friday, whoever went to the opera and entertained the lady is your killer, am I right?'

'That's the thinking,' said Mirza.

'So you don't suspect Seraphine Walker killed Nawaf herself.'

'Not personally. The deceased is a Saudi national who we can see from CCTV footage arrived in traditional dress on Friday. On Monday, CCTV sees him checking out dressed the same but this time he takes care to never show his face to the cameras. We suspect this was his killer but we can't ignore the fact that Walker was on-site that Friday and possibly even arrived with the sheikh. Somehow, she is involved. I know she is. I can feel it.'

'Let me see if I have this right.' Bloom was careful to watch her tone. She was already on shaky ground with the DCI and it would do no good to show any exasperation at their thought processes. 'You suspect Seraphine Walker might be complicit in this crime because the deceased arrived at the hotel with a woman who vaguely matches her description and because she is confirmed to have attended a charity fundraiser there that night.'

'For UNICEF. As if a psychopath cares about troubled kids,' said Rowe with an awkward laugh.

The DCI shot him a look. 'It is my understanding from reviewing the Psychopath Game files that Seraphine Walker challenged her players to a series of tests to detect whether they were indeed psychopaths. Is this correct?' she said.

'It is. But murder wasn't one of the tests.' Seraphine had sent mysterious cards to people she identified as possessing psychopathic traits that read 'Dare to Play?' If they followed the weblink included – which all of them did – they were taken to the dark web and set tasks designed to enable Seraphine to select the best of the best.

'And yet one of the participants, Faye Graham, murdered her husband.'

'A fact that caused Seraphine to reject her from the selection process.'

'Selection for what?'

'Membership of her secret society.'

'And what happened to those who didn't make the grade?'

'They disappeared.'

'Disappeared or *were* disappeared?'

'That's unknown.' It was true that the likes of Faye Graham and Lana Reid, a friend of Jameson's sister, had never been seen again after failing Seraphine's game.

'Didn't you yourself accuse Walker of conducting a cull on those of her kind that she found wanting?' Clearly DCI Mirza had listened to the recordings made of Bloom's showdown with Seraphine as her game was exposed.

'It was a hypothesis.'

The DCI smiled a little as she looked up at the ceiling. 'And what is the purpose of this secret society of psychopaths?'

'Well, that's the million-dollar question.'

'You failed to determine why this woman was collecting fellow psychopaths?'

'We did. We only managed to halt the selection activities.'

'And how can you be sure you did that?'

Bloom acknowledged the point with a brief smile. 'We cannot.'

'Especially now she has been cleared of any wrongdoing.'

Bloom said nothing. It was pointless arguing the point. She, herself, suspected that Seraphine would be back to her old ways soon enough.

'And if you don't know what she was really doing or

why, how can you be sure that murder was not always part of the plan?'

'Because Seraphine ranks those psychopaths who kill lower than she does the rest of us.'

'So she says.' DCI Mirza opened her notebook and flicked through the pages. 'Sheikh Nawaf's killer brazenly lived in the man's hotel room, wore his clothes, and spent his money while his victim's body lay metres away. If those aren't the actions of a psychopathic person, I don't know what are.'

'Maybe. There are lots of motives behind why people do what they do. It's not always down to a dysfunctional personality. Do you have any other theories on who the killer might be? How about the person who won the auction bid? They would have had the opportunity to get the victim alone in the car where he was killed.'

'The guy who won the bid took the chance to drive the car that evening and was seen by multiple witnesses thanking Nawaf and returning to the event.' Mirza's tone was impatient.

'How about prints or DNA evidence, if the killer stayed on site?'

'The hotel received a call from someone claiming to be the sheikh on Monday afternoon, saying he had bed bug bites following his stay. As per hotel policy the room was professionally treated and disinfected,' said Mirza. 'All we have is one print of the deceased left on a bedside light and a partial print of a person unknown. Like I said, the person who did this is smart.'

Rowe said, 'Sheikh Nawaf was something of a

playboy, by all accounts. He often spent a month in London enjoying the freedoms not accessible to a young man in Saudi Arabia. We considered someone might have been offended at how a member of the Saudi royal family was bringing shame on his Muslim faith but that doesn't fit with the killer remaining in Nawaf's room and living the high life.'

'I don't think Dr Bloom needs to hear all our rejected theories,' said Mirza.

Rowe shrank a little in his chair as he went on, 'It has to be someone capable of passing themselves off as the sheikh, so we're thinking someone of a similar height, build and hair colour.'

'Not necessarily,' said Bloom, keeping her tone light so as not to add to Rowe's discomfort. 'Any good con artist will tell you if you act the part people see what you want them to.'

'Isn't that one of the things Seraphine Walker was testing: a person's ability to manipulate and defraud?' said Mirza.

'It was, yes. You've clearly done your homework. But I suspect you asked me here because you're not completely convinced by this theory. You want me to confirm it could be her work but I'm not sure her being at the same venue is enough. In fact, if I know Seraphine, it is a stronger indication that she *wasn't* involved.'

'You don't think she was keeping an eye on her player?' said Rowe.

'She's never felt the need to do that before. In fact, I'd say she's been meticulous in ensuring she is nowhere near any incriminating scenes or events. This woman is highly intelligent and well connected. Even if she wanted to check up on someone, I doubt very much she'd do it herself.' Bloom looked from DCI Mirza to Rowe. 'Look, I get that whoever killed the sheikh was something of an expert con man, someone capable of becoming another character. He didn't simply hide in the room and enjoy the spoils of wealth; he went out in the world pretending to be his victim. But maybe he's a confident killer who knows he can get away with it because he's done it before? Have you considered that he might be a hired professional?'

'Why would a hitman stay in Nawaf's room for the weekend?' said Rowe.

Bloom shrugged. 'Maybe for some reason it was necessary to keep up the illusion that the sheikh was alive.'

DCI Mirza sat back in her chair, thinking. After a moment or two she looked at Bloom. 'In the Psychopath Game were there ever any struck matches used to indicate something?' she said.

'Not that I know of. Why?'

'We found a box of matches on the driver's seat of the Lamborghini. Eight of the thirty matches had been struck and left in a neat stack on top of the box. Have you ever seen anything like that before?'

'I can't say that I have.'

'We have,' said Rowe. 'Six months ago the director of a pharmaceuticals company was murdered outside of his country club and two struck matches were found with his body.'

'That is confidential information,' Mirza said to Rowe.

24

After an uncomfortable moment of silence she turned to Bloom. 'But now you know, Dr Bloom, I may as well tell you we thought nothing of those two matches until we found the eight in the Lamborghini. It just so happens DS Peters worked both cases and now we're wondering if this is some kind of scoring method.'

Seraphine's attendance at the crime scene was one thing but the suggestion that people's murders were being given scores was an altogether different thing. That implied a competition was afoot – or, in other words: a game. She could see how DCI Mirza had joined the dots to Seraphine Walker.

'This is not her style,' said Bloom. 'She's not interested in killers. She wants power, not death and destruction.'

Detective Chief Inspector Mirza moved in her chair to face Bloom more squarely. 'Can you be sure these men were not targeted by Seraphine Walker's game for some reason? These were powerful men with powerful contacts. Right up your psychopath's street, wouldn't you say?'

5

The pub was quieter than Marcus Jameson had hoped for a Friday night. He wanted some hustle and bustle to surround them and release the pressure. He couldn't remember if it was normal to feel this nervous. It had been a long time since he'd dated. His past life with MI6 had taken him around the world and as a young man he had enjoyed the freedom and variety that afforded on a romantic level. But he was out of practice. With any luck the nerves would go when she arrived, but again, he couldn't recall if that's how it usually went.

Truth be told, he had only ever connected with two women on a romantic level and one of them had turned out to be a crazy psychopath. The other, Jodie, might have been the real deal. She had been his closest friend and ally in MI6. They'd worked on many operations together, from Afghanistan to Eastern Europe and Russia, until she had stepped in for him on an assignment one night and never made it back. At the time of her death he hadn't been sure how he felt about her romantically. They had spent one night together, which they both agreed had been a mistake. But in hindsight, there was no doubt he had loved her.

He checked his watch; she was ten minutes late. Hopefully it was an innocent delay. He had no appetite for games. He wanted a beer but knew it was more gentlemanly to wait. Perhaps she would like to share a bottle of wine?

'How did I know I'd find you here.' Augusta Bloom removed her coat and hung it over the back of the opposite chair. 'Are you not having a drink?' She nodded to the empty table.

'I'm waiting for someone, a date. She's late.'

Bloom narrowed her eyes. 'Not . . .?'

'God no. Give me some credit. It's a woman I met online.' He couldn't blame Bloom for thinking he was meeting Seraphine. They had dated briefly before Jameson knew who or what she really was. Then he had stupidly turned to her when Bloom needed help on a recent case and Seraphine's condition for stepping in had been the promise of a date with him. A date he had no intention of keeping because the woman was a manipulative witch.

Bloom sat. 'I won't keep you long then. I've just had a worrying experience with DCI Mirza. They were interviewing Seraphine about her possible involvement in the murder of a man at the St Pancras Hotel.'

'The body in the supercar? I read about that in the news. How is Seraphine involved?'

'I'll get you a drink and fill you in on Mirza's theory, but you're not going to like it.' Bloom left to go to the bar.

Jameson checked his phone. He'd had nothing from the woman he was supposed to be meeting. She was now twenty minutes late. He'd never been stood up before. He wasn't a fan.

Bloom placed a pint in front of him and her usual

soda and lime by her chair. 'The DCI suspects Seraphine is challenging psychopaths again and this is one of her latest tests. They think this murder is linked to another and that both were given a score in the form of struck matches left at the scene. They think she's encouraging people to kill in some kind of sick competition.'

'Oh Lord.' Jameson took a long drink.

'She wanted my input, given I know Seraphine better than most.'

'I hope you told her we charge handsomely for our services and that she can't afford us.'

'She wasn't asking, Marcus.'

'She has no power to make you do her bidding.'

'Of course she does. I let her down on the Gerald Porter case. She can destroy my reputation within the police and I've worked too long and too hard to let that happen.'

Jameson sighed. This was bad. 'Do *you* think Seraphine's behind this?'

'No.'

'Because?'

Bloom shuffled forward in her chair and rested her forearms on the table as she lowered her voice. 'I know Seraphine has killed before but that was a political powerplay. She's not interested in people who kill out of hate and anger. She completely dismissed Faye Graham when she killed her husband, remember?'

'You're saying this can't be Seraphine testing psychos because killers are not the kind of psycho she's after. You know how crazy that sounds, don't you?'

'She was there at the hotel on the night of the murder, attending some charity fundraiser.'

Jameson raised his eyebrows and then let out a long sigh. 'She wouldn't go anywhere near the crime scene. She's too smart.'

'That's what I told Mirza but she's got a bee in her bonnet. I think she sees this as a chance to redeem herself. You know Steve Barker is now an assistant chief at the Met and so effectively Mirza's new boss.' ACC Barker was an old contact of Bloom's who had been pivotal in investigating Seraphine's Psychopath Game.

'Mirza thinks she can impress him by catching the woman he failed to convict?'

'Maybe.'

'OK, but before we discount the theory completely, do we think Seraphine's capable of inciting others to murder?'

'We know she is, but that's not the point. She would never put herself so close to the crime. She didn't need to be there. So why was she? I have a feeling it was just a coincidence.'

Jameson couldn't help the smile. 'Is this a gut feeling?' She always chastised him for relying too heavily on such things. She insisted on the need for objectivity and evidence rather than instinct.

'Marcus, I have never said a gut feeling is bad, just that it needs interrogation. We don't get such feelings out of nowhere. They're born of experience. Your training in MI6 plus your years in the field mean the fast-thinking part of your mind, the part dedicated to efficient decision-making, will flag potential threats or theories that seem to come out of nowhere. But of course that's not true. It's all based on prior experience. On a subconscious level you've seen or heard something that resonates with what's gone before. It's not some magical instinct.'

'You really do take the fun out of everything, don't you?'

'It worries me when officers set their minds to a given theory and stop looking for alternatives. Seraphine has done many things wrong but I don't think this is one of them.'

'Why are you always defending her?'

'I'm not. I said she has done many things wrong.'

'You're always on her side. Why is that? Because you see some of yourself in her?' He knew this would get a reaction. Seraphine had accused Bloom of being psychopathic in nature and for a time he had bought the theory, which was something he knew had hurt Bloom.

He watched his partner sit back in her chair and sip her drink while looking across the room. If he wasn't mistaken there were tears forming in her eyes.

'I made her what she is.'

'You told her when she was a teenager to choose what kind of person she wanted to be and she chose. You didn't tell her to be a purveyor of all things evil. That's on her.'

'She's not evil.'

'Augusta, stop. Stop defending her. It blinds you to the truth.'

6

AJ waited patiently for Zander to finish. It was always this way when the big guy took centre stage. He had opinions, lots of opinions, and he was the kind of well-read pseudo-intellectual who loved the sound of his own voice. There was no way they would have been friends under different circumstances. Funny how a common interest could bind the most unlikely of personalities together.

He liked Lexi, she was a sweetheart, but she rarely spoke up, preferring to listen.

'It's a problem with the West. Ninety-nine per cent of the wealth is owned by one per cent of the population. That's messed up. But what's even more messed up is that people aren't even aware of it. Marx said religion is the opiate of the people but now, today, I'd say it's consumerism. Give people just enough to keep buying plastic crap they don't need and it'll occupy their minds long enough to stop them rising up or asking questions. We need to wake them up and nothing gets an audience's attention like murder. Did you know the press have a saying, "If it bleeds it reads"? What does that tell you about the nature of the masses? Everyone's a rubbernecker. They love nothing more than looking at the misery of others because it makes them feel better about their own crappy lives. And while they're rubbernecking at our work, we can educate them. So we need more targets. A lot more. AJ? Hey, are you listening?'

'I like the coffee in here.' AJ watched people filing in and out of the doorway in a constant stream. It was the kind of place Uncle Bob would have called a caff. It had a lino floor darkened by years of dirty footprints. The plastic tables down one side were attached to the red seats and topped with refillable ketchup bottles and old-fashioned salt and pepper shakers. It served bacon butties, and full English breakfasts with two slices of toast and a mug of tea thrown in for good measure. The corkboard on the wall was full to the brim with business cards for every sparky, plumber and builder in the local area. Some of the cards had fallen off and were now trapped behind the radiator below.

'It's good, isn't it, Lexi, the coffee?' AJ said, trying to draw her into the conversation, but she was having none of it. She wasn't in the mood to bail him out today. The silence felt heavy around AJ. He'd never admit it but these people intimidated him. 'Are you sure *you know who* doesn't know?'

'Leave that to me. I'm making sure of it. But you need to catch up, kid.'

AJ felt the rage fizz and pop inside him like a firework starting to explode. He hated being called kid. Zander and Lexi might be older but they weren't his parents and he wasn't about to let them boss him around. They needed him as much as he needed them.

An elderly man hovered near the table with his mug

of tea and a plate of buttered toast. The other tables were all full and most people had a plate of food in front of them. AJ drained his coffee and stood. Zander would only be on his case if they sat here any longer, and AJ wasn't sure he could hold his temper in check.

'Much obliged,' said the old guy. He was wearing a smart shirt with grey slacks. AJ wondered why such elderly dudes continued to dress that way. Why not come out in joggers and a jumper, or just stay in your PJs. It was only a caff after all, not the bloody Ritz.

He walked to the counter and placed down a fiver, 'For my coffee and butty. Keep the change,' he said to the woman with thinning hair and large round glasses. She didn't even bother smiling any more. The hot drink and bacon butty deal was exactly five pounds and he used the joke every time he visited.

7

Bloom arrived at her and Jameson's basement office on Wednesday morning to find Tyler Rowe waiting outside the door.

'There's been a development and I think I need your help,' he said by way of a greeting.

'Has the DCI sent you?' Bloom unlocked the office door.

'No. I came of my own accord.'

Bloom noted that the young man's hands were shaking as he wrung them together. 'You'd better come in then.'

Bloom gestured for Rowe to take the spare chair next to her desk. 'Before we start, are you sure you're permitted to share what you want to share with me? If it's part of an active investigation—'

'I authorized it with my boss last night. She's fully in support of your input.'

Bloom knew the National Crime Agency was independent of the police with its own authority to investigate serious and organized crime. It provided specialist support to the police but possessed its own separate hierarchy. It was a partnership, in essence.

'Which implies others may not be?'

Rowe swallowed. He looked even younger today than

34

he had on Friday afternoon. 'The DCI has some reservations about it.'

'I see. Well, that's understandable. There is some history there.'

'She wasn't keen on your coming in to observe on Friday but I insisted you were best placed to advise on Seraphine Walker's responses, and I was right. Your reservations made us look at other possibilities. We requested a trawl of the ViCLAS system, that's our database of violent crimes, to see if your hitman theory played out, but nothing came up. So then I sent a request to all our NCA contact officers in various police stations to ask if any had come across murder cases where struck matches had been found at the scene. And that's when things got interesting. I've found three more deaths from the last two years accompanied by a matchbox with struck matches stacked on top, all in the Greater London area.'

'And what does DCI Mirza say about this?' Bloom wanted to check Tyler had followed the right protocol in informing the senior investigating officer before anyone else.

'Her team is looking into it. But she still thinks it's all linked to the Psychopath Game.'

'And you don't?'

'I think . . . well . . . Can I show you?' Rowe took out his notebook and opened it to a list of names that he placed in front of her.

Name	Manner of death	No. of matches
Philip Berringer	Fall from high building	1
Simon Middleton-Moore	Overdose	4
Jeremy Tomlinson	Drowned	6
Keith Runnesguard	Stabbed	2
Sheikh Nawaf al Saud	Strangled	8

'This is in the order of their deaths. Philip's death was ruled as a suicide and Simon and Jeremy's as accidental, but here's the thing: not only do all these deaths have struck matches found at the scene; all of the matchboxes have the word "eye" or the image of an eye on them. That can't be a coincidence, can it?'

Bloom scanned the list. 'It would certainly suggest these deaths may be linked.' Her heart sank a little. She hoped to God this was nothing to do with Seraphine and her people. 'What do you know about these men? Why might they have been targeted?'

'Philip Berringer was a stock market trader who fell from the Roof Bar terrace of his building in September, year before last. One of the officers flagged the struck match left with his belongings in the bar because the bar and terrace were no-smoking areas and Philip wasn't a smoker. Simon Middleton-Moore was heir to a tobacco fortune. He overdosed on some bad cocaine in his own apartment six months after Philip's death. Jeremy Tomlinson was a tech entrepreneur who drowned in the pool of his home seven months after that. He had a high blood-alcohol volume so it was thought he fell into his pool intoxicated.' Tyler was speaking quickly and barely pausing for breath, meaning Bloom had to concentrate to keep up. 'Then we mentioned Keith Runnesguard the other day. He was the pharma CEO who was stabbed in the car park of his country club. That was a month after Jeremy died, and then five months later we have Sheikh Nawaf al Saud who was strangled and left in his car outside the St Pancras Hotel. They are all wealthy men between the ages of twenty-two and forty-five and they all died within a few miles of each other.'

'So five deaths over the past two years with a fairly similar victim profile.'

Rowe coughed before saying, 'I'm thinking we have more than three murders separated by time and with the same calling card, a matchbox with struck matches, implying the same perpetrator.'

Bloom sat back in her seat. A person who commits three or more murders separated by time had an official title. 'You think it might be a serial killer.'

'You see that too?' Rowe's expression showed a mixture of relief and excitement. 'The DCI was pretty dismissive of the idea. She thinks these matches are a score of some kind, but what if they're a count? Philip is number one, Simon number four, Jeremy number six and Nawaf number eight.'

Bloom looked back at Rowe's list of victims. 'So how do you explain Keith? He died between your sixth and eighth victims but only has two matches?'

'Maybe the killer was interrupted or, I don't know,

scenes of crime disturbed the matches, not realizing the number was significant. I think Keith should have been left with seven not two.'

'If you're right, that would mean you still have victims two, three and five to find. That's one hell of a body count. Were the matches displayed consistently, do you know? That could tell you the likelihood of the same or different people having left them.'

'I've checked the crime-scene photographs and in all cases the struck matches were placed on top of the matchbox in the same direction they would have been on the inside, apart from with Nawaf where six were placed this way but then the last two rotated ninety degrees and placed on top.'

'How about Keith's two? Did they look like they'd been disturbed or rushed?'

Rowe shook his head. He knew this anomaly was the chink in his theory. 'But there is the eye theme on the matchboxes.'

'I see you. I'm watching you. Look at me,' said Bloom, thinking out loud.

'Do you agree with me? Could this be a serial killer?'

'It could be. I certainly wouldn't rule it out.' Bloom looked back at how each victim had died. 'Would the same killer use so many approaches, though? There's a marked difference between drugging your fourth victim and stabbing your seventh, don't you think?'

'That's what the DCI said. I think I'm out of my depth with this.'

'Oh, I don't know. You've come up with a sound theory here.'

'I know, but I have no idea what I'm going to do now or how I get the DCI to take it seriously. Do you think …?' Rowe stopped mid-sentence again and reverted to wringing his hands.

'DCI Mirza is an experienced policewoman with a good head on her shoulders. If the evidence is there, she will take it seriously, I'm sure.'

'Can I hire you?' Rowe blurted out the words in a rush.

'To do what?'

'Help me. Behind the scenes, like a mentor? I could talk you through the investigation as we go and you could give me your take, like you have today.'

'Tyler, I'd be more than happy to help you and DCI Mirza but I think you have to clear it with her and officially hire me as a consultant. You can't risk sharing case details behind her back: not only will you lose all credibility, but you could jeopardize any prosecution case.'

The young man looked crestfallen but nodded.

'I know these senior officers can be intimidating at times but take it from me, if you want to earn their respect you have to be brave and stand your ground.'

Rowe took back his notebook and closed it. 'If I'm right, Dr Bloom, and this is a serial killer, he managed to kill eight people before anyone noticed. How do you catch someone like that?'

8

George Shulman turned up the collar on his wool coat before checking his watch. He'd wanted to be home earlier than 9 p.m. *'Even when you're here, you're never here.'* His daughter's words had stung him at the time, but as he entered the park he couldn't help thinking how hard he worked, how everything rested on his shoulders and how bloody ungrateful people could be.

He looked towards his house on the far side of the park. They lived here because of him. They had a holiday home because of him. The private schooling was paid for by him, not to mention the multiple holidays every year.

A branch cracked behind him but he didn't hear it. If he hadn't been so consumed by his growing indignation, he might have noticed that someone was following him, that someone had been following him for a while now. On a normal night he might have sensed a body swiftly approaching or heard their breath. But not tonight. Not until the first dull thud hit the back of his head did he know anything was different about his usual walk home.

The blow was accompanied by a kind of animal sound, something akin to a growl, but George felt more shock than pain.

'You're never here.'

The second blow was an altogether different thing. He heard bones cracking in his jaw and his mouth filled with blood. He spun to see who or what was attacking him and the third strike hit him right between the eyes.

'I hate you.'

He fell to the floor and the dark shape followed, raining down blow after blow. George couldn't work out if the thing was human. It made slavering noises as it struck him with something hard and cold. He couldn't move his arms; they lay heavy and useless on the ground. He gagged as blood flowed back down his throat and the blows kept coming. He tried to say stop, or help, but the only word that came out before the darkness took him was a gurgling and choking 'sorry'.

9

Bloom arrived at New Scotland Yard on Tuesday morning, almost a week after Rowe's visit to the office, having received a call at 7 a.m. from DCI Mirza herself.

'Another man was killed last night and I'd like your take on what we've found as it's . . . disturbing.'

Disturbing. There was a word Bloom never wanted to hear in relation to a crime. In her police career she had worked on rapes, serious sexual assaults, child abuse and murder cases. Truth be told they were all disturbing, but when the police used the word you knew something chilling was coming.

DCI Mirza and Tyler Rowe already sat at the small round table in Mirza's office. The DCI looked exhausted; chances were she'd been up all night. Bloom wondered if the decision to invite her in was down to her or whether it had been Rowe's idea.

She joined them at the table as Mirza spoke.

'Our latest victim, George Shulman, was a millionaire financier who was beaten to death metres from his own front door last night. The autopsy report is not in yet but it was a frenzied and brutal attack.' Mirza nodded to Rowe, who brought a photograph up on his laptop.

Bloom braced herself before sitting forward to study

the photograph. The victim's body lay on the floor. His legs were straight and his arms lay neatly by his side as if he were already in a coffin, but his smart coat was wrapped awkwardly around him and splattered with blood and brain matter. She had to force her eyes to look at what had been his face. If her opinion was being sought on the killer's motive and behaviour, she needed to see all the graphic detail.

'No matchbox or matches were found at the scene but that was drawn on the ground,' said Mirza.

Bloom's gaze moved to the pavement alongside the body where the outline of an eye and three crudely sketched matches had been drawn.

'Is that in blood?' She looked up to meet Mirza's eye.

The DCI nodded. 'What do you make of it?'

'It could suggest a lack of preparation as no matchbox was taken to the scene and that could mean this murder was not as planned as the others. Maybe it happened in the moment.'

'Because a serial killer is escalating?'

Bloom glanced at Rowe. He had clearly been pushing his theory. 'Possibly. That might also explain the added violence.'

'Don't serial killers usually have a set MO? Keith was stabbed, Nawaf strangled and now George has been beaten to death. And how do you explain the other three? Why would a serial killer make his kills look like suicides or accidents only to leave a calling card?'

'I agree it is odd but people are unique. Killers are

43

unique. So anomalies are always possible. I could give you more of a take on how likely this is to be one person if I can look at the case files for each death.'

Rowe nodded enthusiastically at this suggestion but chose not to verbally support it.

'How about the number of matches? Tyler was convinced they were a count and that our stabbed victim Keith should have been left with seven matches not two, but if that were true this latest victim George should have been left with nine matches not three. So that kind of blows the count theory out of the water, doesn't it?'

Bloom could tell the DCI was trying to be open-minded but finding it annoying. She decided to stay quiet and let the policewoman say what she needed to say.

'Is it not more likely, given the differences in how the victims have been killed, that we have multiple perpetrators?'

'You're thinking of those playing the Psychopath Game?'

'Absolutely.'

'You know I have my reservations on that theory, but I can see that it's a legitimate line of inquiry from your point of view.'

Mirza looked down at her notebook and tapped the end of her pencil against it. 'We're thinking these matches, along with the eye imagery, gives us strikingly similar evidence across these six deaths. I've been given the go-ahead to set up a Special Investigation Team to look into the persons or person responsible. Tyler has requested your input to assist with his analysis. Given

this is such a meaty case, I'm comfortable with support-
ing this financially as long as you understand this is my
investigation, and if I feel it pertinent to pursue Seraphine
Walker and her cronies I'll expect your full support.'

'As long as you're open to the idea that this may not be
part of Seraphine's activities. That it might be something
else entirely. Someone who can't stop.'

'Seraphine Walker may never stop. What's the difference?' Mirza looked irritated at the challenge.

'I disagree. If it is her, she will stop once she's got
whatever she wants out of it. Once she's won. But a serial
killer won't. They can't. They will keep killing until
someone stops them – that's how it works.'

Lexi had insisted they talk in private. The cafe wasn't appropriate, she'd said. So Zander now sat in the kitchen of the world's dingiest flat. It was funny how AJ never seemed to notice the tragedy of this place, with its old-fashioned white cupboards bordered with metal handles that ran the full width of the doors and collected all manner of crud in their grooves. He knew Lexi tried to keep it clean whenever she was here but somehow AJ managed to outstrip her efforts with his dedication to chaos. Zander tried to be present in this place as little as possible.

He opened the cupboards, looking for something palatable to eat, but found only half-empty biscuit and cracker packets, their contents now bendy instead of crisp. He rinsed a mug from the drainer and filled it with water from the tap; then he sat and waited for Lexi and AJ to show up. He sensed Lexi was angry about something. He wasn't really interested but he would hear her out. Then he would get on with what he wanted to do: research his latest target.

Lexi and AJ arrived together, and Lexi sounded furious.

'Do you know what AJ has done?' she said to Zander before rounding on AJ. 'Are you going to tell him, or should I?'

Zander braced himself for the news. AJ was reckless and careless. He and Lexi had always known this but they also knew it wasn't without good reason.

'I don't see what the problem is.' AJ's tone was indignant. He could be such a teenager. 'So I didn't take a matchbox. Big deal. This isn't about the matches. It's about the bastards getting what they deserve. Zander agrees with me and you can't tell me what to do.'

There was a silence as Zander waited to see if Lexi would respond. When she remained quiet, he knew she was too angry to speak.

'What happened, AJ?' he said.

'I wore my gloves and I wasn't seen.' AJ's tone remained childlike and stroppy.

'Where?'

'On the street! On the street, for goodness' sake.' Lexi sounded furious. Zander knew her priority was to protect them in whatever way she could. He indulged her much of the time. He didn't really need her help any more, but he knew her well enough to know she needed to think that he did.

'He deserved it. He deserved it!' AJ was losing his temper. 'You can't tell me what to do. You don't know what it's like. These people need to suffer. They need to die!'

'OK, AJ. We are all in agreement. Did you cover your tracks?' said Zander, realizing this could get out of hand if he didn't step in.

'Barely,' said Lexi. 'You can't just go off on your own and attack people without us knowing. Take some

47

responsibility, AJ. This is not about only you. We're in this together.'

'I wore my gloves and I wasn't seen,' shouted AJ again.

Zander knew he had to take control before the argument escalated. He focused on his fingers holding the mug of water. When they curled more tightly around the handle he stood. 'If you say it was fine, I believe you, AJ, but to satisfy Lexi I'll take a look at the street.' Before she could protest, he said, 'I know you think that's risky, Lexi, but better safe than sorry – isn't that what you say?'

Finding a new target would have to wait.

11

Bloom stepped out of New Scotland Yard and looked across the river to where the London Eye slowly rotated. Each capsule on the big wheel could accommodate twenty-five people, providing them with an impressive bird's-eye view of the whole city. On the near side of the river stood the Battle of Britain monument, a striking twenty-five-metre strip of bronze commemorating the pilots who had died during World War Two. Beyond that a wide pavement led to the wall that ran along the River Thames, and on the wall sat Seraphine. She held a hand up to Bloom in a friendly wave.

'How did you know I was here?' said Bloom on reaching her.

'Call it a hunch. I just spoke to one of my police contacts. London has a serial killer. I hope you told them I have no interest in those who kill for pleasure, be they psychopaths or not.'

'Oh, I did. People don't always listen to me though, as demonstrated by the dismissal of your court case.'

'Don't take that as a criticism of your efforts, Augusta. I'm highly impressed by your work but *my* work relies on my freedom. I couldn't afford to be locked up at Her Majesty's pleasure.'

'I thought you were in between careers.'

Seraphine raised her eyes to the sky. 'I had much grander plans for you than rooting around in the psyches of sick killers, you know.'

'Yes, but this work saves lives.'

'A drop in the ocean is never going to quell the waves.' Seraphine rubbed her hands together. 'But I do need a favour.'

'I'm busy.'

'Don't be like that, Augusta. You've needed my help on numerous occasions and I always come running. So it is only fair that you return the favour this time.'

'As far as I can tell, any time you've agreed to help there's been something in it for you.'

'But still. You owe me. Not least for the escape of Gerald Porter.'

Bloom could not argue with this point. When the Foreign Secretary had conned Bloom into helping him escape the custody of DCI Mirza, he had made sure his ex-employer Seraphine was aware of the fact, while simultaneously threatening to take her mysterious empire from her.

'What's the nature of this favour? And that's not me saying yes. I don't want myself or Marcus implicated in any of your crimes even if you do have the power to twist justice in your favour.'

'Can I trust you, Augusta? I always thought I could. I always thought you were the one person I could be totally honest with, but much has changed in recent years.'

'Is this about Porter?'

Seraphine let the question hang in the air for a moment.

'You always said my kind liked to play chess with people's lives. Well, imagine the world is a chessboard. You normals can be the white pieces; I know you like to think of yourselves as the good guys, and my people are the black. I can move my pawns to wherever they may be needed, dispatch my knights, galvanize my bishops and place my very own kings and queens.'

Bloom's heart sank. This kind of wide-scale manipulation was her worst fear about Seraphine's motivation for recruiting fellow high-functioning psychopaths.

'Why?'

'To win, of course. Oh, don't look at me like that, Augusta. Mine and Porter's definition of winning could not be more different. I need to stop him and I need you to help me.'

'How?'

'Porter has recruited twenty per cent of my key people. I can't let him get any closer to fifty per cent.'

'How many people do you have in your club exactly?'

'Enough.'

Bloom folded her arms.

'All you need to know is that for every member invited to join we get access to their organization. Many people work for us without ever knowing why they are doing what they are doing or for whom. It's surprising how rarely you normals question your bosses.'

'Because it's professional and social suicide in many cases.'

Seraphine looked to consider this for a moment as if the idea had never occurred to her; then she said, 'I'm fairly sure someone on the inside is helping Porter, feeding him information on my activities. I need you to find out who.'

'Oh come on, you have the means to do that yourself, I have no doubt. Why do you really need me?'

'I recruited some of the smartest manipulators and fraudsters in the world. I'm not arrogant enough to think one of them doesn't know me well enough to be able to hide this from me.' Seraphine flashed Bloom an almost apologetic smile. 'Truth be told, Augusta, you are the only person in the world I can trust right now.'

'That's a pretty damning indictment on your organization, isn't it?'

Seraphine shrugged. 'Once I've cleared the dead wood we will be back on track. So will you help me?'

'No. You need me here proving you're not part of these murders. The DCI is not going to give up on her theory that you're behind this and you hardly gave them a strong reason not to suspect you in there.'

'I can have DCI Mirza moved. I can scupper their investigations.'

'And let more people die as a serial killer runs free?'

'And why would you think that matters to me?'

Bloom placed her hands on the top of the wall next to where Seraphine sat and watched the London Eye's almost imperceptible motion. 'I try to think the best of you,' she finally said, echoing Jameson's criticism from their conversation in the pub.

'Is there some advantage to that? Would it not be more prudent to expect the worst?'

'Prepare for the worst and hope for the best. Isn't that what they say?' Bloom met Seraphine's gaze and for a beat the two women held eye contact.

'I have never needed anyone. You understand that, don't you, Augusta? But if I want someone to do something for me, I won't give up until they do it. Especially if they are the right person for the job.'

'And you know that no matter how much you might want me to do your bidding, I am not and never will be one of your puppets. I think I've made that perfectly clear.'

Seraphine slid off the wall. 'So the answer is no. You won't repay the debt you owe me.'

'Not in this way, no.'

'An interesting decision.'

Bloom watched Seraphine walk away. It had been a surreal conversation. Less tense than their recent interactions, closer to their old counselling sessions in tone. The change in behaviour concerned her. Either Seraphine was genuinely afraid of Gerald Porter – which was entirely feasible; he was a powerful enemy – or she was playing some new game: one Bloom was in danger of becoming a pawn in. The idea again brought the image of a chessboard to mind. Seraphine and her people were attempting to affect world politics but to what end? Psychopaths were all about personal gain. What would they be prepared to do to secure their own power or financial success? The options made for a depressing list: with people positioned all over the world they could incite wars, support terrorist acts, restrict resources, disrupt societies or, worse still, increase poverty, prejudice and death rates.

She was right to refuse to help these people. She could not bear to be a part of such monstrous ideologies. So why did she feel guilty for saying no? And why did she have the nagging feeling she was missing something?

12

Zander walked towards Hans Crescent at the side of Harrods, taking in the grandeur of the world-famous store's marble fascia and green canopies. An IRA bomb had exploded outside door 5 of Harrods in 1983 and Zander slowed to read the names of the three officers and three civilians listed on the memorial plaques. He remembered learning in school that the IRA were evil terrorists who did not hesitate to kill innocent people. Only later, when he was an adult, did he discover that there was more to it than simply baddies versus goodies. The Irish Republican Army had a clear mission and good reasons for resorting to violence. The upper-class establishment of the defunct British Empire would not listen and they would not leave Northern Ireland. Zander had no problem with people taking back power under such circumstances. So what if people lost their lives in the pursuit of a good cause; losing your life quickly was not the worst thing that could happen to a person. Plus it had all been so civilized compared to the terrorism of today where passenger planes were flown into buildings jam-packed with people. In those days the IRA would call first and tell the authorities where they had left their bombs, giving police a fighting chance of saving lives.

As he took a right turn on to Basil Street he wondered

if it would be fun to do something similar. They could tip off the police as to the location of their next attack, see if the plods could stop it. The tip would have to be cryptic, or late enough to ensure the police had no chance of success. Zander liked the idea of sending panic through a whole shift of officers but he knew Lexi would never allow it. And he knew better than to challenge Lexi.

He took a left turn and walked to Hans Place Garden where AJ had beaten their latest target to death.

He slowed as he came to the wrought-iron gate into the park. The gate was shut and on the other side, through the trees, he could see a small white tent had been erected over the section of the path. Zander turned his head to look at the surrounding houses. They were a good distance away and the tent was under the cover of the thick trees which grew around the circumference of the small oval garden. Unless someone had been standing at the fence, it was unlikely they'd have seen anything.

Lexi was furious with AJ for taking what she saw as unnecessary risks. It had been the same when AJ had attacked the guy outside the country club. But that had all turned out fine and Zander felt sure this would too. AJ might be young and reckless but when it came to their work, he followed the same drill as Zander. First they identified a target, then they learned their habits before deciding on the best place to make them pay. AJ liked to search online. He was younger than Zander and more attuned to the digital landscape. Zander preferred a more personal touch. He knew where the type of people who deserved to be punished spent their time and he enjoyed infiltrating their worlds. He didn't even have to look for the targets, they usually volunteered themselves with a sly put-down here, a smug aside there or a flashy show of wealth. They might as well be holding their hands up high in the air like an over-eager schoolgirl and shouting, *Me, me, please pick me.*

Lexi was obsessed with the clean-up and making sure they were invisible. Attacking a target outside stressed her out as it reduced the time available for covering their tracks. Ever since that first time, she had drilled into them the importance of gloves. But what she really liked to do was follow them in and clean the scene herself and AJ was making that hard for her.

Zander watched a man leave his home and make his way along the pavement.

'Any idea why the park is shut?' Zander said when the suited man passed by.

The man frowned. People in London rarely chatted on the street. 'Someone was attacked. It's off limits for a while.'

'Must be serious if they've shut the park.'

The man was past Zander now and walking in that no-nonsense city manner that said, *Get out of my way.*

'Anyone see what happened?'

The man did not respond. Their interaction was done. Zander placed his hands in his trouser pockets and walked slowly around the oval road. Someone else might come out of their house and be more talkative. He knew

Lexi would say he was being stupid for spending too long here but he didn't care. The walk would give him time to think. He needed to make the next target something big. He'd enjoyed his time in the St Pancras Hotel but it hadn't moved them forward. People needed to know the truth about the kind of well-dressed man you see in adverts driving up a winding road in his fancy car, or doing business and greeting friends while wearing his fancy watch. Such people were admired and it was Zander's job to open everyone's eyes and show them just how selfish and smug their idols really were.

13

Nadia Mirza sat at her desk with her eyes closed. She was used to sleepless nights, not least because she had a two-year-old son at home, but lately they were taking their toll more than usual. She didn't know what to make of this growing set of murders. When the struck matches had linked the Saudi prince's death at the St Pancras Hotel with the stabbing of a pharmaceuticals CEO, her gut had told her this was her chance to win everything back. The murder of two such high-profile people was bound to be linked to organized crime or terrorism and her new boss, ACC Barker, had agreed. When she'd told him Seraphine Walker had been at the St Pancras Hotel the very night the sheikh had been killed, he'd asked her to review the woman's file as he'd thought she'd been planning something big. And the Psychopath Game file had not disappointed. She'd learned that Seraphine Walker wasn't looking for any old psychopath, she was hunting for the most intelligent, the most cunning and the most calm. In short, the high-functioning kind capable of hiding their true nature from everyone around them. Mirza had had no idea psychopathy was so prevalent in the general population; that there were lawyers, surgeons and business leaders out there lacking empathy and conscience.

ACC Barker had told her Seraphine Walker had evaded justice on a technicality, something he felt sure was down to Walker having recruited psychopaths within the UK justice system.

And still the question remained: what was the woman planning? If it was organized crime, that meant anything from cybercrime to trafficking drugs, firearms or even humans. If it was terrorism, they could be attempting to influence international governments or threaten national security. The murders of two such wealthy individuals must provide a clue. Perhaps Seraphine Walker was involved in market abuse, insider dealing, bribery or corruption, and these men had either been used or they presented an obstacle. Maybe they were potential whistle-blowers.

Nadia had felt excited for the first time since the scandal.

She knew people had been envious when she had been assigned the prestigious MOD secondment only months after returning from maternity leave, but she had always been a fast-tracker and her bosses knew that. The scandal with Porter's escape had been embarrassing and bruising. People had felt they had been proven right: she should never have been given that job.

But now her chance to redeem herself was looking less and less likely. If this was a serial killer, chances were she'd be in for a rocky ride. If the newspapers caught wind of it, she'd be harassed and pressurized and if, God forbid, she couldn't find him, her reputation would be destroyed.

The knock on her door jolted Mirza's eyes open.

'Sorry to disturb you, ma'am,' said Fleur Morgan. 'I need to tell you something.'

Mirza braced herself for the latest round of petty team complaints she had become accustomed to as a line manager; the 'he said, she said' stuff that had no place in a professional workplace and yet was ever-present.

'Go on, Fleur, but make it quick. It's a busy day.' The sooner she could get her office back to herself, the sooner she could rest her eyes again.

But seconds later Nadia Mirza was wide awake. What Morgan had told her changed everything. This just might be the break she needed.

14

Bloom arrived at the office to find the Matchbox Murder case files already in her inbox. After checking her other emails she started with the first victim, Philip Berringer, intending to work through them in order so any escalation would be apparent.

On finishing this first file she stood and wiped clean the whiteboard. Then with a blue marker pen she wrote each victim's name across the top, and under that their age, occupation and marital status. She filled in the details she had learned about Philip beneath that. In green she wrote notes on his character, such as the fact that he was described as happy and stress-free prior to his apparent suicide. She knew family and friends were not always privy to a loved one's inner thoughts but given this was now a suspected murder she felt it worth noting. Under that she recorded in black how and where he had been murdered, the kind of matchbox (Bulls Eye Matches) that had been left and the fact that only one struck match had been found. The different colours would hopefully help her to easily see similar kinds of information and register any patterns.

Moving on to Simon Middleton-Moore's case file, the first photograph she opened gave her the familiar feeling of dissonance she had become accustomed to when she had worked with the police. Simon's flat looked neat and organized. The contemporary art on the wall was vibrant and colourful and the grey corner sofa looked like the perfect place to curl up and relax. But in the midst of all the ordinary was the jarring sight of Simon's dead body. The only sign that he was not sleeping was the large stain on his trousers where his bladder had emptied, probably as he had died. A separate photograph showed the close-up image of a Bird's Eye Diamond matchbox on the coffee table with four struck matches lined neatly on top.

Bloom wrote on the whiteboard that, according to the report, there were no signs of a struggle or forced entry. Friends had been over that evening but according to their statements they had left him alive and alone around midnight. They said no drugs had been taken during their visit but they had been drinking vodka cocktails. Bloom looked at the photographs of Simon's flat again. The kitchen was clean, with no glasses, bottles or signs of food anywhere to be seen. Had this young man really tidied up so meticulously after his friends left and before his killer arrived to fill him with a lethal dose of drugs? And why had the concierge not reported another visitor?

She wrote on the bottom of the whiteboard in red pen: 'How did the killer get in?' Both Philip and Simon lived in buildings with a reception so whoever entered should in theory have been recorded doing so.

There was little detail in the file of the third victim Jeremy Tomlinson. The wealthy bachelor was pictured fully clothed and face up in his large kidney-shaped swimming pool. Bloom flicked through the notes. No one reported being with him on the night he died and he wasn't found until the pool cleaner arrived two days later. He had been three times over the drink-driving limit so case closed. She studied the pictures until she found one of a gold matchbox. It sat on the work surface in a kitchen that looked so immaculate she suspected it was never used. On top were six struck matches lined up side by side. Rowe had added a note to say that under the matches the box had an embossed image of an eye on it.

The matchboxes had clearly been left on purpose to show police that these deaths were linked. Was this a killer showing off? Or did it speak to the motivation or manifesto of an individual or group?

Keith Runnesguard's file was a lot more disturbing. He lay face up by the side of his Range Rover in the car park of his country club. His face was frozen in an expression of shock, making it clear that this was a man who had seen the horror of what was happening to him in those final moments. But despite his shocked expression, Keith's eyes were closed. That jarred somehow. As far as she was aware, eyes often relaxed open at the moment of passing, so had someone shut them? She read through the police report. He had not been found until over an hour after his death. Rigor mortis would have set in by then. She checked back to Simon's file and noted that his eyes had also been closed, as had Jeremy's and Nawaf's.

She stood back and assessed the board.

To Bloom, the attack on Keith felt similar to the latest one on George Shulman; both were more brutal than the ones on Sheikh Nawaf, Philip Berringer, Simon Middleton-Moore and Jeremy Tomlinson. Was there something about Keith and George that made the killer more angry?

And then there was the brazen way Nawaf's killer had moved into his victim's hotel suite. Was this the killer becoming bolder and more confident in living out his fantasies? And if so, what were those? Being rich, powerful, admired?

'Find anything interesting?' Jameson carried his cycle helmet and the cleats on his shoes clicked against the wooden floor as he came to stand alongside her. He smelled salty and Bloom could feel the heat from his body.

'We have another victim. Beaten to death last night in Knightsbridge.'

Jameson whistled. 'Is that what convinced Mirza to let you in on it?' he said, looking up at the whiteboard.

'I think ACC Steve Barker might have had a hand in it. Rowe told me Barker was there when he suggested they bring me in as an advisor.'

'And Steve was never going to block that. He's a big fan of yours.'

Bloom ignored Jameson's attempt to tease her.

'Go on then – are you going to tell me what you've found? I can tell you've spotted something.'

Bloom took a moment to gather her thoughts. 'What strikes me is these people were killed in a manner that points to a lavish lifestyle. George was beaten outside his

Knightsbridge mansion, Nawaf was strangled in his supercar and Keith was stabbed outside his exclusive country club. Then we have Jeremy who drowned in his private pool, Philip who was pushed off the top of a fancy apartment block, and Simon who was administered a drug overdose in his luxury apartment.'

'You suspect this is driven by a hatred of the rich?'

'Or envy. After all, the killer tried on Nawaf's lifestyle for a weekend. I think, coupled with the image of an eye at every scene, that strengthens the idea we have a single killer who has some issue with the victims. I suspect he is trying to punish or expose them in some way, but we need more victim insight. What kind of people were they and how might they have come to the killer's attention? What might they have done to anger him?' There had been little Bloom could write up in the green ink. The background on the victims said little of who they had been as people, what their loved ones might have loved about them or their enemies might have hated. Instead, the information gathered related to last-known movements, close associates, potential enemies or recent arguments. 'The problem is we're under strict instructions from DCI Mirza to conduct a desk analysis only. She wants to stay in control of any witness interviews.'

'Makes sense. She won't trust us after we aided and abetted Porter's escape.'

'I did that. Not you. But thanks for the support.'

'Hey, we're a team, aren't we?' He walked to his chair

and sat to remove his shoes. 'Let me take a look through the case files, then I'll run a few errands.'

'Errands?'

'You're the one with the expertise needed to do the desk analysis. My skills lie elsewhere so I say we stick to our strengths.'

Bloom smiled at him. This was what she enjoyed about their work as independent investigators. They had the autonomy to do things their own way.

Jameson took a quick shower and read through the case files while eating a banana followed by a granola bar. Forty minutes later he was ready to head out.

'Just to confirm: are we also considering Seraphine is behind this?' he said as he put on his jacket.

'I have no doubt DCI Mirza will be pursuing that line of inquiry but I'm concerned that this is something more personal, especially given the escalating violence. I think someone out there is angry and they're getting angrier.'

15

Jameson loitered on the pavement outside the St Pancras Hotel with a folded map of London he was pretending to study. When it came to witnesses, the sooner you could speak to them after the incident the better, so it made sense to start with Oscar Dunne, the bellboy who had quite literally uncovered Sheikh Nawaf's body.

Oscar's social media pages had been easy to view. There were multiple pictures on Instagram and Facebook so Jameson knew what the young man looked like and he also knew Oscar aspired to a career in the theatre. That was something he could use.

His phone rang and he saw it was his sister. 'Hey, Claire,' he said, figuring he could kill some time talking to her while waiting to spot Oscar.

'Hi, Uncle Marcus.'

'All right, Soph, everything OK?' he said to his eldest niece. He would never admit it but Sophie was his favourite. He loved her younger sister Holly, obviously, but Sophie had held a special place in his heart since she'd first grabbed his finger as a baby.

'Mum says stop ignoring her messages and come over for tea.'

Jameson laughed. It was typical of his sister to use Sophie to badger him. 'I will, Soph, I've just been busy.

Tell your mum some of us work full time.' Jameson's sister was a teacher so he knew that would wind her up. He was forever ribbing her about all those holidays.

As Sophie began to tell him about a new recipe she'd learned to cook at school that she wanted him to try, Jameson saw Oscar Dunne walk down the long forecourt of the hotel with his parka coat covering his uniform.

'That sounds ace, Soph. Count me in. I'll have to go now, honey. Tell Mum I'll text her later,' he said before hanging up and following Oscar over the pedestrian crossing and into Pret A Manger.

This case felt exciting in a way most of their others had not. There was something about the immediacy of an ongoing police investigation, coupled with the chase, that really had the juices flowing. It felt more positive, more productive.

An hour later Jameson headed over to Hans Place Garden where he had read George Shulman's house overlooked the park in which he had been attacked. Oscar the bellboy had been a breeze: a bit of banter about how working at a hotel was hardly following your dreams followed by referencing the recent body in a supercar mystery and the budding playwright couldn't resist the chance to gossip. Jameson mentally filed away the pertinent points to share with Bloom as he walked. He also planned to take a walk by Simon Middleton-Moore's apartment building later as it was not too far from where George had been attacked. He knew it was a long shot, as Simon had died over a year ago, but you never knew what helpful details might come to light.

But first he had to pull off the trickiest investigation of the lot. Wealthy families like the Shulmans were traditionally private and on the back of George's murder they would no doubt retreat even further from public life, maybe even escaping to some holiday home in the sun. There was a short window of time to try and speak to them leading up to the funeral.

He'd considered the options for how to introduce himself as he'd finished his coffee in Pret. He needed something that would avoid alarming George's widow – so a journalist was out of the question – and that also wouldn't alert the police, and specifically DCI Mirza, to his activities. He knew from his life in MI6 that people in any given social class responded best to those they saw as similar and so he settled on a work colleague, someone new enough to the company to not have met Mrs Shulman yet. He had called George's employer and had a nice chat with Lucy the receptionist. He told her someone from the company had called him the week before but he couldn't recall the guy's name, all he remembered was the caller was new to the business. Lucy was clearly very good at her job. She immediately told him only two people had joined in the past six months: another receptionist and a junior account manager, Seb Baxter. Jameson asked to be put through to the latter. Once young Mr Baxter answered Jameson changed tack; without any introduction he said he was organizing George's funeral and wanting to know who from the company should attend. Had Baxter worked closely with George? Did he know the family? The answer to both questions was no and the conversation was done before Seb Baxter had a chance to think anything was amiss.

Finally he had called into Harrods on his way past and bought a small hamper containing a bottle of claret, English breakfast tea and indulgent caramel and sea salt biscuits. It had set him back a bit but all in a good cause. That's what expenses were for.

The Shulman residence was a grand five-storey townhouse with a gated doorway. Jameson rang the bell and waited. The park behind had a small police A-board by the gate requesting that any witnesses to an incident that had occurred on Monday evening contact them urgently. After a few moments Jameson heard a click and a young female voice said, 'Yes?'

'Hi, hello, sorry to bother you. I'm Seb Baxter; I worked with Mr Shulman. I just wanted to drop something off for the family to say how sorry I am.'

There was a pause and then a buzz before the door behind the gate opened and a teenage girl stepped out. Her eyes were red and puffy and she was dressed in pink pyjamas. 'You knew Daddy,' she said, her accent the plummy pronunciation of good breeding and probably an expensive private school.

Jameson refined his own accent. Sebastian Baxter was likely of a similar vein. 'By reputation mainly. I'm new

71

but I heard great things and . . .' He paused, then followed an instinct: 'I lost my dad a few years ago.'

'I'm sorry,' said George Shulman's daughter, no doubt out of politeness more than sympathy.

'Is your mother here? Maybe so I can—' He held up the hamper.

'She's my stepmum and she's not seeing anyone. I can take it. Thank you.' The girl opened the gate.

Jameson kept hold of the hamper, knowing as soon as it changed hands that door was closing.

'How are you doing? The first week is awful, I remember. The shock of it. Dad's was a road accident. I know it doesn't feel like it now but it does get easier, I promise.' He smiled at the girl. She could be no older than fifteen.

'Not for me.' She shook her head. 'We had a row on Sunday. I told him . . . the last thing I told him . . .' The girl began to sob and Jameson instinctively placed the hamper on the floor to put an arm around her shoulder. She leaned into him and continued to cry until he felt his shirt getting damp.

For the next twenty minutes the two of them sat on the front steps of her house as she confessed her regrets to a stranger. She told him how she'd accused her dad of never being there, even presenting him with a diary of all the important things he'd missed in the past year: her birthday party, her school piano recital, her parents' evening. The last words she'd said to him were that she hated him because he obviously didn't love her enough. She knew this wasn't true, of course. She was an angry, hormonal teenager who ordinarily would have had a lifetime to apologize, to make it right and to some day chuckle with her old man about her teenage temper tantrums. But the killer had taken all that away. Jameson's blood boiled. They had to get this guy, and fast.

16

Lexi sat on the yoga mat and folded her long legs into a lotus position with each foot resting on top of the opposite knee. Her new crimson leggings felt silky against her skin and matched her painted toenails. She loved how her body felt when she did her yoga: so flexible and elegant.

Her nightmares were back. Only last night she had dreamt of her mother hiding in the corner, her head between her knees and her voice loud as she tried to drown out the sounds. Sounds that would bring any other mother running to help. For some reason her mother always chose to sing Beatles songs even though she knew barely any of the real lyrics. It irritated Lexi that such light-hearted melodies could be used to drown out such horror. In the dreams Lexi would try to reach her mother, to pull her arms apart and drag her to her feet. To make her protect her child as a mother should.

After a few moments she slid her arms forward across the mat, letting her legs uncurl and flatten out behind her until she had seamlessly moved into the cobra position with arms braced directly below her shoulders and her head raised high. The combination of precise movements and regular breathing calmed her as nothing else could. Zander and AJ's new hobby was taking its toll.

There had been a time when she'd wished she could be free of them but their lives were too entwined now. They were family because no one else understood what they had each survived and why they needed someone to pay for their trauma.

Lexi moved into an upward dog and then a downward dog as she tried to pinpoint the reason the nightmares were back. She couldn't do what Zander and AJ did. It wasn't in her nature, but that didn't mean she ever tried to stop them. She simply took care of the details, educated them on how careful they needed to be and, most importantly, cleaned up after them. She was their insurance policy, their guardian angel. Even with AJ's latest attack he'd asked for her help. She'd been lucky that it was dark and no one had disturbed her as she made sure everything was tidied up and nothing incriminating had been left behind. But something told her they didn't care enough any more. She suspected that Zander wanted people to know what they were doing. She had fought hard against the matchboxes. He had left the first on a whim and the second as an in-joke but it wasn't long before he changed his story. There was no point doing what they did if their activities didn't teach the world something, he'd said. AJ was an entirely different matter. His rage was on another level and she feared it wouldn't be long before he was out of control.

How would she protect them then?

And what if Sandy found out . . . well, that did not bear thinking about.

17

'How's it going?' Jameson walked back into the office and found Bloom at her desk surrounded by printed documents. She glanced up, her eyes lingering for a moment on his hair. He could see she looked tired. He should encourage her to take a holiday after this. She'd had a rough year since Seraphine had come back into her life.

'Were your errands a success?'

'Possibly. Oscar Dunne, the bellboy at the St Pancras Hotel, told me Nawaf was offering a drive of his supercar to anyone willing to pay for the privilege on the Friday night. He'd asked Oscar to hold on to the cash for him but keep it quiet. When Nawaf never came to collect, Oscar says he sealed it in an envelope and pushed it under his room door.'

'How much are we talking?'

'Thousands. The guy was asking for bids upwards of five hundred pounds a time and took five or six people out.'

'So the last person to take him up on that could be our killer?'

'They drive away. The killer pulls over in some dark alley and strangles him. All he has to do then is drive back in the dead of night and put the cover on.'

'Where did he get the cover from?'

'That we don't know. It could be a good lead for Mirza though — if it didn't come from the rental company, someone might have bought it that day.'

'I'll flag that to the DCI. Anything else?'

'You mentioned he'd arrived on Friday with a tall blonde. Oscar's suspicion from the way the woman was dressed was that she was a "lady of the night" – his term, not mine. An assumption strengthened by the fact that a second woman paid a visit to Nawaf's room on a different night.'

'But Nawaf would already have been dead, according to DCI Mirza.'

'So was our guy simply copying how Nawaf lived or are these women involved in some way?'

'Nawaf was not averse to flaunting his wealth if this offer to drive his fancy car is anything to go by. Is that the case for all the victims, I wonder? Have they been targeted because they behave in a similar way?'

'I managed to speak to one of the neighbours in Simon's fancy apartment block – he was the guy who died of an overdose – and she said she'd seen him the morning before his death, and that he was upbeat and looking forward to something exciting happening later that day.'

'You think there's something significant about that?'

'Could have been a date with someone who turned out to be his killer.'

Bloom nodded.

'I've asked her to pass my number on to the family so hopefully I can get more information from them.'

'And who do they believe they're calling?'

Jameson switched to an Australian accent and loaded his voice with emotion. 'Jasper. I'm in bits about Simon. I flew in yesterday from Oz. I want to pay my respects and I need to get my dad's watch back from Simon's apartment.'

'I wondered what was going on with your hair.'

Jameson immediately ruffled the slicked-over style to return to his messy curls. 'I also discovered Philip Berringer's building has an apartment for sale so I'm booked to view that tomorrow morning, and I'm speaking to the manager of Keith's country club later in the week about an article I'm writing on the Top Ten Clubs for the city's millionaires.'

'You're enjoying yourself, aren't you?'

'Not entirely.' Jameson sat and rubbed his eyes. 'I spoke to George Shulman's daughter. She's in a state, poor kid.'

'That must have been a tough conversation.'

Jameson acknowledged the observation with a shrug. 'And her dad wasn't out partying or doing drugs like Nawaf and Simon. It sounds like he was a workaholic family man rather than a bachelor playboy.'

'That's interesting.' Bloom walked to the whiteboard. 'There's a definite distinction between the stabbing of Keith and the beating of George compared to how the others died. Not only are they the only ones that occurred outside, they are considerably more violent. And, like George, Keith was married with children whereas Nawaf, Simon, Jeremy and Philip were all bachelors.'

'What are you thinking?'

'At first, I thought it was something to do with Keith and George, that the violence they faced was because they'd angered the killer more, but now I'm thinking it might be something more fundamental. Maybe Keith and George were killed by someone different altogether.'

'So Mirza was right about this being some kind of competition?'

'Possibly. But that's rare. I've been doing some research and although there's been a couple of cases where killers were reported to have competed, when you look closer that's not really what's going on.' She checked the notes she had written on her pad. 'There was the case of Mark Goudeau and Dale Hausner who killed nine and six people respectively over a fifteen-month period from 2005 to 2007 in the US in an apparent attempt to beat each other's body count. But in truth there was no overt competition or communication between the men. Only the reports in the press acted to spur each killer on to beat the competition.'

'What about the likes of Ian Brady and Myra Hindley, or Fred and Rosemary West?'

'Psychologically that's a different thing entirely. Those couples acted to validate and encourage each other, and they mostly killed together.'

'Could that be happening here?'

'I don't know. I think I need to speak to Mirza. I only hope she doesn't see it as further evidence of her own conviction. Whoever's doing this wants the police to know the deaths are all connected, otherwise they wouldn't be leaving these matches or references to eyes. That worries me. It means they want to be noticed and if they think the police are oblivious to their message . . .'

'They'll up the ante,' Jameson said, finishing her thought.

Shareen Dubeck climbed into the back of her driver's car the same way she did every night after work. It was a perk of her high-powered City job. One that she now took entirely for granted. In the early days she had felt unworthy, embarrassed even at having the likes of Lee drive her around the city, but she had soon become accustomed to the convenience of it. So much so she paid little attention to the man himself or the exact make and model of the car. He was there – same place, same time – every morning and every night. What was there to pay attention to?

After responding to a few final emails on her phone, she sent a list of priorities to her PA for the following day and then sat back to have a minute of relaxation before arriving home hopefully in time to call the kids at their dad's house and say goodnight.

'You know this is technically a workspace so you can't smoke in here, Lee,' she said, seeing that he had a box of matches lying on the armrest between the two front seats.

After a few moments he met her gaze in the rear-view mirror.

'I brought them for you,' he said.

That was when Shareen finally noticed the differences. Not her usual car. Not her usual route home. Not Lee.

Tyler Rowe felt anxious as he walked to the office. He had sent the Matchbox Murder case files to Dr Bloom after their meeting yesterday morning but heard nothing back. And now DCI Mirza had called an early-morning briefing, which meant something significant had happened, or Dr Bloom had found something he'd missed. When he joined the rest of the team, he noted Dr Bloom wasn't here yet. Hopefully he'd get a chance to sound her out before Mirza called on him. He didn't want to get something wrong. Lives literally depended on it and he had never had such an awful responsibility resting on his shoulders.

As the DCI entered, Rowe noted that the contents of the whiteboard had changed. The list of victims had been joined by a photograph of Seraphine Walker.

'Morning, all.'

'Ma'am,' the group chorused.

'I've spoken with the superintendent and agreed we should change the scope of our investigation because I received some rather disappointing news about Dr Bloom yesterday.'

Rowe sat up in his chair.

'I have to be honest with you all, guys. I've had deal-ings with her before in which I suspect she assisted a high-profile suspect to escape custody.'

This was the history Bloom had alluded to between her and the DCI, the reason Mirza had resisted bringing Bloom in. The scandal was well known, already police legend: Mirza had messed up big time and let someone important escape. Everyone knew it was Gerald Porter, the former Foreign Secretary, but it had never been officially confirmed.

'Fleur, can you tell the team what you saw after Dr Bloom met with Tyler and me yesterday morning?'

'She was talking to Seraphine Walker outside of this building.'

'And how did you describe what you saw to me, Fleur?'

'They looked intimate. They were deep in discussion, heads together.'

The DCI pointed to the new photograph of Seraphine on the board. 'I think we have to consider that Dr Bloom might be trying to steer our investigation away from her friend. I've been working it through all night and not only did she actively try to stop us from pursuing Walker, saying murder was not her style, she then came up with the idea of a serial killer being responsible. And then we find all these other victims. Coincidence? I think not.'

Rowe thought about speaking up and saying he had been the first to suggest a serial killer but something told him this was not the time to challenge the boss.

'Wasn't she key to the investigation into Walker's Psychopath Game?' said DS Peters.

'Indeed. She worked closely with ACC Barker, which is why I spoke to him and the super last night. I think we have to consider that Dr Bloom might have been compromised.

It may not be that she is working with Seraphine Walker but that doesn't mean she isn't being used.'

There was silence in the room.

Rowe tried to stop his leg from shaking. *Shit, shit.* He had invited her in, insisted she could help them.

'I want us to revert our efforts to investigating how Seraphine Walker and her people might be involved. We need to stop focusing on murders in the gutter and look up to see what someone might have gained. I do agree with Dr Bloom on one point: I don't think Walker would kill for kicks. I think her crimes are more highbrow. White-collar crime is a lucrative market. All our victims are from the world of the rich and powerful. So I want to know: were they killed to cover up something they had done for Walker, or to convince others to do her bidding? Or do their deaths give some advantage to her business? Are they the victims of organized crime?'

Rowe watched the team all making notes. 'What about the matches?' he said finally. His voice sounded pathetic even to him.

'I think they are left intentionally to make us think what Seraphine Walker wants us to think – that some crazed individual is doing this. Whether Walker is testing people or tasking them, I don't think it's beyond imagination that she might coach them to leave clues at the scene intended to throw us off the scent. Inviting Bloom on to the team played right into her hands. I don't know if you're aware but Dr Bloom counselled Seraphine Walker when she was a teenager. This is why Bloom was able to see the truth of the Psychopath Game. But here's what I'm thinking: that insight goes both ways. Walker knows Dr Bloom too. And that means she knows how to play her.' On seeing Rowe's frown, DCI Mirza moved closer to him. 'This is not your fault, Tyler. It was my call.'

'Do we need to investigate Walker's activities in general then, her fellow psychopaths and their activities?' said Fleur Morgan. 'Because that's a big job and I don't know if we're resourced for that.'

The DCI was shaking her head. 'The NCA and MI5 have a team tasked with that. We can feed in anything we find to them. I simply want us to uncover what links our victims have to Walker. We have a strong new lead. The owner of a wealth management company has contacted us to say that Keith and George were both clients of theirs. This could be a critical find. Does Seraphine Walker have any links to this business? There has to be a reason why this company connects two of our victims.'

Mirza ended the meeting by saying she intended to keep Dr Bloom on the team as she didn't want to raise any suspicion with Walker. They would continue working with Bloom on the serial killer theory until they were able to prove otherwise. They were to treat her as normal but avoid sharing anything sensitive.

Tyler Rowe remained in the briefing room after everyone had left. He was not sure what to do next. He didn't disagree entirely with the DCI's suspicion that Seraphine Walker might be playing them, but he also didn't want them to forget that this could be a crazed killer on the hunt for new prey.

20

Bloom entered the office space assigned to Mirza's newly created investigation team at 10 a.m., as agreed. On the wall they had a similar whiteboard display to the one Bloom had created, only this one displayed photographs of the victims and the matchboxes found. There was also a picture of Seraphine. Down one side was written each victim's name in order of their death along with the number of matches found with their body, similar to how Rowe had written it out in his notebook, but this time vertical lines had been used to represent each match left.

Philip Berringer	I
Simon Middleton-Moore	IIII
Jeremy Tomlinson	IIII II
Keith Runnesguard	II
Sheikh Nawaf al Saud	IIII IIII
George Shulman	III

Mirza introduced Bloom to the team as a consultant assisting Tyler Rowe and the NCA. It was a clear positioning tactic to reduce Bloom's influence. Essentially, she'd been billed as an assistant to the assistant. She didn't take it personally; such politics were familiar and she never complained about being in the background. It was the best place to observe things from.

She sat back and listened as the team talked through their investigations so far. They had discovered some of the same things Jameson had, which was reassuring. They knew multiple guests at the charity event had paid to drive Nawaf's car and were looking into who the last person was. They had not managed to find the woman who had visited Nawaf's killer on the Sunday night but they had established that the car cover was standard issue. Bloom wondered if the killer had known that before their attack because that would indicate research and planning rather than spontaneously taking advantage of an opportunity. They were also trying to trace the origin of the matchboxes which they had pictured on the wall. They all looked to be fairly vintage, so the theory was the killer could be acquiring them from the same seller. Finally they discussed the autopsy on George Shulman. His death had been caused by fifteen separate strikes from a metal pole of some kind around 15 mm in diameter. The pathologist also confirmed that the body had likely been posed. She had found that two of his fingers had been broken, one quite severely, but they had been straightened out by the attacker so that George's hands lay neatly on the ground.

The DCI looked at Rowe and Bloom for the first time. 'Any thoughts on that?'

Rowe looked like a rabbit in headlights. 'None of the other bodies were posed.'

'I'm not sure that's true,' said Bloom. 'I noted that

Simon, Keith, Jeremy and Nawaf's eyes were closed but my understanding is that the eyes often relax open at the point of death.'

DS Peters spoke up. 'Keith's eyes being closed always struck me as weird given the rest of his expression.' Bloom recalled that Peters had worked on Keith's stabbing originally, which is how they had spotted the matchbox link when Nawaf's body was found. 'That's another eye-related clue then?'

'Perhaps,' said Bloom. 'From looking briefly at the pictures of George's body I'm not sure the eyes were even visible any more—'

'So the straightening of the hands might be something the killer did instead,' said Mirza. 'That's a good shout. I'm not sure the pathologist had flagged the closed eyes. Can you speak to her and get an opinion?' she said to Peters, who nodded.

Something about the straightening of George's fingers and posing of his body brought to mind the neatness of Simon's post-party apartment. Bloom jotted a quick note for herself.

An officer Bloom didn't know described how a wrapped Tiffany jewellery box had been found in the pocket of George's overcoat containing a necklace inscribed with his daughter's name. Bloom recalled Jameson's conversation with the daughter and her guilt over arguing with her father. She looked up at the photographs on the board. These men had been stolen from their families. Families who would spend the rest of their lives trying to come to terms with why it had happened to them and how they could live with it. It was bad enough when people were told family members had died from an accident or illness, but to have their loved ones taken on purpose added another level of unfairness that made the families even less capable of moving on.

'If the killer didn't take the jewellery, that's another indication this is not about stealing from these men,' said Rowe, having recovered his confidence a bit. 'The killer had a chance to take not only belongings but cash from most of the scenes but he chose not to. That's probably significant. He's targeting rich men but not for their money.'

'It could be *because* of their money though,' added Bloom. 'They were all killed in a manner that pointed to extreme wealth, be it in their own private pool or swanky hire car or in the exclusive gardens outside of their London mansion. I think our killer or killers may have stalked their victims and picked out exactly where to attack them. The more I looked at the files, the more I sensed they were sending us a message.'

'Right, I'm confused,' said Mirza, taking a step towards Bloom and barely containing her irritation. 'You said killers, plural, and that *they* are sending us a message. Are you dropping the serial killer idea now? Because I thought you were sure it had legs?'

'Not dropping it, no. Expanding it,' said Bloom. 'I think the differences between the murders are the most interesting factor. Like you said, why is it that so many methods have been used? In particular, why are some of them close-contact kills such as stabbing and beating while others are more distant kills such as an overdose or pushing someone off a roof?'

'What does that tell you?'

'I think there's a good chance the person who killed Keith and George enjoyed the process of killing them. He took out his anger on them and most likely watched their last moments. But with the other victims I think the killer might have been more interested in the outcome of them dying rather than the death itself. I think there's a strong possibility you have two killers working in parallel.'

Rowe had been silently listening, the frown on his forehead increasing as Bloom presented her thoughts. After a few moments his posture changed and he spoke in an almost apologetic way. 'Look at the matches. If they're tallies of two separate killers that works,' he said, pointing at the list on the whiteboard. 'If Philip, Simon, Jeremy and Nawaf are more detached kills their numbers run in sequence, one, four, six and eight; then the two emotional kills, Keith and George, are numbered two and three.'

Bloom was pleased Rowe had spotted this as it was all the more powerful coming from the guy on the inside. But the rest of the team looked entirely disinterested, which was odd. In fact, now she thought about it, the energy in the room had been off all along.

'Of course that's bad news really,' said Bloom. 'It means you have at least five missing victims. Numbers two, three, five and seven from one killer, and one from the other. That's eleven murders in total.'

'Is that so?' said Mirza and Bloom had the familiar feeling she was missing something.

21

The following morning, Jameson followed the wide pathway between two immaculate lawns towards the entrance of Canary Wharf's newest high-rise luxury apartment building. He looked up to the external terrace on the top floor from where Philip Berringer had fallen to his death, then moved his gaze to the ground in front of him and tried not to picture Philip's smashed-up body.

He was here to view a vacant three-bed apartment. As the show home for the building, it was the last unit to be sold and the estate agent had told him they had already had twenty viewings and three full-asking-price offers. Clearly the suicide of a resident hadn't distracted buyers from the lure of the river views and central location. Jameson had replied that he was a cash buyer willing to pay more for the right place in the right location and this was the perfect location. The estate agent's tone had shifted immediately and he'd been offered a viewing the next day.

At the door he checked his reflection in the window. He'd had two obvious choices for portraying the kind of high roller who might live here: designer suit or dressed-down casual. He'd chosen to dress down. In his experience, men with real money didn't feel the need to show their wealth via their clothes. They could afford to be contrary in that way. The guy in jeans and a jumper in the Michelin-starred restaurant was most likely the richest person in the room. Accessories were a different matter of course, and so to accompany his tan chinos and casual shirt he wore a Rolex.

'Mr Jameson, welcome,' said an attractive woman in her fifties as he entered the lobby.

'Marcus, please,' he said. He had given his own name because he had no presence on social media, a consequence of his previous life, so even if she googled him she would find nothing. And an air of mystery might even add to his gravitas.

She introduced herself as Diane and led the way to the lifts. On the way up to the 21st floor she described the facilities available, from a pool and gym to a restaurant. Finally, as she opened the door to the apartment, she explained that residents automatically gained membership to the club on the 36th floor.

The space was impressively luxurious with its floor-to-ceiling windows on both walls of the corner plot revealing a breathtaking view of the London skyline. It had been decorated in black and white throughout with the kind of modern furniture that made it feel like any five-star hotel. Even the large vases of lilies looked too perfect. The table had been set for four people but Jameson expected that four people in here would feel crowded. Square footage was not what you were paying for. You were paying for location, amenities and the brag factor.

'I understand there was an accident here just after it opened. Someone fell from a balcony?'

'Oh yes. That was very sad.'

'Did he fall from his apartment? I have children. I'm not living in a death trap.'

The woman's cheeks flushed a little. 'I don't believe he fell. It was . . . on purpose.'

Jameson held her gaze, keeping his expression serious.

'Not from his apartment. From the terrace in the, erm, the, erm, members' bar.'

He walked towards the door. 'I'd like to see that.'

Diane kept her chatter light and cheery on the way up. She asked him a few times what he thought of the apartment but he held his tongue. He wanted her to feel intimidated and desperate enough to talk.

The entrance to the bar was via a keypad. Diane typed in the six-digit number and the smoked-glass door opened to reveal another black-and-white space punctuated by vases of lime-green flowers and large bowls of green apples. On the far side of the room a single resident sat reading. He glanced up as Jameson and Diane entered, saw nothing of interest and went back to his paper. Outside, the terrace was more narrow than Jameson had expected: a strip of grey, less than a metre wide, with barely enough space to fit a chair. Its glass balustrade was a little over a metre high. Jameson walked to the closed glass doors to look out.

'He climbed over that?'

'There was a full health and safety investigation. The balustrade is a safe height. It's not possible to fall over.' Diane tried to lead him away, pointing out the two private rooms attached to the bar area where you could have smaller gatherings.

'But you can climb over it. Like I say, I have children.'

'He used a chair,' the resident said, looking up from his paper. 'Carried it out and stepped up on to it.'

'Did you see?' Jameson took a step closer to the guy.

'Nobody did. But they found the chair out there.' The way the man's eyes flicked to the bar before saying 'nobody did' made Jameson wonder if that was really true.

'I assure you it's perfectly safe, Mr Jameson. There are a number of children living here.'

'So long as you don't give them access to chairs on the balcony,' said Jameson. Not only was this a good way to pump for the information, it was also his get-out clause for not wanting the apartment.

'There are cameras out there now and the police are happy with things.'

'I don't think anyone could be happy with that particular turn of events.'

Diane glanced to the bar where a young man had appeared. 'Mr Jameson, Marcus, please, have a drink on us? Let's sit and go through the final details.' She gestured to the young man, who began to make his way over.

Diane sat and laid out the apartment pack on the small table. 'It's a beautiful apartment. The nicest of the lot in my opinion.'

'I'd want a full refit.'

'It was redecorated last year and to a very high standard.'

'Not to my standard though.' Jameson couldn't deny he was enjoying himself. 'Coffee please, espresso,' he said to the barman.

'Thank you, Laurence. Just a water for me, please,' Diane said.

'I'd need a new kitchen and the bathrooms redone.'

Before Diane could respond the man across the room reacted to something the barman had said.

'I pay a lot of money to not be asked such things. Your job is to remember people. I suggest you do it.'

The young barman scurried away, glancing back a few times at the resident who glared after him.

'What's that about?' Jameson asked in a low voice. He could see that Diane was looking exasperated. This viewing was not running smoothly from her point of view.

'It's nothing. As I said, I have three offers on the table and—'

'What was that about?' he repeated, a little louder.

Diane sighed a little. 'We have a couple of apartments that the owners rent out with Airbnb. Those visitors sometimes try to enter the members' areas. But as you can see it is strictly managed.'

Jameson looked again at the scowling man who was shaking open his *Times* newspaper and then folding it to a new page. He imagined such high rollers didn't take kindly to being challenged about their legitimacy in a building they'd paid millions to live in. He couldn't help but smile. Poor Laurence the barman. He was only a young lad.

Ten minutes later, when the espresso was done and Diane's hard sell was starting to repeat itself, Jameson excused himself to visit the bathroom. He wanted to walk through the space and get a sense of how someone might get in and out unseen. There were cameras on the balcony now, Diane had said, but none in here of course. That wouldn't go down well with the highly private clientele. The Airbnb fact was interesting. It meant you didn't have to be staff or a resident to be in the building. He wondered if the police had followed up on anyone staying in the apartments on that basis at the time of Philip's death.

The bar was a small corner space with only two fridges. Restocking must require leaving the room completely as there were no side doors leading to storage areas. So whoever had been working the night Philip died could have been out of the room for a decent amount of time.

As Jameson washed his hands, the resident from the bar entered and nodded hello.

'Is it worth the price tag?' Jameson said, drying his hands on a small square towel.

'You looking to buy?'

'I'm always on the lookout for a good investment. How long have you been in?'

The guy carried himself like so many people who feel they've made it in life. He had a small stain on the front of his white shirt and Jameson wondered if that was why Laurence had asked if this man was a member. Maybe he thought a real resident would not be so careless as to spill something. As if such people were different from the rest of us, more special, as opposed to simply having access to more cash.

'It's very exclusive.' The guy threw his small hand towel in the waiting basket.

'You haven't been affected by the suicide scandal then? I expect that dropped the price tag for a while.'

'Not at all.'

'It must have caused a stir in here. There must have been gossip.'

The man smiled and walked to the door. He was giving nothing away and that was fair enough. These people saw this as a club. One Jameson was not yet part of.

Diane continued with her sales pitch when he returned to the table but it was a half-hearted attempt. She was experienced enough to know he was not showing any buying signals but he had to admire her professionalism for seeing the meeting through. She took him through to the private dining rooms where she said they had chefs on staff to create a menu of your choosing. Then she took him back through the bar and asked if he would like to view the leisure club. As she collected her paperwork Jameson took another walk to the doors for the terrace. Surprisingly for the time of year they were open, so he stepped outside into the spring air. The wind alone told you how high you were without the need to look down, but he stepped right up to the railing and peered over. The top of the glass rested above his waist. He was 5 feet 10 inches and Philip had been an inch shorter. Pushing someone over here would take strength and most probably speed. Jameson didn't buy the chair story. He'd seen a photograph of it in the case file and it looked to him like a piece of theatre to suggest suicide. He had no way to prove it but he guessed the killer had placed it there after the fact. If Jameson had wanted to throw

97

someone over here, he'd simply alert them to something below, something that would naturally make them step to the barrier and lean over it a little. Then, with a good deal of speed, he would lift their feet upwards and backwards to tilt them forward. As soon as their centre of gravity shifted enough, physics would do the rest.

'Mr Jameson?'

He turned and smiled at Diane, then returned inside without explanation.

'Great view,' he said to the resident, who had been watching him.

'Are you planning to buy?' The man sat with his legs spread wide and his elbows resting on his knees. The paper hung from one hand, its edge curling as it met the floor.

'Not exclusive enough for me,' Jameson said, playing the man's words back to him in a purposeful slap-down. He had travelled the world and seen the scale of poverty and the desperation it wrought first-hand. These people didn't know they were born.

22

Zander walked through the city alone. Life could be loud and busy with AJ and Lexi around, which only made these moments so much more pleasurable. When he had a new target, he liked to focus his mind on the job at hand. It was his favourite part of the process: the chase. And the targets were becoming easier to find. Take this latest one. He had landed in Zander's lap out of the blue. A smug man in a Rolex volunteering himself for the position with one distasteful comment.

The chase had begun immediately. Zander had followed him, hoping to be taken to his place of work, or even better home, but the guy was slippery. It had started easily enough as Zander trailed the target on to the tube and off at Bank station, but after that things became trickier. Zander followed him into M&S; he assumed the man intended to buy lunch, but he had simply walked in one door, across the store and out of another. The man did the same again in a large branch of Boots and then a hotel. Zander had relaxed at that point, thinking this was where the target was staying; he slowed and began to take in the details of reception, where the lifts were, how many staff he could see. And then he realized the target was not slowing. He had walked across the lobby to the side entrance and was exiting. Zander had sped up, feeling infuriated. It was as if the target knew he was there but of course he couldn't. The pursuit went on until they reached Primark on Oxford Street where Zander became surrounded by large groups of shoppers that were impossible to pass. By the time he exited on to Tottenham Court Road the target was nowhere to be seen.

Zander had been disappointed but not at all despondent. The chase in the real world might have faltered but online would be a different matter altogether. He had the man's name. Mr Jameson. Marcus. He'd heard the woman say it. AJ would find him. He wasn't as skilled as Sandy, but he was a quick learner and Zander could tell he was getting better. So it was just a matter of time before they knew where the target worked, where he lived and his buying habits. Then Zander could begin to immerse himself in that other world, watching and learning until he knew enough.

The memory arrived vividly as always. He never knew what triggered it: some sound or smell of the city most likely. He was aware of people around him crossing the road but he remained motionless on the pavement. He could almost feel his mother's hand tugging him along the street as he had looked up awestruck at the houses around them. He recalled the wide pavements free of litter and the smell of grass and flowers. He had never smelled nature like that in the city. His world had always smelled of petrol fumes, takeaway food and rotting rubbish. They had arrived at a glossy red door in a tall house full of huge windows and his mother had rapped on it until her knuckles reddened. He remembered pulling at her other arm. Wanting them to walk on. Afraid of what might happen when that door opened. And then it did.

A man in a shirt and tie filled the space, his aftershave filling Zander's nostrils with a thick, spicy scent.

'You need to take him.'

His mother's words had Zander pulling harder in the opposite direction, but somehow she gained the super strength to yank him forward and push him between herself and the man in the doorway. Zander desperately clung to her fingers as she tried to wriggle them free.

'I can't deal with him. He's too much trouble. You have to take him.'

The man never looked Zander's way. His voice was calm and a little amused as he said, 'You wanted the brat. You made your bed, so lie in it. And for the record my bed is comfortable as hell.'

'You've got all this and you give your child nothing. What kind of father are you?'

'You want a better life? Get off your arse and work for it. Everything I have I've worked for. You and your kid are entitled to none of it.'

'He's your kid too. You total bastard.'

'I think you'll find he's the bastard.' The man closed the door and despite his mother's desperate knocking he never reopened it.

Eventually she'd given up and walked away. Zander had hurried to follow her. Somehow, she broke free of his hand and now she strode away without looking back. Zander had to run to keep sight of her through the busy crowds. At one point he lost her and had to make a choice at a busy junction about which way to go. He decided to trust his instinct, a decision that had served him well ever since. A few roads later he began to recognize where he was, but by the time he reached the house his mother was already inside. If he hadn't found his own way home, he was never sure she would have come looking for him. In fact, she never really looked at him again. She looked past him or through him but never at him and Zander knew why that was. The man had called Zander a bastard and although he had no idea what that meant he knew it was bad. Nothing was ever the same after that.

Someone pushed Zander off the kerb, which brought him out of his trance.

He continued walking, thinking how everything bad that had happened was a result of that day: the fault of the man behind the red door.

23

Augusta Bloom was cleaning her kitchen for the third time that day. Jameson had convinced her to take Friday off and rest. She had intended to go for a run and then head to the supermarket but instead she had made excuses and stayed home. Her head felt full and she craved some kind of escape: the ability to step out of her life for a short while to regain perspective. It wasn't simply the Matchbox Murder case. Their last case, which had seen her go undercover in the Artemis cult, had exhausted her physically and emotionally. She had been deprived of sleep and food but that had not been the worst of it. If it hadn't been for Jameson, a lot of people would have died, herself included, and so now she was hiding in her house.

She opened the fridge and sighed. She really should have made that supermarket trip. Toast and butter would have to do. She placed a couple of slices of bread in the toaster and sat down to read the papers she had picked up the day before. Both had articles on George Shulman that she wanted to read. DCI Mirza had stressed that they should focus their attention on the two most recent murders. This was where they would have most opportunity to identify their killer or killers, so she wanted to get more of a sense of who the victims had been.

Bloom didn't disagree with the woman, but she had a strong feeling Mirza was holding something back. Not only had she been even more distant with Bloom in the last team briefing, Bloom had not missed the glances passing between police officers when she had spoken up. And then there was the real elephant in the room. No mention had been made at all of Seraphine or how these murders might be linked to the Psychopath Game, despite the fact that her picture had been pinned up on the investigation-room wall alongside those of all the victims. Bloom simply didn't buy that an officer as intelligent and experienced as Mirza would drop one of her theories so completely.

She finished the last bite of toast and answered her ringing phone.

'Somehow that bitch got me arrested,' Jameson said.

Bloom moved quickly across her kitchen to grab a paper and pen. What had Seraphine done now? She knew there was no one else he would speak of with such venom.

'What for?' she said with pen poised.

'Murder.'

24

The cafe was quiet. Only one other person sat reading the *Daily Star* with a large mug of tea.

'Have you nothing to say about it?' said Lexi.

Zander could feel her irritation. She was looking to him to rein AJ in. She thought the lad was losing it, but Zander saw something different. He saw an apprentice hitting his stride. Yet, sure, they were different: Zander's strength was in his intellect and his ability to melt into any background whereas AJ was all about muscle power.

'You worry too much, Lexi. I checked out the gardens. They were not overlooked.'

'But anyone could have walked through at any point.'

'But they didn't, did they?'

'Why can't you see this is getting out of control? If AJ gets caught how long do you think it will be before they discover us, too? Before they find out what you've done to Sandy?'

'Don't talk about me like I'm not here.' AJ picked up his half-eaten sandwich and took a large bite.

Zander let him eat. For some reason AJ couldn't get enough of the greasy bacon and builder's tea here, which made it a good place to talk to him. He was less likely to strop off in a temper when he had his favourite food in front of him.

'Zander?' said Lexi, impatient for him to react.

Once AJ had swallowed his latest bite, Zander said, 'Mate, I am loving your work, you know that. Between us we could really teach the world a lesson, but Lexi's work is no less important. If we want to keep doing what we're doing we have to work with her. You know that. You have to let her know what you're planning so she can be prepared. It's not fair to expect her to clean up in a panic.'

The thin-haired woman with the large glasses came to the table and collected AJ's empty plate. She also picked up his mug of tea.

'Hey, I'm still drinking that.'

'I'm closing up. It's gone four.'

The man reading the *Daily Star* took his cue and stood while folding up the paper.

'I'm not finished,' said AJ, staring at the woman. 'Put it down.'

The woman hesitated, her brain sending up a flag for danger.

'Put it down.' AJ slammed the side of his fist on the table.

'All right, fella, calm down,' said the *Daily Star* reader.

AJ made a move to stand, his hands balled into fists.

Zander took over. 'Sorry. It's fine – take the tea.' He placed a five-pound note on the table for AJ's food as the woman scurried away. Then he made eye contact with the *Daily Star* reader, who stood with arms folded across his chest. He was a big man, clearly capable of looking after himself. Zander gave a short nod before saying, 'One of those days.'

The man unfolded his arms slowly but didn't move to leave. He was staying to make sure the waitress had company.

Zander walked to the door, knowing AJ had no choice but to leave with him. AJ might not like it, but Zander was the boss and that wasn't changing any time soon.

25

'What have you done to Marcus?' Bloom asked when Seraphine answered.

'I said you both owed me and I would come to collect.'

Jameson had filled Bloom in on the fact that Superintendent Ned Nesbitt had sent officers to collect him from his London home to take him in for questioning. Nesbitt was an old friend of Bloom's in the Scottish Police. She'd called on him for help when she and Jameson were investigating Artemis, a women's rights group with a mysterious retreat site near Inverness. At the climax of the Artemis stand-off, Jameson had shot and killed a guard working for the group, who were threatening Seraphine's life. Seraphine had initially corroborated Jameson's version of events but yesterday she'd changed her story, telling Nesbitt that she couldn't be sure of the timings and that perhaps Marcus Jameson had come into the room intentionally to kill the man. It was a claim that Nesbitt could not afford to ignore. Jameson would need to be questioned under caution and it would be his word against Seraphine's because the other people who had been in that room were dead.

'He owed you a date, not a murder conviction. I thought you cared for him.'

'But *you* owe me.'

'And what does Marcus's arrest have to do with my debt?' Before she'd articulated the question, Bloom knew the answer. 'Don't tell me. He's a ransom.'

'Like I said, I tend to get what I want. But don't worry – once you have successfully paid me back, I'll make sure they drop the charges.'

'What is it you want me to do?' Bloom sat heavily on a kitchen stool.

'Gosh. No hesitation. No request for time to think about it. You really do have a crush, don't you?'

At that moment Bloom heard someone push something through her letter box. She walked to the hall and saw it was a thick, brown A4 envelope.

'You should have received my instructions,' said Seraphine before hanging up.

26

The basement office was dark and cold. Not that AJ minded. He loved coming in here and using all this stuff. It was awesome.

He flicked on the light switch and the bare bulb in the middle of the room lit up the brick walls and stone floor, both coated with dust and cobwebs. Evidence that Lexi never came down here. At the far end of the room sat Sandy's desk with four screens set up, two on a stand at the back and two on the desk itself. AJ switched on the small fan heater under the desk and sat down. Then he powered up the two desktops and typed in Sandy's passwords. It had taken AJ a while to figure them out but once he had, it had confirmed something major: he could be a match for Sandy's skills.

The four screens laid out on the desk began to load up with the various applications AJ had been using regularly. His hunting ground. He couldn't tell Zander and Lexi about his latest victim. They had made it clear that mothers were out of bounds. But as soon as he'd seen Shareen Dubeck's picture he couldn't stop himself. It was something about the blondeness of her hair, the pointiness of her nose and those eyes: dark brown eyes that he'd stared into as she'd fought for her final breath. Eyes he'd imagined belonged to someone else entirely.

He'd remembered to take a matchbox this time, but in the end he'd chosen not to leave it. What the others didn't know couldn't hurt them.

He pulled the sleeves of his favourite old hoody over the palms of his hands to keep them warm. His tracksuit bottoms were worn on the knees but comfy to work in and he had tucked them into his thick football socks. Not that he had ever played football in his life.

He spent a couple of hours going over the same ground he'd already covered. He wanted to be sure he hadn't missed anything. He wasn't having much success with Zander's latest target. Zander preferred to find his own people, but it was up to AJ to fill in the blanks. He found details of where the target lived, worked and socialized. It was disturbing how much of your life was captured digitally. Which only made the fact that AJ couldn't find *this* target all the more infuriating.

When he could go no further, he knew he had to speak to Zander.

He walked back up the stone stairs to the kitchen.

'Are you sure you heard the name right?' he said as he made his way to the sink.

He took Zander's silence as confirmation.

'How about the others I told you about?' AJ had offered up a few alternatives, the types he knew Zander liked but Zander wasn't biting.

'If you're not up to it . . .' Zander's voice was calm and he let the point hang.

'Don't be angry with me. It's not my fault. I've looked everywhere. The problem is Marcus Jameson is not an uncommon name. I can find lots of bank accounts, mortgages, loans, pensions, et cetera, but there's no way of knowing which of these is your guy. There's nothing to cross-reference it with. You usually give me a business name or an address or a club they're part of. I know you said he's rich but without knowing how rich it's a needle in a haystack.'

AJ opened the fridge and the smell of blue cheese hit his nostrils like a punch. He gagged and closed the door. For a few seconds he took in deep breaths of air to try and hold off the urge to throw up. It wasn't the smell that made him want to retch; it was the memories associated with it. His stepfather had described himself as a foodie even though he'd probably never set foot in a decent restaurant in his life. He was the kind of guy who wore cheap suits and knackered old shoes he had to polish to cover the scuffs. He had a naff job in sales and was always promising the next pitch would make them rich. But it never did. On a weekend he would buy a large block of blue cheese which would sit on the kitchen table festering and stinking up the place. He insisted it tasted best that way. He would wash it down with bottle after bottle of red wine and then, when he'd satisfied his lust for food, he'd look to satisfy his lust for fresh meat: namely his stepson.

The guy would reek of the disgusting mouldy cheese as he insisted to Mother that the boy needed punishing, before forcing him up to his bedroom. And there in a place decorated with posters of Transformers and superheroes he would force himself on AJ, breathing rapid stinky grunts into his face as he repeatedly told him he deserved it for being an ugly little shit whose own father couldn't even love him.

AJ fought off the memories with rage. He had found this to be the most effective tactic. Rage at his stepfather for being a perverted bastard but most of all rage at his father for letting it all happen. Fathers should be there for their kids. They'd brought them into the world so they should protect them. He'd always imagined his dad was some superhero who would some day come and prove his replacement wrong. But the guy had never stepped up. Choosing to live a life with holiday homes and swimming pools and fancy sports cars by the garageful. When AJ had been told this reality, that's when his rage really took hold. How could someone be so blind to the horror they had left behind? If he could have met the man before he succumbed to cancer how he would have enjoyed ramming a stake in his heart or watching his brains splatter on the floor. He would have told his father as he watched the lights go out in his eyes that *he* was the disgusting shit unworthy of love.

When AJ returned to the basement the computer screens had all gone to sleep. He hit a few keyboard strokes and fired them up. Zander wanted this target and AJ realized he'd missed something obvious. A route to finding the target's contact details: the estate agent.

AJ's smile spread wider as he said to the cold, dark room, 'Time's running out, Marcus Jameson, you disgusting little shit. We're coming for you.'

27

Bloom paced back and forth. The contents of Seraphine's package were laid out in five neat piles on the top of her kitchen island. They contained airline tickets, transfers and accommodation details for four countries Seraphine wanted her to visit. She would have less than twenty-four hours in each location to make contact and sound out Seraphine's psychopath there. First, she would travel to Latvia, followed by France and then on to Vatican City and Cyprus. Vatican City was a surprise but then Seraphine had said her chessboard included bishops, and when it came to seats of power few matched the Catholic Church for reach and longevity. It was a whistle-stop tour of some of Europe's highlights, but this was no dream holiday or great adventure. This was truly dangerous. Then again, given the kinds of activities Seraphine might be involved in, Bloom had to acknowledge that at least she wasn't being asked to travel to the likes of Syria or Afghanistan.

According to the United Nations, there were currently 195 countries in the world. If these were Seraphine's squares on a chessboard, Bloom wondered how many dark players the woman had. Hundreds? Thousands? It was estimated that 1 per cent of the world's population possessed significant levels of psychopathy, which gave a pool of 70 million people for Seraphine to fish from. It reminded Bloom of a recent article she had read in the *Guardian* which suggested that the Freemasons, one of the world's most infamous secret societies, had over 6 million members worldwide. Was this the kind of influence Seraphine wished to emulate? Bloom wouldn't be surprised.

The final pile on her kitchen island contained notes from Seraphine on how Bloom should play things when meeting her people. It made for a depressing read. They could not know Bloom came at their leader's behest and they were all well aware of Bloom's previous efforts to halt Seraphine's work. Also, to make things just a little trickier, they all knew Bloom had assisted Gerald Porter in his recent escape. In short, these people saw her as an adversary.

She read Seraphine's final paragraph again.

Use it to your advantage, feign allegiance to Porter, tell them he has enlisted your help. If they are loyal they will report back to me, plus they will be less likely to harm you if they think you are with Porter.

Less likely to harm you.

Why me, Seraphine? she thought. *Is this revenge? Is this how you finally get rid of me?*

Bloom knew the idea didn't carry much weight. The psychopathic mind is too logical to let an emotion like revenge overcome a tactical advantage. Seraphine needed to know who was betraying her, which meant she needed Bloom to succeed.

She picked up the phone.

'Why would they speak to me?'

'You will understand when you get there.'

'What does that mean?'

'It means you have to trust me as much as I'm trusting you. I have given you the details of some of my most critical people. It is information you could easily use against me. Augusta, these people are too smart to say anything that implicates them, but you hear more than what people say, you hear why they say it – I'm relying on that.'

'Hence having Marcus arrested for shooting Stephen Green without provocation. Something you and I both know is not what happened.'

'He will be relying on you too.'

Bloom was in a trap. The option to never negotiate with blackmailers was out of the question. Despite Seraphine's attraction to Jameson, Bloom knew it would not stop her from protecting her business interests. That would simply not be rational. If Bloom didn't do this, or at least make it look like she was, Jameson would go down for murder, she felt sure.

'And what about the serial killer case?'

'You do know there is some clever technology around these days that enables you to work remotely. Plus I'm not sure the detective chief inspector will miss you as much as you think.'

'Charming.'

'Oh come on, Augusta, you can't be critical to every case you work on. But you are critical to Marcus's future. We all have things to gain and lose here. And I've always thought that together you and I could be unstoppable.'

Bloom felt a little sick. She had spent the past year fighting against Seraphine's attempts to draw her into whatever Machiavellian activities she was orchestrating and now she was willingly going to help her.

'Just . . .' Seraphine fell silent for a long moment. 'Just . . . remember Marcus is relying on you.'

28

After a gruelling few hours of interrogation from Superintendent Nesbitt's detectives, Jameson was dropped off at the end of his street by a patrol car. He had texted Bloom during the journey to say he was on his way home and he would fill her in on the details later. He didn't fancy going through the whole interview again just now.

He'd been informed by Nesbitt's team that Seraphine had called the superintendent to change her statement about the shooting of Stephen Green. Green had been providing security for Paula Kunis, the leader of the Artemis cult that he and Bloom had investigated earlier in the year. He was an ex-special forces soldier who'd had a gun to Seraphine's head when Jameson arrived. His memory of the event was clear, as it was every time he had taken a life. Jameson was not the kind to coldly carry on without looking back, despite his training. Every death at his own hands played like a mini-movie in his head. Movies that interrupted his thoughts at random: never invited and never welcome.

Green's final moments played out for him now, including Seraphine pleading for her life. *'Please, please don't shoot. Tell him not to shoot, Paula. I'll do anything. I'll give you anything. Please. What do you want? I'm begging you. PLEASE!'*

He had pulled the trigger instinctively, as trained to do when there was a direct threat to life.

Superintendent Nesbitt had questioned him about it personally the next day. They had been in regular contact in the hours leading up to the event and Nesbitt knew Jameson had been critical in resolving a high-risk situation. 'I've spoken to the CPS,' Jameson recalled the superintendent saying. 'They say given your background and the self-defence nature of the shooting they do not see any value in pursuing charges.'

But now Seraphine had changed her account. Suddenly she was claiming there had been no threat to her life. She had told Nesbitt the group were simply talking when Jameson walked in and shot Green without reason or provocation. It was a claim that naturally required the superintendent to speak to the CPS again, who requested that the incident be reinvestigated. As a result, they'd reinterviewed Jameson and had taken away his passport.

Members of the superintendent's team had travelled down specially, having requested an interview room from the Met. Technically if the crime was committed in Scotland they could have insisted he be reinterviewed there as their jurisdiction was distinct to that of the English police. They had been keen to point this out as if, despite the fact that he was under arrest, he should be somehow grateful.

He expected Seraphine had hoped for a night or two in the cells but thankfully Nesbitt was a pragmatic man who saw no need to detain a suspect unless absolutely necessary. Jameson's version of events was straightforward and unchanging, plus he had volunteered it immediately to police at the time. All of this counted in his favour. Or at least, he hoped it did.

He took out his phone to text Bloom again, to let her know he would call tomorrow, but before he had the chance to type a word something caught his attention. It was the little things which often set off his spider senses. The car that had pulled into the road behind him was travelling a touch too slowly. In and of itself that wasn't too troubling. It could be one of his neighbours preparing to park. But there was also the figure he'd briefly seen as he'd passed the side road. A lone man walking swiftly in his direction and dressed from head to toe in black. Again this could be innocent. But something told him it was not. A fact confirmed by a quick glance back at the approaching car. Inside he saw that the driver and a rear passenger both wore balaclavas.

He knew what would happen next before it happened. The car would pull alongside him but wouldn't stop as the rear passenger door nearest to the pavement opened and the third man, approaching from the side road, would jostle Jameson in and quickly follow. Jameson would then be pinned between two men and unable to escape as the car increased speed and drove away. It would take a matter of seconds.

There was no time to run. The car was already at his side with the rear door opening. The only defence he had was to brace his hands against the car roof as he felt strong arms shove him from behind. It was no use. His abductor jabbed him hard in the side and his body's natural reflex to arch away from the blow weakened his frame. The man placed a hand on Jameson's head and roughly pushed him into the car shoulders first. The passenger began to help, gripping Jameson's right arm and the back of his neck. By the time the car began to accelerate he was exactly where he predicted he'd be.

His companions were well-built and muscular and could no doubt handle themselves.

'All right, chaps?' Jameson said as light-heartedly as he could.

They didn't respond. They simply placed the seatbelt across his chest and took his phone before placing handcuffs on his wrists and a dark hood over his head.

As they drove Jameson thought about his SERE training with MI6. It stood for Survive, Evade, Resist, Extract. The idea was they gave you the skills to not only evade capture but also to stay quiet when interrogated. The training itself had been entirely practical. He had known it was imminent but it had still been a surprise when he was apprehended at his local gym after a two-hour bike ride and hauled to the training facility, still sweaty and dressed in Lycra. He'd been deprived of sleep for forty-eight hours and then taken to a room for questioning. When he failed to answer the questions to his interrogator's satisfaction he was forced to climb into a barrel buried in the floor that they then covered with a lid. With his knees folded to his chest and his arms pinned to his side his panic had risen in time with the water seeping in from below. He had been pretty sure they wouldn't let one of their newly trained assets drown, it was only a test, but even so, could he really be certain? That feeling of panic was what they wanted to create, the principle being to build your mental toughness. You started to view torture tactics as survivable and you learned coping mechanisms.

He let his eyes move out of focus inside the bag and then back again. It was the mental trick he used to take himself into that alternate mindset: the one of survival. Stay calm; keep control; be alert.

He wondered if Seraphine was to thank for his current predicament. She would find it amusing to have him accused of a crime and then make him disappear so he became some kind of fugitive, reliant on her to save him. He also expected she would enjoy the game of 'You be the prisoner; I'll be the captor'.

The car stopped and his door opened. He was released from his seatbelt and pulled out by a firm hand. The same hand kept hold of his bicep as they walked out of the cold and into a building. He could see nothing. The floor beneath him felt smooth, like polished wood or lino.

'Take him through,' said a man's voice before Jameson was led a little further into the building. When his hood was removed he found himself inside a small, internal room with no furniture. The door was shut and locked behind his captors. On the floor stood a small bottle of water and a cheese sandwich. Both were sealed in their packaging but he was not foolish enough to consume them. It didn't take much to inject something into such things. Instead he sat on the floor in the corner opposite the door and waited.

29

Once Bloom had cleared security at Heathrow on Saturday morning, she bought a green tea and found a quiet corner of the departures lounge to make a call.

Superintendent Ned Nesbitt answered on the second ring. Bloom liked the efficiency of the man.

'I can't say I'm surprised to get your call, Gusta.'

'With all due respect, I wish I didn't have to call you, but I need you to know that Marcus Jameson is innocent.'

'It's not looking good.'

'Well, she's very good at what she does. She'll have covered every angle.'

'She as in?'

'Seraphine Walker.'

'Oh aye, Marcus pointed the finger at her too. Didn't your case against her just fall apart in court?'

'I'm sure you know better than I that you can't always believe the conclusions of the justice system.'

'I know you of old, Gusta, but I have to ask. You don't have the blinkers on about this guy, do you?'

'You know how critical he was to defusing that situation with Artemis. He's a good man. All I ask is that you fully look into the validity of her claims. Seraphine Walker is an accomplished manipulator and has no issue with lying to get what she wants. Marcus, on the other hand, is one of the most trustworthy men you could hope to meet.'

Nesbitt agreed to keep an open mind, which was all she could hope for.

Bloom hung up and considered calling DCI Mirza to say that she was going away for a few days but decided on balance it was unnecessary. As Seraphine pointed out, she could work virtually if needed and Mirza was not her boss.

On the flight to Riga International Airport, Bloom reread her background notes on the man she needed to meet. Despite the anger she felt about Seraphine's tactics in making her take this trip, she had taken the woman's advice. She'd emailed the target's assistant last night requesting a private audience to discuss a psychological study she was undertaking on people in power. Seraphine had suggested using this same tactic for securing meetings with all four of her people and Bloom felt highly sceptical about the likelihood of it working. Unsurprisingly, there had been no reply up to the point of take-off, and on touch-down when she checked her mail again she found there was still no reply.

It was eleven fifteen as her plane taxied to the airport building and her flight out to Paris was booked for six twenty that evening. With a two-hour check-in time that gave her only five hours to convince Koen Laukums to speak to her.

She opened Google on her phone and typed in his name. He was an attractive 56-year-old man with neatly cut fair hair and steely grey eyes. He was also Latvia's recently elected president.

How the hell would she secure a meeting with this man?

She knew his official home was within the ancient Riga Castle on the banks of the River Daugava. Her plan was to catch a taxi there and speak to security on the gate. She might need a better reason to see their most senior politician than some research project though. She might have to name-drop Seraphine or even Gerald Porter. Perhaps that would motivate the man to speak to her. She wished she had Jameson to call. He would no doubt know someone who knew someone who could get her in. But she couldn't tell him what she was spending her weekend doing. He would go ballistic. Seraphine might have overestimated Bloom's ability to do what she asked without Jameson's help.

She was still pondering on the futility of her task as she walked through arrivals to find a smartly dressed chauffeur holding a card with her name on it.

'I'm Augusta Bloom,' she said on reaching the young man.

'Welcome, doctor,' he said in a thick Latvian accent. 'We have been expecting you.'

30

Jameson listened to the sound of water dripping somewhere in the walls. The room he had been left in was a
small square painted white with a polished concrete
floor. It had no furniture and nothing hung on the walls,
so he had no potential tools to defend himself with. His
right thumb tingled with pins and needles. He rotated it
a few times to try and get the blood flowing. He needed
the bathroom but he also knew this was the adrenaline
so he could ignore it for a good while yet. Another skill
to thank his training for.

*Keep calm. Control your breathing. Control your thoughts.
Remember everything.*

The bottle of water and cheese sandwich remained
untouched despite his hunger. He wondered what Bloom
was doing. He had no doubt she would be on the case to
get the charges against him dropped. Bloom knew
Seraphine had a hand in his arrest so she would have contacted her by now and tried to find out why. He had
watched his partner undergo some personal trauma over
the past year, but his admiration for her tenacity and ability to read people was unwavering. He knew he could not
have a better person on his team than Augusta Bloom.

He also knew it might be way too late for her to help
him.

If Seraphine was the next person to walk in he'd be furious but also on some level relieved. At least with her he felt confident she only wanted to play games; she didn't want him dead. Others might not be so kind.

He thought about the various people he had pissed off over the years. The men and women he had interrogated in the likes of Belmarsh, the people whose secrets he had ferreted out and passed on, the friends he had made with the sole intention of some day betraying them. It was a long list. But none of them really scared him. There was only one adversary who did that. Jodie's killer. Not the man who'd actually shot her. Jameson had arrived in time to chase that bastard down and deal with him. The man he was afraid of was the one who'd ordered it.

He and Jodie had worked closely for three years on a deep-cover assignment that ultimately led her to a meeting at a cafe in Serbia. It was a meeting Jameson should have attended but, owing to a bout of food poisoning, Jodie had gone in his place, never to return. Following her death he'd gone on a rampage of revenge for six months, hunting down anyone associated with the group they'd been meeting with that day. He'd exposed and ruined as many of them as he could, revealing their identities to the countries they spied within, informing on their criminal activities to the authorities or, when neither of those were possible, simply sending an anonymous letter to their spouse revealing who they were really married to. But no one had ever given him enough to find the man responsible. And so he'd walked away.

Mic drop, Marcus out.

He should have requested witness protection but he hadn't been prepared to lose his sister, his nieces or his parents and so he'd simply turned on his survival mindset: when the day comes, I'll deal with it and until then why worry?

What worried him now, in this cold, hard room, was that the day had finally come. He heard the lock on the door release and sat up a little straighter in his corner. The only factor in his favour right now was that whoever was on the other side of that door needed him alive. If this was an out-and-out revenge thing, he'd be dead already. So they wanted him to tell them something, or to do something for them, and he could work with that.

He watched the door open and the last person he expected to see walked in.

31

Riga's medieval castle was an impressive yellow and white building with towers at each corner. The red tiled roof and green copper-topped spire stood out proudly against the blue sky. A fire had sadly damaged part of the building in 2013, but it remained the place where the country's president worked and met dignitaries.

Bloom was taken inside without any of the security checks she had anticipated and led to a grand office where Koen Laukums awaited her. He was taller than he looked in photographs and loomed large over her as they shook hands. She was not offered any refreshments, but water was provided on the small table next to the chair Laukums asked her to take a seat in.

He walked back around his wide desk to sit across from her. A display of power, no doubt.

'I did not expect this to be so easy,' she said, because walking out of the airport and being brought directly here was an entirely surreal experience that called for comment.

'My assistant received your email request,' he said in perfect English. 'I was intrigued by the nature of your research.' The small smirk on the president's lips told Bloom this statement was untrue. She guessed he'd brought her here to find out exactly what she was up to, given what he knew about her background with Seraphine and her recent dealings with Gerald Porter.

'Successful people have always been a fascination of mine. I think psychology has been remiss in focusing most of its research on broken aspects of the human mind such as mental illness or behavioural problems. Why not study the healthy, effective mind? There is more there for most of us to learn from, wouldn't you say?'

'Your statement assumes that most people are not prone to mental illness or behavioural deficiencies.'

'Do you disagree?'

Laukums pursed his lips for a moment and narrowed his eyes. 'I think that *you* disagree.'

'Because of my profession?'

'Because you didn't come here on a research trip.'

'Oh, but I did.' Bloom reached for a pad and pen from the bag at her feet. 'Is it OK if I ask a few questions?' She smiled at him and waited for a nod. 'I noted that you joined the government in Latvia only three years ago after a lifetime living and working in Russia. Is that accurate?'

'I grew up in my father's homeland not far from Moscow, but I am Latvian born. My mother's family are all from here and she insisted this was where she gave birth.'

'And now you are their president. That's quite the rise. How exactly did you achieve that?'

'Hard work and a bit of luck.' His smile was broad and full of humour. She could see he would easily be mistaken for a warm and considerate man.

Bloom looked around the elaborately decorated room.

This felt too easy. Why would this man be so willing to see her and answer her questions? She was missing something. Perhaps if she cut to the chase she could figure it out.

'Would you define meeting Seraphine Walker as a bit of luck?'

He sat back in his chair and folded his arms. 'What is it that you want, Dr Bloom?'

'I recently had some dealings with our former Foreign Secretary in the UK, Gerald Porter.' She paused to see if that would gain a reaction but Laukums simply continued to smile at her. 'He and I are of the opinion that Seraphine's organization needs to be stopped.'

'And what does that have to do with me?'

'I have it on good authority that you are a critical member. What I don't understand is what people like you get out of it.'

'People like me?' The President of Latvia rose slowly from his desk. Bloom thought he might be about to throw her out or worse, but then he fetched a book from the shelf behind him. After a few moments he said, 'When Machiavelli wrote *The Prince* in 1513, he did so with the full knowledge that politics has always been a game of deception, treachery and crime. He said any ruler should be excused their deeds, even their most deadly deeds, if the intention and result are beneficial.'

'Yes, but beneficial to whom?' She wasn't sure if he was saying that she should expect a level of deception and treachery in politicians or that Seraphine should expect it from her members.

Laukums flicked through the pages of *The Prince*. 'You come to my country, to my private office, and tell me you wish to take away my power, all the time knowing full well the kind of man I am.' He sat again, placing the book on the desk in between them and looking her in the eye. Charm gone. Mask down. 'Do you know why you feel able to do that?'

Bloom was stumped for a second. She was unsure why she felt able to come in here and have this conversation. In her past life she had done such things with the full back-up of the police, and since leaving their employ and working independently she'd had Marcus Jameson, a skilled ex-secret service man, at her side. But here, today, there was no one. And yet she had to acknowledge her lack of fear even in the face of that psychopathic stare.

He continued, 'I do not believe you are in league with Porter. From what I have heard of you, I think you would have spotted the truth of him immediately and distanced yourself from any association.' Laukums held her gaze until she felt the sizzle of adrenaline.

No Porter, no protection. She should be afraid.

She concentrated on staying very still and not looking away.

The president's laugh was large and booming. He patted the book a few times with the palm of his hand. 'The reason you are not scared of me, Dr Bloom, is in the answer to your own astute question. Who benefits?'

'You mean Seraphine or Gerald Porter?'

'Do I?' The charm was back on full power. Laukums's

eyes sparkled with it and he became animated, amused and, although she hated to admit it, attractive. 'Why did Seraphine go to so much effort sending out those Dare to Play cards and risking our whole endeavour?'

'To show off.'

'Oh, you can do better than that. No matter the nature of our childhoods or our characters we always want to either impress our parents or prove them wrong, don't you agree?'

'I don't see Seraphine caring one bit about the opinions of her mother or father. What I'm interested in is whether you think Seraphine is on the right track with her current plans.' Bloom needed to avoid being distracted by his word games. She had one priority here: to determine whether Laukums was Seraphine's suspected mole or not, so she could save Marcus.

Laukums emphasized every word as he said, 'Why was she showing off?'

Bloom knew the answer but she had never said it out loud before. It had felt too arrogant.

After a few moments of prolonged silence under the weight of the president's unwavering stare, Bloom said, 'To try and impress me.'

'You liberated her. Handed her the tools she needed to make her true nature something that could help her rather than hold her back.'

Bloom began to get a sense of something that had bugged her for many months: what glue might be strong enough to hold together a fundamentally anti-social collection of people.

'And she in turn liberated you and that is why you follow her, is it? Because you and your associates are creating a world that benefits your kind?'

'Oh, you are getting warmer, Dr Bloom. So much warmer.'

Back at the airport, awaiting her flight to Paris, Bloom reflected on Laukums's words. Was he saying she felt safe with him because he revered her as the person who had in some way liberated Seraphine? Prior to their counselling sessions all those years ago it was true that Seraphine had had no clear sense of why she was different. She could feel it but she couldn't explain it or name it. Bloom had helped her to do that. Explained how her emotions were not as alive as those of her friends. How she might not feel love or guilt or empathy like others do because she was quite simply wired up differently. But that didn't make her any less valuable or credible so long as she used her intellect to make the right choices. At the time Bloom had been fascinated by psychopathy. It had been the topic of her PhD and she had felt sure it was an entirely necessary evolutionary branch. It ensured the human species had individuals brave and bold enough to do the things other people find too scary or too damaging, like exploring the unknown or stepping in the way of danger. Her views on this had not entirely changed but she had to admit Seraphine's activities were making it hard for her to keep telling herself that psychopathy in and of itself was not a recipe for being bad.

Her short visit with the President of Latvia had been

enlightening. She couldn't say for sure whether he was fully in support of Seraphine, but she did detect a dismissive tone when the man spoke of Gerald Porter. That could be a red herring, of course. As a senior politician he was no doubt a man who knew what to say to have his desired impact. She would be foolish to take things at face value. What she did feel sure of, however, was that President Laukums believed Bloom had been pivotal in enabling Seraphine to become what she had become by encouraging her to embrace her psychopathy. In turn, Seraphine had gone on to similarly liberate and elevate others like Koen Laukums. So did these people feel grateful in some way to Seraphine, and by association Bloom? Perhaps that was what Seraphine had meant when she'd said Bloom would have no trouble securing meetings with her people.

But only those still loyal to Seraphine would feel that way, surely. Any whose allegiance was shifting towards Porter would feel differently. In fact, they might see harming Seraphine's liberator as the ultimate way of bringing Seraphine down and, if Seraphine's suspicions were correct, at least one of the four people Bloom had been sent to see was already on Porter's side.

32

Gerald Porter stood in the doorway and smiled at Jameson. It was a self-satisfied kind of smile, closer to a sneer than a greeting. His thick red hair was ruffled and unkempt. Jameson had read somewhere that the former Foreign Secretary messed it up purposely to give himself a man-of-the-people image. In contrast his blue suit was tailored and sharp, his white shirt bright and his pink tie clashed horribly with his hair.

'Marcus Jameson. I have looked forward to meeting you for a while now.'

Jameson remained seated on the floor and tried to suppress the fear snaking through his veins. Bloody psychopaths. He was more than done with being stuck in a room with these people.

The man paused to pick up the water bottle from the floor, open it and take a long drink. Proving that Jameson was foolish to have not done the same, no doubt. Porter then screwed the top back on and continued to twist it back and forth as he watched Jameson.

'Take the sandwich too,' said Jameson.

'It's not poisoned.'

'I'll eat when I get home, thanks.'

'*If* you get home.' Porter's sneer returned.

Jameson stretched his legs out flat on the floor and

folded one hand over the other in as relaxed a manner as he could, considering the handcuffs; then he raised his eyebrows.

'One of the advantages of being the Foreign Secretary is that you get to look inside the files of MI6, and I found some very interesting things about your time there, Mr Jameson.'

'I've no doubt.' Jameson was determined this man would not use him in whatever war he had with Seraphine. At the end of their last case in Scotland, Seraphine had shown Jameson and Bloom a letter from Porter informing Seraphine that he was intent on taking her sublime idea and making it his own. Porter had ended the letter with the challenge *Dare to Play?*, which is how Seraphine had tempted psychopaths to join her in the first place. Clearly the game was now afoot and Porter was looking to make Jameson part of it, but no matter Jameson's distaste for Seraphine he would not play any part in their rivalry. The consequences of that were simply too high. The woman would be unbearable.

'There were some questionable activities in your last few months with MI6. You betrayed many of our friends for your own benefit.'

Jameson knew Porter referred to the contacts he had exposed as spies to their families or other governments as he pushed to find the man responsible for Jodie's death.

'I admire the venom you invested in hunting down those responsible for the death of Jodie Sinclair and I can't help but wonder if you'd have been that bit more tenacious had you been in full possession of the truth. You see, doctors who treated Jodie found she was nine weeks pregnant.'

Jameson felt something shift in his gut. But this was not the time. He needed to keep calm, control his breathing and, most importantly, control his thoughts. It was time to put the professional barriers up.

'So?' Jameson shrugged.

It was Porter's turn to raise his eyebrows. 'I'm beginning to see why Ms Walker likes you so much.' Porter stooped on to his haunches so he was almost at the same level as Jameson. 'Not yours then?'

Jameson forced a smile. 'Unlikely.'

'Even so, if I told you who had Jodie shot, what would you do then?'

'Not my problem any more.'

'Really? You wouldn't want to wreak your revenge and see them pay? I can help you with all of that.'

'You've seen my files. You know this little interrogation routine won't work on me.'

'And you know you've never faced me.' Porter picked up the cheese sandwich. 'Enjoy your hunger and your thirst. I'm excited about us working together. Aren't you?' he said, before leaving and locking the door behind him.

Jameson sat perfectly still. He knew if he moved, he'd throw up.

Jodie had been pregnant.

Please God, no.

33

Bloom arrived at Charles de Gaulle airport just after 9 p.m. to find no chauffeur waiting for her this time. She caught a taxi to the hotel Seraphine had booked, half expecting a message from tomorrow's target to have been left at reception or in her room, but there was nothing. She checked her emails but found no reply to her request for an audience with Madame Miriam Chevalier, Minister for Europe and Foreign Affairs in the French government. It appeared not all of her targets were going to be as easy to track down as Latvia's president.

She took a quick shower and changed into a grey cashmere jumper and black trousers before heading down to the restaurant for food. Fortunately, other Europeans ate their evening meals later than the British, and there was no point visiting France if you weren't going to enjoy its superior cuisine.

The stylish and modern hotel was situated not too far from Quai d'Orsay on the left bank of the Seine where the minister was based. The hotel bar was decked out in mustard and grey with gold-rimmed round tables topped with small vases of delicate white flowers. It bordered a leafy interior courtyard which looked to be a lovely place to sit but was empty this evening. A few businessmen sat on the soft grey chairs reading papers or checking their phones, each accompanied by a glass of wine or beer. She looked ahead to the dining-room entrance where the maître d' stood awaiting his guests. She hoped they did French onion soup; it was her absolute favourite and never more delicious than when prepared in its home country.

'Charlie?' She stopped as she caught sight of a familiar face.

The man looked up, squinted his eyes and then opened them wide in surprise. 'Goodness gracious, Augusta. Is that you?' He stood and they greeted each other with a kiss on each cheek.

'What are you doing here?'

'Meeting with suppliers. I come every month.' Charles had always been boyish in looks but it had been a decade since she'd seen him and the filling out of his face and small wisps of grey scattered among the chestnut hair at his temples made him look all grown up and very much a man. 'Join me, please,' he said, moving the second soft grey chair at his table towards her. 'What brings you to Paris?'

The waiter came to her side allowing her to dodge Charlie's question.

'Still a whisky drinker? Not sure they'll do a Scottish malt here but I'm sure they stock some fine bottles.'

'*Soda au citron vert, s'il vous plaît,*' she said, requesting a lime and soda and taking a seat.

'Always the sensible girl,' Charlie said with a wink and a laugh.

In that moment he looked so much like his brother,

Gregory, that she reached out a hand towards the waiter. *'Pardon, un petit whisky, merci.'*

Her ex, Gregory Levensworth, had been a man of light humour and high intellect, careful and considerate; what some might call a match made in heaven for Bloom. A soulmate. But all that was far in the past now. She had not seen or heard from him in years.

The waiter enquired about the lime and soda, which she cancelled. She needed a stiffer drink for this.

'How's Olivia and the children?' she said.

'Oh, she's delighted to finally have the big house and stables she always coveted. Did you hear that Pops passed?'

'Yes. I am sorry. I sent your mother a card.'

'They'd have appreciated that, thanks.'

They as in his mother and Greg.

He continued, 'Ma said she wanted to see us enjoy our inheritance, so she sold the estate and bought a little cottage nearby which meant Olivia got her stables and the kids got a pool. So everyone's happy.'

'What did you get?' She wanted to ask if Greg had a new home filled with a family.

'Peace and bloody quiet at last.' He laughed and it was like hearing his brother again. 'I see you've been doing some interesting work, getting your name in the papers.'

She knew he was referring to the Seraphine Walker case. 'I seem to attract it lately.'

'I recall Sylvia saying that once. "My Augusta attracts darkness like a light bulb attracts flies," she said.'

'My mother said that?'

'Yeah, at that garden party we had once, the one at Greg's house.'

The speed at which he said his brother's name told her she would not be learning anything about Gregory in this conversation. She remembered that garden party vividly. She had not long turned thirty and Greg was encouraging her to leave the police and go into private practice. 'We'll get you somewhere on Harley Street,' he'd said. 'It'll be more steady work.' By which he really meant safer work. She had thought her future was set and yet now it felt like a lifetime ago.

When the silences became longer and the small talk was exhausted, she repeated how lovely it was to see him, then they stood and repeated their double cheek kiss before saying farewell.

Bloom continued on to the dining room to enjoy French onion soup followed by the cheeseboard. She had made notes on Madame Chevalier which she tried to read between courses but she was distracted by bumping into Charlie and found it hard to concentrate.

Eventually, back in her room, she managed to focus her mind on the job in hand. She read that Chevalier was a member of the Republican European People's Party, part of France's far right. She was a lawyer by qualification whose views in her early career had proved controversial, particularly her support for using military strength to quell civil unrest. But over recent years she appeared to have softened and the controversy around her had all but disappeared.

Bloom considered what that might mean: an outspoken psychopath in a position of power suddenly becomes a diplomat. A change which appeared to coincide with her association with Seraphine, Koen Laukums and the rest. Was that because Madame Chevalier didn't need to make waves any more because she had found a better way to push her agenda? Or was Seraphine holding her back until some critical moment when the full force of their collective callousness could be unleashed?

This was another question she needed to find an answer to. Alongside uncovering what hold Seraphine had on these people, she needed to find out what they were doing, or planning to do. Helping Seraphine to stop Gerald Porter might not be the best course of action, even if it was her only way of clearing Jameson's name. If Seraphine planned something globally devastating, stopping that would have to take priority.

Later in bed, her head swimming a little from the whisky, her thoughts turned once more to Gregory Levensworth. She fell asleep to thoughts of garden parties, pastel cupcakes and holding hands in the sun.

34

The view from Seraphine's HQ was impressive at night. Looking out, she could see down a brightly lit Constitution Hill to Buckingham Palace on one side and on the other across Hyde Park to the inky black Serpentine.

'Who took him? Where did they take him? How did we not know someone was planning this?'

For the first time in a long while Seraphine felt the urge to hurt somebody. In her teenage counselling sessions with Dr Augusta Bloom, the psychologist had warned her that people with Seraphine's particular personality – the psychopathic kind – were prone to confuse love with possession. She knew there was some truth in this. Marcus and Augusta were hers. She might play with them and tease them but no one else was allowed to even think of causing them pain.

'Well?' She looked at Clive Llewellyn and Stuart Lord, two of the most talented members of her inner sanctum.

'He was dropped off at the end of his street by a patrol car but never reached his front door. Somewhere in between he disappeared,' said Stuart Lord. Lord was one of Seraphine's more recent recruits: a man with a shady history in petty crime and drug dealing who'd ended up living off his successful fiancée and working as a shelf stacker in Asda before Seraphine showed him his potential. Now he was adept at working their underground sources and had become an influential player in the crime world.

'We have a Ford Focus on CCTV moving slowly along the road about that time but there's no indication it stopped. He could have decided to run. He has the skills.' Clive Llewellyn was one of her most highly educated psychopaths: a corporate lawyer with connections across business, politics and the aristocracy.

'He wouldn't run, he's too . . . upstanding. This has to be Porter. Is he using MI5 to do his own bidding?' As the UK's Foreign Secretary Gerald Porter had been the top of the tree for all secret service agencies.

'Maybe. The trail's gone cold.'

'How? The whole point of infiltration is that we know what is going on. First Porter manages to hide from us in the basement of the MOD's main building and now you're telling me he's made Marcus Jameson disappear. This should not be possible. I haven't dedicated my life to this for people to run rings around us. Somebody somewhere knows something. I want everyone on this. Everyone. Is that clear? If Marcus comes to any harm, I don't need to tell you how badly people will suffer.'

Seraphine walked to the window and watched the cars snaking through the street below.

Porter had dared her to play his game, much as she'd dared the likes of Llewellyn and Lord when she had recruited them. Porter was testing her. But she was not some naive recruit as yet uneducated about the power her psychopathic nature provided. She was mature and highly evolved. The queen of their particular branch of the species. To be tested was an insult. She had nothing to prove. And she would not play the games of a lesser opponent. She would play her own game – as always.

35

Bloom awoke early in her Paris hotel room. She checked her emails for a response from the office of the French government's Ministry for Europe and Foreign Affairs, or Miriam Chevalier herself, but found neither. It was Sunday so there was no need to check in with Jameson but she was surprised he'd not been in touch to update her on his arrest. Nesbitt had told her he had been released on Friday night so she knew he hadn't been charged yet. She considered texting him but didn't want to risk him calling her back. As soon as he heard the international dialling tone he'd be asking questions and she did not fancy hearing his reaction to her flying out here at Seraphine's behest. He would be furious even if it was for his benefit. Instead, she took her notepad and pen to the dining room and reflected on the Matchbox Murder case as she ate fruit salad and drank hot water with a slice of lemon.

She came across the note she had written for herself in Mirza's team meeting about George's straightened fingers reminding her of Simon's very tidy post-party apartment. Finishing her breakfast, she headed back to her room and opened her laptop. She scrolled through the various crime-scene photos, and when she studied Simon's more closely she saw why the neatness had jumped out at her. The open-plan kitchen and living area resembled those seen in a kitchen magazine. The jars of pasta and rice on the shelves were displayed in size order and separated by exact distances. Three mugs were positioned neatly by the kettle with matching handle positions, and the two tea towels hanging on the oven handle were folded so precisely you could be mistaken for thinking one was a reflection of the other.

Turning her attention to the photographs of Jeremy's kitchen and pool area she found everything looked pristine and organized there too; from the four sun loungers lined up precisely at the same angle and equidistant from each other, to the mugs on the kitchen shelf positioned perfectly in a matching set. Even the post on the kitchen island was stacked in a size-ordered pile. This could be explained by the bachelor having had a cleaner but the magazines on Simon's coffee table were similarly arranged according to size. Even in Keith's Range Rover she noted that a number of files and papers on the back seat had been stacked in the same way.

Bloom sat back. She thought again about how Keith had been carrying a sports bag in one hand and a suit carrier in the other. If that was something he habitually did when visiting the country club after work, arriving in his suit and leaving with the carrier, it was feasible that his killer had observed this. He would know if he attacked Keith when his arms were full there was less chance of him fighting back, hence less chance of the killer being scratched and leaving skin under fingernails or being hurt to the point that he bled. All this suggested the killer was capable of taking careful precautions when

148

carrying out these murders. Right down to knowing how a hotel would react to a report of bed bugs with an in-depth clean of the room, effectively removing all traces of previous residents. But the closed eyes, straightened fingers and overly neat crime scenes felt different to good planning and preparation.

A knock at the door interrupted her thoughts. It would be room service, no doubt, as it was checkout time. She quickly packed away her laptop, then grabbed her case and coat, taking one last look around to make sure she'd not forgotten anything before opening the door.

'Dr Bloom?' The French Minister for Europe and Foreign Affairs walked purposefully into the room causing Bloom to move back and to the side to let her pass. 'You can wait outside,' the minister said to a man in a dark suit who stood in the doorway.

Miriam Chevalier stood with her back to the window. She had the kind of elegant put-togetherness that came so easily to Frenchwomen. Her navy-blue outfit was tailored and yet feminine, her hair was perfectly styled in an asymmetric shiny black bob and her nails manicured in French polish.

'How did you know I was staying here?' Bloom felt just a touch frumpy in her trousers and jumper as she hung her coat back on the wall hook.

'*Ce n'était pas difficile.* I understand you wanted to speak to me. Why is that? I do not buy this research story.' Miriam Chevalier's French accent was made even more impressive by her slightly husky voice.

'I want to speak to you about Gerald Porter.' Bloom

figured it was best to get to the point with a woman such as this. She sensed Chevalier wouldn't have the patience for any other strategy. 'He and I believe Seraphine Walker needs to be stopped.' This was risky but she had no time to think of a clever alternative.

'I know something of you. I know you are the person who tried to stand in Mademoiselle Walker's way in the UK. Why would Gerald Porter trust you?'

'Because I'm the person who enabled his escape from custody. I'm the reason he is currently free.' Bloom had anticipated this kind of challenge so was ready for it.

'This makes no sense to me. Why would you do that?'

'He asked for my help with a personal matter and in our time together he convinced me that he was the only person who could stop Seraphine. That appealed to me.'

Miriam Chevalier smiled just a little. 'I do not know of anyone Mademoiselle Walker admires in the world other than maybe you. To use you against her is quite, quite cruel.'

Bloom could tell the woman was impressed despite her words. Was that because Chevalier admired Porter? And was that enough to make her the mole? She needed to do more digging.

'He has long admired you and wanted me to tell you he hopes you will see the future as we do.'

'Mademoiselle Walker has been useful to me.'

'You joined Seraphine's organization for a reason. Would you be comfortable with Mr Porter taking charge if he could offer the right incentive?' This was the question Seraphine needed answering.

'The advantages for me would be equivalent, as far as I can see. It is the world which would feel the difference but I can't say I care about that.'

'That's a great philosophy for a politician.' Bloom spoke the words before taking time to think. It was a rare occurrence for someone of her careful nature. But such egotistical bias from people in power hit a nerve.

'Monsieur Porter is a politician too, is he not?'

Bloom felt relieved that the woman had chosen not to bite. 'Do you agree with us that Mr Porter would make a better leader?'

Madame Chevalier walked back to the door.

'I believe we are done.'

Bloom checked out of the hotel five minutes later as she pondered on her brief chat with the French minister. As predicted by Seraphine, Chevalier had said nothing to incriminate herself or show any allegiance to Gerald Porter. However, it was the unspoken things that told Bloom more. Despite not buying Bloom's research story she had made the effort to travel to her hotel room. Why? Was it curiosity or a defensive move? The minister had spoken highly of Seraphine as someone who had been useful to her – was this genuine or an attempt to deflect suspicion? Then there was the refusal to answer Bloom's question about whether Porter would make a better leader. It was an understandable choice but it also begged the question why – if Miriam Chevalier supported Seraphine completely – she hadn't simply answered 'absolutely not'.

36

Before making her way to Charles de Gaulle airport to catch her onward flight to Rome, Bloom found a small cafe from where she could make a few calls. The waiter delivered her *café crème* as the call to DCI Mirza connected. Bloom mouthed, *'Merci,'* before speaking into the phone.

'Nadia, it's Augusta.' It was the first time Bloom had used Mirza's first name but it was her long-held philosophy that the sooner she could deal with police officers on first-name terms, the sooner the effects of status were reduced. Bloom found officers worked best with her when they did not see her as either junior or senior to them. Plus, Nadia Mirza was behaving coldly towards her and Bloom wanted to force some change in that.

There was a brief pause, maybe while Nadia Mirza considered insisting she be addressed by her professional title, but then she said, 'Augusta. What have you got for me?'

Bloom liked the woman's no-nonsense approach.

'I think our killer, or one of our killers, might suffer from a form of obsessive-compulsive disorder that compels them to create order and neatness in the crime scenes. If you look at the photos, you'll see every scene is overly neat and precisely organized.'

'Are you suggesting they might be tidying up?'

'Exactly. OCD is a condition affecting those who suffer from anxiety; the obsessive behaviour acts as a means of controlling their world.'

'Could the victims not be the neat freaks? Maybe that has something to do with why they were targeted?'

'I did wonder that, but I think the specific style of organizing and ordering items such as putting post and magazines in size-ordered piles, ensuring cups and chairs have equal spaces between them and that they sit at the same angle, is more likely to be the manifestation of one person's coping strategy than something common to a pair or group. And that implies our killers are attending the scenes together.'

'They can't both have OCD?'

'It's entirely possible that two separate killers might suffer from a condition like OCD, as most serial killers have experienced the kind of childhood trauma that triggers it, but the chances it would manifest itself in such a consistent way across the scenes of crime are slim. Are you married, Nadia, or living with a partner, if you don't mind my asking?'

'Yes, why?'

'If I visited your home, would I see a difference between how you and your other half tidied a room, or let's say made the bed?'

Nadia Mirza snorted a little. 'You sure would.'

'This is the truth of all people, isn't it? We all have a unique approach and someone with OCD is no different, just much more exaggerated.'

'I see. Could this be coached in? Could someone be teaching the killers to do this in exactly the same way?'

'It's possible, I suppose, but—'

'Fine. I'll make a note.'

Mirza hung up and Bloom sipped her coffee. The DCI had sounded more irritated than appreciative of this latest insight. Bloom knew Mirza had had reservations about bringing her in on the case initially but then she had personally authorized it. Had she felt backed into a corner by her boss, Steve Barker, because of his friendship with Bloom? Or had Bloom done something to annoy her? It crossed her mind that the DCI might know that Jameson had been speaking to their witnesses. That would be enough to anger her, but Bloom felt sure if that was the problem Mirza would have simply taken Bloom to task. Whatever was bugging her was something the policewoman felt she couldn't directly address.

Thinking of Jameson reminded Bloom that she should call him but instead she rang Seraphine.

'How's life as a spy suiting you? Marcus would be proud.'

'I'll let you know when I've met them all. Miriam said something interesting. She observed that the world would feel a different impact depending on whether it is you or Porter in charge. You said something similar when we met by the Thames, that his idea of winning was nothing like yours.'

'Is that a question, Augusta?'

'Two questions actually. What are you intending to do, and how would Porter being in control change that?'

'Why do you need to know?'

Because I'm scared I created a monster. 'I think it would help me in my conversations.'

'I'll think about it. I've already allowed you to see more than I should.'

'If you really want my help, Seraphine, tell me what you're doing. Or are you worried I'd refuse if I knew the truth?'

It was odd how different their conversations were these days. The usual mocking tone had gone from Seraphine's voice and Bloom could almost hear Seraphine's fourteen-year-old self in the more reticent manner of communicating. It had always impressed Bloom back then how thoughtful and serious Seraphine had been. She'd appeared, on the surface at least, to be genuinely listening to Bloom's advice and mulling it over. It had been a shock and a massive disappointment to discover the adult Seraphine had become some manipulative mastermind of criminal activity.

'I'll think about it. Did you enjoy your stay at the hotel? Meet anyone interesting?'

Bloom placed her cup down, fearing what was coming.

'I mean, I could have booked you into any hotel in Paris but I chose one frequented by a friendly face.'

She meant Charles Levensworth. Gregory's brother. How did Seraphine know about them? Not even Jameson knew the history of her personal life and he knew more than most.

'Don't be angry. It was simply a little thank you from me.'

Bloom had no headspace for this little revelation right now. 'When are you planning to sort out this situation with Marcus?'

Seraphine was quiet for a beat. 'Situation?'

'His arrest for shooting Stephen Green. You and I both know that's on you.'

'Can you tell me who my mole is yet?'

'Not yet but while we're on the subject, what's the point in my approaching them covertly if you're letting them know I'm coming?'

'I am not letting them know.'

'You told Miriam where I was staying, Seraphine. That's hardly keeping things low key.'

'I most certainly did not.'

'She came to my hotel room.'

'Are you really so naive as to think one of my people could not find where you were staying?' The mocking tone was back in Seraphine's voice.

'Why are these people so keen to meet me? I barely contact them and they send cars to the airport or find out where I'm staying and turn up at my door. That makes no sense, Seraphine. You said on the phone in London that I would understand once I got here. What did you mean? What are you not telling me?'

'This is not the time. There are more pressing matters.'

'Than making sure I continue to help you to test out your people? What else could possibly be more pressing for you right now?'

'My world is more complicated than you could ever imagine.'

Bloom was feeling angry now. 'Don't insult me, Seraphine. I am out here doing this for you. The least you can do is tell me the truth about why your powerful contacts around the world are willing to meet me. Laukums hinted that my reputation as your liberator might be a factor – is that it? Is that why they are willing to meet with a total stranger at the drop of a hat?'

The pause on the line lasted a few seconds before Seraphine said, 'No, Augusta. It is because you are not a stranger. They all know you well.'

'What does *that* mean? They've been spying on me?'

'Not in the way you might think.'

'I suggest you start talking or my next flight will not be to Rome, it will be back to London.'

For a few moments there was silence on the line and Bloom thought she was not going to get an answer, but then Seraphine sighed and said, 'Are you sure you want to know this?'

37

It had been forty-six hours now since he'd last eaten and Jameson felt the familiar light-headedness that went with hunger. More worrying were the hours that had passed since his last drink. That had been a coffee when he was taken for questioning on Friday afternoon, now forty-two hours ago. Why hadn't he opted for water? Coffee was a diuretic often leaving you less hydrated than more. He'd had to urinate in the far corner of the room as the discomfort had become too much to bear. Humans could survive for approximately three days without water. No doubt Porter knew that and would be prepared to take it to the wire.

In the hours since Porter's visit Jameson had tried to work out where he might be. The building was old, probably a 1960s or 70s construction that had a certain public-sector feel about it. An old council building or the like. They had travelled for around thirty minutes from his home in Wembley so given the average speed of traffic they were probably somewhere in a radius of ten to twenty miles. Not that working any of this out would help. He had no phone; that had been taken off him after he was forced into the car. His only option was to negotiate his way through whatever came next, whenever that might be.

He tried not to think about Jodie and the pregnancy. He needed a clear head. But it was hard not to. The timings were right. The baby could have been his. Not that he kept tabs on Jodie's activities. She might have been sleeping with someone else but she was a professional and they were in deep cover so he thought it unlikely. She wouldn't let her guard down that way. He wondered if she'd known about the baby. By week nine there must have been some obvious signs. He hadn't noticed her suffering from any sickness or being overly tired, but then again, Jodie was a professional.

The child would have been seven years old by now. Would he be playing football with them in the park or driving them to ballet lessons? He knew if the child had been his he'd have insisted on playing an active role. Maybe he and Jodie would have left MI6 together and made a go of it as a family.

When the door unlocked an hour or so later, he was trying to imagine what his life would be like if he'd never met Augusta, and subsequently Seraphine.

'Have you worked it out? I expect a smart chap such as you won't take long to join the dots even when faced with a good dose of denial.' Porter entered, clutching a fresh bottle of water.

Jameson frowned. Was Porter suggesting he knew who was behind Jodie's shooting already but was in denial about it?

His mind worked it through at hyper-speed. Who would he be in denial about? His employers? Could MI6 have been behind it? That's a concept he would struggle to get his head around. He had his reservations about the British secret service but they would never, ever, turn on their own. It was unthinkable. And he wouldn't be in denial about any legitimate enemies so it would have to be an associate, someone he was close to. Someone he didn't want to consider might be behind it, even if there was clear evidence of their capability. That left only one person.

'If you're trying to imply that Seraphine was responsible for Jodie's murder, that would be terribly convenient, don't you think? Seraphine had no idea who I was back then, so you're stretching, Porter.'

He and Bloom had established that Seraphine's Psychopath Game had been running for a while before they became aware of it a year ago. Indeed, they both felt sure the woman had chosen to show off her work to her old mentor once it was all but complete. But he had left MI6 six years ago and Jodie had died six months before that. It seemed unlikely that Seraphine would have been in any position to be masterminding the kind of organized network he and Jodie had been investigating back then. Plus the group they were looking into were trafficking migrants, with many of the women being sold into sexual slavery. Seraphine would never touch such a disgusting business.

The certainty of this conviction surprised him. He hated Seraphine. She had used him and hurt his family. And Bloom's continued determination to try and see some hidden good side irritated the hell out of him. And yet here he was, having his own gut feeling that some things were simply too bad for Seraphine to touch. Maybe Bloom was on to something after all when she said the woman would not participate in serial murder.

Porter shrugged. 'It was worth a punt.' He was leaning against the wall, slowly sipping water from his bottle. His oversized gut tipped over the top of his trousers and strained the bottom button on his shirt. Jameson had no time for men who did not respect their own body enough to stay fit and healthy.

'Why don't you stop pissing about playing mind games and tell me what you want.'

'Drink?' Porter held out the half-drunk bottle.

Jameson shook his head, well aware this might be a life-and-death choice. If Porter walked out and left him alone for a further twenty-four hours, he'd be in trouble. But there was no way he was showing weakness before their negotiations had even begun.

'Why am I here?'

'You wrecked lives and relationships trying to find out who was behind Jodie's death, not to mention sabotaging your own career. That kind of anger doesn't go away. You bury it. It's still there festering inside you. Waiting.' Porter paused to sip some water. 'I can give you a name. I know who it was. I'll even help you get your revenge, if you like.'

'And what is the price for this deal with the devil?'

'Nothing your training and recent experiences won't make light work of.' Porter's smile was different from the public version he showed in media interviews. It was a sneering thing closer to a snarl.

Jameson stayed quiet and squared his shoulders as he held Porter's gaze.

'I need you to kill Seraphine.'

38

Bloom stared out of the plane window at the land below. It was a short flight to Rome, only two hours. Her head pulsated with a strong headache that had begun during her conversation with Seraphine and worsened with every passing minute.

'Are you sure you want to hear this?' Seraphine had asked during their call in the cafe, and then she had delivered her body blow. 'The final step for those who were to become my most powerful collaborators was to infiltrate your life without your knowledge.'

Bloom had been in part appalled and in part incredulous. 'I have never met Koen Laukums or Miriam Chevalier before in my life,' she had said.

'You think that because they are very good at blending in. But you met your neighbour's tenant, Karl, back in 2015. He would smile and wave, ask how your day was and share some light-hearted anecdotes. I believe you once told him he brightened your morning with his cheery smile.'

The possibility that this had been Koen Laukums, or that the future French minister had been a fellow commuter who caught the train into the city, was preposterous. And yet she couldn't be sure it was not true. She did remember a few regular commuters on her train. The businessman with an endless collection of red ties and the young student who insisted on doing her make-up within the crowded carriage, an activity that always made Bloom anxious when it came to the application of eyeliner and mascara; one jolt of the train and that could be a nasty eye injury. As she forced herself to recall the regular journey, she felt sure there had been no one who could have been Miriam Chevalier. Then she remembered there was one woman she would occasionally chat to. This was rare in London; most commuters go out of their way to avoid speaking to others, but this particular woman had once dropped a bag of shopping and Bloom had come to her aid. It had broken the ice and for a few months they had passed the time of day whenever they were in the same carriage. Bloom couldn't recall what she looked like now or if her accent had been French. It was years ago. Jameson would not have such trouble. His skill at recognizing and remembering faces was phenomenal, but she, like most normal people, had a flawed memory for such things. Part of her wanted to believe Seraphine was bluffing and playing some kind of joke at her expense, but the trouble was she did remember the neighbour's tenant Karl and the fact that his smile had brightened her day.

Seraphine had been entwined into her life for so much longer than she had known – at least two years before the Psychopath Game had come to her attention, if Karl and the woman on the train really had been Koen and

Miriam. But Seraphine had also known about her ex, Gregory, and his brother, Charles, and Bloom's relationship with Greg had ended a decade ago. Had Seraphine been spying on her even then? The thought of it made her want to scream. Her personal freedom and privacy were critical to her. She didn't let people get too close for a reason. Spending your life analysing others made you paranoid about how people might view you; plus, once you knew how much darkness was out there, it could make you want to close your doors and hide away.

All this time she had felt free and in control. But this had been an illusion. In truth she had been stalked, tracked and manipulated by an invisible group of people. What had they seen her doing? Where had they followed her to? What private parts of her life had been studied and analysed as if she were some experimental subject? It didn't bear thinking about. It would drive her crazy.

As the plane came in to land, she wondered if on some level she had always felt Seraphine's presence lurking in the shadows. Maybe that was why she guarded her privacy so strongly. On some primal level had she always known?

39

'Kill her yourself.' Jameson crossed his legs and leaned against the wall. This discussion was over. The man was an idiot if he thought Jameson was some gun for hire. He'd spent Friday afternoon assuring Superintendent Nesbitt's team of his innocence in one murder case; he wasn't about to mess up his chance of living a free life now.

'I can give you the person who murdered the woman you spent six months trying to avenge. The person who killed her unborn child. Your unborn child.'

'Not my child.'

'You keep telling yourself that, son.'

Jameson's muscles tensed. He focused on relaxing his shoulders and breathing steadily. 'If you want her dead, kill her yourself.'

'But it's much more fun to watch the man she loves doing it. That way she dies twice.'

'She doesn't love me. You people are incapable.'

'We can love as keenly as we hate, Mr Jameson.' Porter took three strides across the room so that he loomed over Jameson on the floor. 'And trust me: we can hate.'

Jameson slowly raised his eyes. Porter stood with his feet wide and his hands on the back of his waist, elbows out, making his frame as intimidating as possible. It reminded Jameson of silverback gorillas with their fists on the floor and their shoulders hunched: ready to rumble. In contrast, Jameson kept his body relaxed in a show of insolence.

'If you don't do it,' Porter said in a low, quiet voice, 'I will kill all the women you care about, all the women in your life.' He unscrewed the lid of the water bottle and poured the remaining contents over the floor. Some of it splashed on to Jameson's trousers and it crossed his mind that he could suck up the moisture. 'I will start with Augusta Bloom and then I will kill your sister Claire, followed by that scraggly foster kid Jane she's taken in and finally your nieces Sophie and Holly. Sophie's your favourite, isn't she? So I'll make that one last. I'll let you watch.'

Jameson clenched his jaw. Bloom had told him once that a psychopath's favourite pastime was to find out what a person cared about most and then purposefully destroy it. Porter had done his research. Despite all Jameson's training in how to resist coercion and pressure, the women in his life were his Achilles heel.

'I thought that might convince you. Shall I assume we have a deal?' Porter stepped back. He looked triumphant.

Jameson watched the man walk to the door. He wasn't a silverback. Gorillas were a proud and impressive beast. This man was a snake, as slippery and toxic as any cobra.

'Porter?' Jameson said as the man opened the door.

Porter paused and half turned his head.

'Just remember, you asked for this.'

40

Zander was frustrated. There had been a flurry of press interest around AJ's attack in Hans Place Garden but nothing yet to suggest any of their kills were linked. Zander wanted the kind of national panic that went with the likes of the Yorkshire Ripper. He wanted these men to think twice about whom they insulted. He wanted them paranoid and pitiful. And that would only happen if Zander and AJ got the attention they deserved.

He knew what the problem was. Lexi. She was too good at what she did. She had convinced him that masking the kills was a priority and in the beginning he'd agreed. He'd even felt proud when no one even suspected his involvement. But AJ had changed everything. He attacked with a passion that made it impossible for people to ignore. It made Lexi nervous but Zander felt inspired. Hence his prolonged stay in the St Pancras Hotel. He had no interest in a blood-and-guts kind of kill so he figured making it obvious he'd been there was the next best thing.

Zander greeted the concierge. He knew it was risky coming back here but he couldn't help it. Every so often he'd rent out the Airbnb for a couple of days and enjoy the peace and the luxury.

This was how he should be living.

The apartment was small but nicely furnished in modern minimalist furniture. His favourite item was the wing-backed chair and footstool in front of the floor-to-ceiling window. He enjoyed sitting there and watching the little people below.

He thought about where it had all begun: the moment when he'd found his true calling in life. He could never understand what the point of his existence was. Where was the value in being anonymous and invisible? If you exist, surely you should be present and able to make your mark on the world?

For a couple of years before that moment in the bar with Philip Berringer, he had tried to live the life he wanted virtually. He'd paid to join an exclusive millionaires' platform called MoneyMakers, using funds he'd raised through online poker, which it turned out he had a talent for. MoneyMakers provided exclusive membership deals such as access to discounted supercars or luxury yachts, real-estate opportunities and virtual conferences where the wealthy could share their tips and tricks. But by far the best part of it for Zander had been the forum. They called it the ShareSpace but it was essentially a chat room for the rich. People would brag about their latest purchases by asking for advice on what extra features to buy, or promote their latest ventures in the hope of investment from like-minded people. Zander had spent hours honing his identity in this world. He presented himself as a self-made man with a Lamborghini and an ex-model wife who drove him crazy with her outlandish spending habits. He asked for advice on which Omega watch to buy and spent an enjoyable few months discussing a possible shared venture with two other members, only to drop out last minute blaming existing business pressures. And then he'd seen an apartment for sale in an expensive block in Canary Wharf and, in passing, he'd said he was thinking of buying it as a bolthole from the family. Philip Berringer had replied to say he already had one and Zander was welcome to come and take a look whenever he was in the city.

In the days that followed Zander had come back to the invitation numerous times. Could he do this? Could he go and actually live out his new identity in the real world? If he prepared well, there was nothing to say he couldn't. And so he'd bought an expensive suit, new shoes and some designer sunglasses, again using his poker funds. He'd had a haircut and even trimmed his nails before setting off to view his new millionaire friend's home, feeling more alive than ever before.

He could never be sure what had given him away. It might have been the style of the suit or the way he spoke but within seconds of meeting the casually dressed Philip in the lobby, everything started to unravel. Philip gave him the tour as promised, even taking him to the lounge on the 36th floor for a drink, but there was something about how the spoilt brat looked at him – as if he knew Zander was an out-and-out fraud.

That meeting changed everything. He had felt accepted online, as though he was finally with his people, but in the real world he realized he would never belong.

They would always think they were better than him, just as his father had. And so he needed to teach them a lesson.

A few days later he had rented this place for the first time. He could only afford the one night but it was all he needed. Philip had told him how he liked to have a quiet drink in the bar early evening on the weekend. The smug bastard had been surprised to see Zander, and the flash of disgust on his face when Zander said he had bought the apartment was the final nail in the man's coffin.

After that, it had been easy.

And now it was time to turn up the volume even more. Grab even more attention so that when they struck again, everybody would take notice.

Speaking of striking again, AJ had played a blinder. He had hacked the estate agent's computers and managed to find the address and contact number left by Marcus Jameson when he booked a viewing at this place.

Another smug, moneyed dickhead who would come to regret ever insulting him.

Bloom arrived at the hotel Seraphine had booked for her in central Rome not long after 8 p.m. Her room was decorated in mint green and beige and had a view of St Peter's Basilica. There was a well-stocked minibar and also a tray of complimentary water and fruit.

She removed her shoes and hung up her clothes for the next day. She had changed tack when making contact with the next psychopath. Cardinal Francis Sousa was the 75-year-old Vice Dean of the College of Cardinals. The email she had sent from the airport departures lounge in Paris had dispensed with the facade that she was a researcher sounding the cardinal out for Porter. Instead, she had used the message to test the validity of Seraphine's claim. She read the sent item again now.

From: Augusta Bloom   15:08
To: Cardinal Sousa
Subject: I believe you know me

Your Eminence,

I need to meet you urgently to discuss a sensitive issue.
I will arrive in Rome this evening. Please let me know the best time and place to come and see you in the next 24 hours.

Best wishes
Dr Augusta Bloom

Bloom's desire to find out if Seraphine's claims were true now outweighed any intention of assisting the woman in ferreting out her mole. She could not imagine for one moment that a senior member of the Catholic Church in his seventies would have taken time out from his duties to stalk her. If he had spent time in the UK it would have to have been as a senior priest and, as she was not a religious woman, there was no chance their paths could have crossed.

There was no reply to her email so she googled the cardinal and began to research his career. Born in Portugal in 1943, he had been a late entrant to the Church. Unlike his contemporaries, he had not been confirmed in his pre-teens or gone on to become an altar boy. Rather, he had joined a seminary in his late twenties, making it all the more impressive that he had risen to the highest-most levels in Rome. There was little detail on his career up until he was appointed as a cardinal in 2013. She read that he had become a firm favourite of the Pope, who then promoted him to his current exalted position a year ago. The write-up went on to explain the honour was all the more powerful due to Sousa's struggle with cancer three years prior, which he had overcome through a combination of faith and a medical miracle.

Bloom looked out at St Peter's Square, the headache from the plane returning with a vengeance. Cancer treatment would require an absence from Church duties for a significant period of time. Enough time to have participated in Seraphine's game? Enough time to have travelled to the UK? Enough time to have stalked her?

42

The Piazza del Sant'uffizio was quiet apart from a few cyclists and the odd car making the morning commute. Bloom had circled St Peter's Square on foot and followed Via Paolo VI alongside the four-column-deep Doric colonnades. She had read that this curved border to the square represented the maternal arms of Mother Church. The sun was still rising and the shadows from the columns reached out like long fingers seeking out the faithful. It was impossible not to feel humbled and in awe of the place.

The piazza formed part of a network of streets which circumnavigated the smallest country on the planet. Vatican City was walled and accessible only via the official visitor entrances, although St Peter's Square could be walked around freely when no events were occurring.

Cardinal Sousa had emailed late the night before suggesting they meet for a morning stroll. *Dr Bloom, how delightful to hear from you*, he had written, so it was clear that he did indeed know her. Bloom had felt a little sad that a man of his age should be still up and working at 11 p.m.

As she waited by the Vatican souvenir shop, she tried to imagine what she should expect. She had never met a senior member of a Church. Prior to today she would have felt under pressure to portray her best self in the presence of such a committed and devout person, but this was no ordinary man of God. She was intrigued to know whether his motivations were purely manipulative – after all, with the Church came power and access to everyone's secrets – or whether he saw people like himself and Seraphine as God's intentional creations, thereby making his faith and vocation genuine.

At the far end of the street an army truck was parked and two soldiers with machine guns stood on the pavement. Bloom wondered if this was normal or if something was happening here today. She had only visited Rome once before, in the early days of dating Gregory. They had queued for an hour to access the Vatican City tour and it had been worth every minute to marvel at the works of Michelangelo, da Vinci and Bernini. She recalled waiting to enter the Sistine Chapel, listening to the recorded message from the speakers explaining that the chapel was a holy place and silence was compulsory, only to realize this was an impossibility for pretty much every person who stepped into that room. Visitors instinctively gasped and whispered to their loved ones as they pointed to sections they recognized in the iconic ceiling. At regular intervals the guards at the doors would demand, '*Silenzio!*' and the room would fall quiet until the next wave of visitors stepped in, gasped and began to whisper.

Bloom realized she was smiling at the memory and for the first time in an age she felt a pang of regret. She had told herself many times over the years that she had been young and naive in her assumption that life would follow a set path of meet, marry and have children. In the aftermath of her relationship with Greg she had vowed never to be so foolish again, but standing here, in the shadow of God's presence, she wondered if she had ever been truly happy since.

The sight of Cardinal Sousa approaching pushed aside all memories of Gregory. He wore a long black robe with red buttons, a wide red sash and a red skull cap that covered the top of his white hair. The skirt of the robe kicked out in a graceful flourish as he walked her way. Bloom rarely felt intimidated by people in power but something about the nobility of his clothing had her wondering if she was supposed to bow or kiss his hand on greeting him.

He slowed a touch as he neared. His eyes were a deep brown and they held her gaze for a touch longer than was polite. Bloom knew this was a common habit of those personalities who lack the empathy to know what makes others feel uncomfortable. She also knew his position and experience would have taught him to control such a tendency, so his choosing not to do so was another sign that Seraphine's claim was correct: the man knew who she was and also that she knew his true nature.

'Augusta,' he said. He held out both his hands and she gave him one of hers which he clasped tightly between them. 'Welcome. It is wonderful to see you again.'

His voice was soft and raspy with a deep Portuguese accent, and there was a slight emphasis on the word 'again'. Bloom felt a chill. She had studied photographs of Sousa online last night and felt certain that their paths had never crossed but standing here now she knew she had been wrong. His face was thinner in real life, his nose longer and his cheekbones higher. In the photographs he had looked like a kindly old grandfather, but in real life he gave off the energy of a man decades his junior. His eyes were alert and his smile a distinctive one-sided slope.

'You knew my mother.' Her words sounded distant, as if someone else had spoken them.

'An impressive lady. Very accomplished.'

Sylvia Bloom's Alzheimer's had arrived quickly and without much warning, but there had been signs. In the year before her diagnosis Sylvia's lifelong scientific sensibilities had given way to a more spiritual outlook. One of the reasons for that was the priest she had become friendly with in her home town of Harrogate. Bloom had met the man a handful of times when she was home visiting her mother. He had not been dressed as a priest then, although his black trousers and dark jumpers had hinted at his profession. Bloom had found him pleasant enough. He did not appear to be forcing religion down her mother's throat, which would have concerned her. He came over quite simply as a man chatting with a friend. Bloom thought back to when that was: 2014 most probably, the year before she met her neighbour's tenant Karl and the woman on the train, three years before Seraphine's Dare to Play cards began to appear.

'My mother treated your sister, didn't she?'

'My brother. He married a British woman and adores

176

your National Health Service. When he needed heart surgery your mother was recommended. She saved his life.'

'Recommended by Seraphine?'

Sousa smiled his lopsided smile and bowed his head.

'I don't recall you having such a strong accent.'

Sousa released her hand to place one of his own over his chest. 'I try my best to fit in wherever I go.'

I bet you do, thought Bloom, knowing psychopathic personalities often made effective mimics as they learned to hide their differences from the rest of the population.

'Shall we walk?' His accent sounded less pronounced now, perhaps to demonstrate his skill to her.

They began moving away from the basilica and St Peter's Square.

'So you were only there to test me, is that right? You had no real interest in my mother.'

'It was *I* who was being tested, and spending time with Sylvia was no hardship.'

Bloom recalled one of the staff at her mother's nursing home saying that a vicar had visited on a couple of occasions. Bloom had thought nothing of it then, assuming it was someone from the local C of E church, but of course not everyone knows that Catholics are called priests not vicars. Maybe there had been a real friendship, or maybe he had been pumping her for information.

'Why did you visit her in the home?'

'Like I said, she saved my brother's life. I owed her a debt of gratitude. You look sceptical.'

'I'm trying to work out if you sound like a true man of God because you are one or because it serves you to be.'

'I can hear that you are displeased with me.'

'You used my mother – why would I feel anything other than displeasure? If she had known who you were and why you were there . . .' Bloom felt her temper rising and reined the emotion back.

They walked in silence along a busy road as the wall of Vatican City became more distant on their right-hand side.

'What made you play Seraphine's games? Don't you have enough power and influence in the world already?'

Sousa's laugh was soft and deep like his speech. 'You disapprove of our recruitment methods.'

'I expect I would disapprove of all your methods if I knew them, but yes, I am intrigued why someone such as yourself would lower themselves to such arbitrary challenges.'

'Nothing worth doing is without challenge. Such measures were necessary and still are, especially for those who are yet to open their eyes to their own potential.'

'You mean those psychopaths who do not know they are psychopaths.'

'I prefer the term logicians rather than psychopaths. It is less value-laden.'

'Logicians?'

'It is better, no?'

There was a truth in the fact that those of a psychopathic nature see their own lack of emotional richness as a strength. Indeed, this appeared to be Seraphine's manifesto: that she and her kind were more capable and competent than normal people because they were unhampered by feelings. Bloom felt more of Seraphine's motivations slide into focus.

Bloom said, 'So you have been involved with Seraphine since before you met my mother?'

The cardinal nodded. 'We originators helped realize her vision.'

'Originators?' Bloom saw it clearly now. The people she was meeting – the people Porter was trying to poach – were Seraphine's first wave, the ones who helped her to build her start-up organization.

'Was Gerald Porter an originator?'

'No, no.' Sousa frowned a little. 'Mr Porter came later.'

'Do you know him?'

'Why do you ask?'

'He is the reason I'm here. He and I believe Seraphine's plan is flawed and needs to be stopped.'

Silence fell between them again and Bloom watched the cardinal's robe flick out and fall back, flick out and fall back.

'He worships a different God.'

'How do you mean?'

'I mean that in the universe there are forces for good and forces for evil.'

'Are you referencing religion or *Star Wars*?' She knew Jameson would have been proud of this little retort.

'I mean that selfishness is but one of the faults we are all destined to fight.'

'I'm sorry, I don't mean to be rude but isn't it true that those of a psychopathic nature see the world in terms of what it can give to them? And isn't that fundamentally selfish?'

'Those of a non-psychopathic nature are not so different. We arrive into life alone, leave it alone and see it through only our own eyes.' Sousa smiled warmly at her. 'Even acts of great goodness, of altruism and charity, have some personal payback, don't you agree?'

'The smug factor, you mean?'

The cardinal's low chuckle was a pleasing sound and Bloom realized she was enjoying talking to this man. She imagined he made a surprisingly good priest.

'Did you really come here on Gerald's bidding?'

Was it wrong to lie to a priest? Even a psychopathic one? She decided to stay quiet.

'Because I think that would be very sad, for Seraphine.'

'You mean the woman who's been stalking me for goodness knows how long and using me to test her people? I'm not sure that deserves any sympathy.'

'Seraphine did not wish us to meet you as a test; that is not what she values you for.'

'I'm not sure I understand. I thought I was the final test you all had to pass before she let you into her gang. She said you had to infiltrate my life without my knowledge.'

'Because she wanted us to see what she saw.'

'Which is?'

'Your desire to see the good in every person you meet.'

'I'm not sure that's true. My job requires me to judge people all the time.'

'And yet you do so without judgement. You do it with

an objective eye on why someone behaves how they do.' The cardinal stopped as they reached the high wall of Vatican City again. Over the top, the dome of the basilica could be seen and the wall was bordered with long vertical slits at regular intervals like the arrow slits of a castle. 'It was not about fooling you. It was about educating us.'

That was the last thing Bloom expected to hear this morning. She had been bracing herself for all manner of shocking or frustrating insights into Seraphine's organization but never did she imagine she would learn this: that Seraphine had been using Bloom as some kind of exemplar. But why? How did that fit with their hiding in the shadows and espousing the virtues of Machiavellian politics?

43

Jameson awoke on his sofa with his arm attached to an IV line that hung on a stand next to him. When he moved his head it pounded and the room began to spin so he lay back for a moment. The hours that followed Jameson's last conversation with Porter had not been pleasant. The dehydration had kicked in at a serious level, making him dizzy and confused. He'd attempted to leave the room numerous times, bruising his fingertips as he'd scraped at the locked door. He'd also called out for help until his throat was sore and the words would no longer come. Eventually he slumped to the floor and passed in and out of consciousness, each time waking to the confusion of trying to work out where he was as his brain struggled to function.

And now he was home.

This was another message from Porter: not only can I get to you, I can end you quietly and secretly so no one will ever know, and if I can do this to a person trained to survive, imagine how easy it will be to take defenceless women and children like your sister and your nieces.

Jameson realized he was dealing with a particularly brutal kind of bastard.

He slid his feet off the sofa and sat up – slowly, allowing the dizziness to pass. His house keys had been in his pocket so whoever had delivered him home would have had no hardship getting him inside, but the alarm had been on. He reached out to switch on the table lamp. It stayed dark. They'd cut the power. Figures. He removed the IV and went to fetch water from the kitchen. His phone was gone. He'd have to report it stolen. He opened the drawer and removed the new Pay As You Go one he kept for emergencies. He opened it up and checked the charge, then he called the emergency number for his electricity company to request his power be reconnected. While he waited for them to arrive, he'd catch up on his sleep. And then he needed to speak to Augusta and his sister.

44

Bloom trotted to catch the cardinal up. This trip was becoming disturbingly personal. The tentacles of Seraphine's activities reached right into the heart of her life. It had been going on for years, a decade maybe or even longer.

Fifteen years ago, at age fourteen, while being counselled by Bloom, Seraphine had lured a young drug addict to a remote railway bridge where they had swapped clothes and jewellery. Not long after that, the drug addict was killed on the tracks below, her body decimated by the high-speed train, leaving everyone to believe that Seraphine was dead. How long before she had been back on her feet enough to start infiltrating Bloom's life? No more than five years, if she knew about Greg.

Bloom realized she had unwittingly put her mother in harm's way. It felt as though her world was tilting on its axis and her only option was to keep moving forward and hope she didn't fall.

As she reached Sousa, she decided that if she wanted the truth she needed to start telling it. 'It was actually Seraphine who sent me here to see you. To check if your allegiance was moving to Gerald Porter.'

Sousa looked her way. His expression was amused. 'She always said you would come around.'

'I have come around to nothing. She had my friend arrested to blackmail me. She sent me to see Koen Laukums and Miriam Chevalier and tonight I'm supposed to fly to Cyprus to meet the major general in command of the British Forces out there. But I am done being used and I want answers.'

'And you expect me to give them to you?'

'You've been more plain-speaking than anyone so far, plus you owe me for how you used my mother.'

'You think that such an emotive argument will work on me? I thought you knew better.'

'I'm treating you without judgement, Cardinal Sousa. I'm speaking to your humanity, not your psychopathy. You are logical – you said it yourself. Seraphine came to me for help despite my having stopped her activities successfully in the past. Why would that be?' Bloom felt conflicted about whether Seraphine had genuinely turned to her because she was the only person who could help or because the woman was up to something.

'You are asking the wrong question.'

They passed a couple walking in the opposite direction, who bowed and spoke in Italian to Sousa. He placed his hands in a prayer position and said something that sounded like a blessing in response. The couple looked entirely delighted and moved away with large grins and excited chatter. The cardinal was a rock star to some people.

'What is the right question?'

Sousa paused alongside a large walled-up entrance. The doorway was surrounded by carved stone. He pointed to a round medieval tower beyond, topped with a ring of windows.

'This is one of my favourite structures here. It was converted into an apartment by Pope John XXIII, who resided there in the final years of his papacy. What a wonderful experience that must have been.'

Bloom could only imagine the decadence of converting the interior of this large stone cylinder. It spoke of the wealth and privilege afforded to those at the helm of the Catholic Church. She could understand why such an organization would hold an appeal for the likes of Francis Sousa.

'Should you try to stand in our way . . .' Sousa said as Bloom gazed up at the tower.

Her eyes moved slowly back to his. 'I never expected to be threatened by a priest.'

'One of our core remits is the issuance of threats. We threaten hell and damnation and the loss of the Lord's love on a daily basis. But that is not what I meant here.'

'What are you threatening me with then?'

The street was quiet. There was a restaurant a little farther along but it was closed. In between were a couple of apartment buildings. She couldn't see any people but that didn't mean they weren't there. A man such as this would not dare to harm her here. It was too public. Plus he was old and probably not as strong as he thought. She was not a tall woman but she was fit and more than thirty years his junior. All of this was no real defence, she knew. Despite the cardinal's impressive outfit, softly spoken words and seemingly gentle ways, there was something familiar in his cold, hard stare.

'You misunderstand me. I am telling you that the right question to ask is, "*Should* you try to stand in our way?"'

'Because some harm will come to me if I do?'

'Augusta, you are doing the very thing that every psychologist, psychiatrist and criminal investigator does when faced with a psychopath or a sociopath. You are stereotyping. You are valued by Seraphine because you have faith that people can choose who they are despite the cards they may have been dealt. Do not forget that.'

A large black car pulled up to the grass verge and stopped. The driver was a Swiss Guard in his distinctive blue, red, orange and yellow Renaissance-style uniform. Swiss Guards were the military unit assigned to protect the Pope. He climbed out and opened the rear door nearest to the cardinal and Bloom.

'Our time is at an end, I am afraid.' Sousa once more took one of Bloom's hands in his own. 'A true pleasure.'

'Wait.' She spoke quietly so the guard would not overhear. She did not want to embarrass or out the cardinal. He had said and done nothing in this conversation to warrant that. In fact, he had been surprisingly helpful. 'Why shouldn't I stand in your way? And how about Porter, are you intending to align with him, and if not why not?'

'After our conversation, do you really think Seraphine sent you to me because of Porter or ... because she wants you to discover something of greater importance?'

The old man bowed his head and climbed into the back seat of the car. The guard closed the door, returned to the driver's seat and drove slowly away, leaving Bloom alone in the road.

Should you try to stand in our way? she repeated in her head. Not a threat but an enquiry, a request to think carefully before deciding.

But how could she decide if she had no idea what they were doing?

45

Jameson's first stop had been Bloom's home, and when she wasn't there he had come here to their office in Russell Square. What he had to tell her was not a conversation for the phone.

The place was locked up and in darkness. He had been the only one in on Friday and the note he'd left for Bloom on her desk saying he would be in a little late on Monday morning was still there. Untouched. He picked it up and looked around. It was Monday evening. Where was his partner and why hadn't she been into the office?

He'd last spoken to her on Friday afternoon after Superintendent Nesbitt's officers arrived unannounced at his flat. They'd insisted he bring his passport with him, and as he'd fetched it he'd made a quick call to tell Bloom that Seraphine had stitched him up for some reason. In his time with Nesbitt's team, and then at the mercy of Gerald Porter, he'd imagined Augusta first working tirelessly to release him and then, when she realized he had not returned home, organizing a search for him. But it appeared she might have done neither of these things.

He dialled her number on the Pay As You Go phone but it went straight to voicemail. *Where was she?*

He had a horrible feeling Gerald Porter might know the answer.

He looked up the number for DCI Mirza on his laptop and called her. When she answered he could hear the chaos of family life going on in the background. A dog was barking and a child was squealing. He couldn't tell if this was in delight or as part of some toddler's tantrum.

'Sorry to interrupt you at home,' he said. 'I wanted to check if Augusta has updated you about the Airbnb apartments in Philip Berringer's building?' It was the only thing he could think of as a reason to be making the call. 'I discovered some of the residents have been renting them out for a couple of years now and I wondered if Philip's killer might have used one. It would be a clever way to move in and out of the building without suspicion.'

'Funnily enough, your partner omitted to mention this when we spoke.'

Bingo. 'You spoke to Augusta? When was that?'

'Yesterday. You two should turn up the team communication.'

Jameson apologized, explaining he'd been engrossed in another case and Mirza said she'd ask the team to look into the Airbnb angle before hanging up.

So Bloom had been OK yesterday if she'd spoken to Mirza but she hadn't been into the office today. That was not unusual in itself. She sometimes chose to work remotely when she wanted to concentrate on something. He was an insatiable chatterbox and he knew that drove her crazy sometimes.

She might well be fine. No need to worry until necessary. Suppressing the image of Bloom sitting in the corner of her own improvised cell, he rang his sister Claire. 'Hey, sis, what you up to?'

Claire filled him in on the family's various mini-dramas, from Sophie's latest pre-teen tantrum to Jane's new love interest. Jameson listened and asked the appropriate questions when pauses came, but his head was not really in the conversation. He had to find a way to convince his sister and the three girls to go into hiding. He'd been running through the options all the way to the office. Claire would not want the girls knowing something was wrong. The best option was an impromptu holiday somewhere, but his sister wouldn't tolerate the girls missing school without good reason and it wasn't half term until next week. The only option he had was to tell her the truth, or at least a version of it.

His sister's foster daughter, Jane, had been the first person to alert him and Bloom to Seraphine's Psychopath Game last year when her mother Lana went missing to play it. Lana was nowhere near the calibre of Seraphine's other players, but had been selected because of her proximity to Bloom via Jameson and his sister Claire. In the course of their investigation, Jane had been kidnapped by her mother and threatened by Seraphine before eventually being returned safely. But it was an experience that Jameson knew had made his sister especially protective of the teenager.

When Claire had finished telling him about the neighbours posting a letter through the door requesting that the family keep the noise down, he took a breath and just said it: 'I'm sorry, Claire. Seraphine's back on the scene and I think she might come after Jane.'

46

'Uncle Marcus!' Sophie ran down the path and launched herself into his arms.

'All right, poppet.' Jameson wrapped his arms tightly around his eldest niece. 'When did you get so big? You'll be taller than your mum soon.'

Sophie grinned at him. She loved nothing better than being told she was growing up. Funny how you spent your childhood desperate to be older only to spend the rest of your life wishing you were young again.

Claire stood in the doorway, drying a mug with a tea towel. Despite the smile and cheery, 'Hello, bro,' he knew her well enough to detect she was unhappy with him. And rightly so.

His brother-in-law was out at the back of the house digging up one of the flower beds. He raised a hand in greeting as Jameson entered the kitchen-diner. Sophie had bounced upstairs to fetch her sister, Holly.

'You know where the kettle is,' Claire said as she continued to dry up the dishes and put them away. 'If I'd known you were coming over I'd have saved you some shepherd's pie.' She looked him up and down. 'You're looking too skinny again. Is that because of her?'

Yes and no, he thought. A weekend without food and

water had taken its toll and this was indirectly down to Seraphine.

'You want one?' he said, lifting the teabag.

'Go on then. Dan will too. He was supposed to do the garden yesterday but it rained non-stop.' She dropped her volume. 'We've got the new climbing frame coming for Holly's birthday, so he needs to make space.'

Jameson mentally checked the date. His youngest niece's birthday was on Wednesday. Claire would be reluctant to go anywhere without Dan until that had passed.

'How about I buy you all a trip to the seaside for her birthday?'

'Why would we want to go to the seaside?' Claire was no fan of sand and salty air. He should have known he'd get such a response.

'All right, well, a forest lodge then. With a hot tub.' He placed her tea by her side. 'All expenses paid. Once-in-a-lifetime offer.' He grinned but she stared him down.

'This is not funny. Even if Dan and the girls were up for it, Jane won't be. She's all about the new boyfriend now. She's eating at his parents' tonight.'

Jameson drank tea as he watched Dan digging. He should probably offer to help.

'Have you ever tried making a teenager do what they don't want to? That's a tough call when you're their actual parent, but when you're not . . .' She let the point hang.

'You're the closest thing to a real parent she's ever known. Don't put yourself down.'

'Why would Seraphine come after Jane again? Lana's out of the picture.' Lana was a woman who for years pretended to be in the military, leaving her daughter with Claire and Dan while she was deployed overseas, when in reality she was living a double life. She was also one of Seraphine's rejected game players. She hadn't made the cut and since then no one had heard from her. Hence his sister and brother-in-law applying to become Jane's foster parents.

'Sis, you know I wouldn't ask if I didn't think it was important.'

'Holly's having a sleepover at the weekend. She's been planning it for months. Going away will break her heart.'

He watched Claire press her lips into a flat line just like their mum used to when one of them had annoyed her. Their mother had not been a shouter. When he or Claire had been naughty as kids, she would go quiet, sometimes going for whole days without looking at them or speaking directly to them. It was a powerful punishment that rendered the recipient totally powerless.

'Can we just talk about it?'

Claire faced him and folded her arms. 'How long do you expect us to go into hiding for?'

'What's this?' Dan entered through the bi-fold doors. His face was smeared with mud and he was wiping his hands on an old cloth.

'Marcus wants to pay for us all to go on holiday.'

Dan laughed.

'I'm not joking.'

Dan closed the door. 'Why on earth would you do

that, Marcus? Feeling guilty about abandoning your family for months on end?'

Claire said, 'Seraphine's back.'

Dan became momentarily still before he turned the lock on the doors and then crossed the room to close the door to the hallway.

'This is the first you've mentioned it?' Jameson said, surprised that Claire had not filled her husband in immediately after their phone call.

'I was hoping it was one of your practical jokes.'

'I don't joke about that woman.'

'You'd better tell us what's going on.' Dan joined his wife, putting the cloth down on the work surface before placing his hand over hers.

'At the beginning of the year, Augusta investigated a women's rights group that turned out to be a cult. While she was at one of their retreats the whole thing imploded. I won't go into it but something happened and I messed up.' He wrapped both hands around his mug. 'I asked Seraphine to help.'

'What? Why the hell would you—'

'Let him speak,' Dan said, interrupting Claire.

'I needed someone impervious to their mind-controlling tactics to find out what was going on and she seemed like a logical solution. I know, I'm an idiot, you don't have to tell me.'

They were interrupted by Sophie and Holly, the latter dressed in a whole series of scarves tied around what looked to be a frilly swimming costume.

'We're hungry. Can we have a snack?' They both

flopped on to the armchair and immediately began arguing about who sat down first.

'Girls, stop arguing and go up to your rooms. I'll bring you some snacks,' Dan said.

After a prolonged negotiation over whether biscuits, chocolate and ice cream constituted snacks or not, an agreement was reached that they be served a bowl of fruit with a pot of yogurt each. The girls left happy with the outcome and Dan set about selecting fruit from the bowl to slice up.

Claire picked up the conversation as soon as the girls were out of the room. 'What the fuck, Marcus? You should be staying the hell away from that woman after everything she's put you through.'

'I know, and I'm sorry. Believe me, it was my only choice at the time.'

'So, you asked her for help and now, what, she's planning to mess with the family again?' Dan began filling two bowls with sliced apple and orange segments.

'She says I owe her one and need to return the favour.'

'What's that got to do with Jane?' Claire said.

Jameson and Dan exchanged a look.

'What?' said Claire. 'What are you both not saying?'

'I think Marcus means if he doesn't do what Seraphine wants him to do, she'll come after Jane,' said Dan.

'What does she want you to do?'

'You don't want to know.'

'Of course we do. If you want us to up sticks and hide for God knows how long we want to know how easy or difficult this task is to do, don't we, Dan?'

Dan was looking at Marcus with his hands flat on the table either side of the two snack bowls. After a long moment of silence, he looked at his wife.

'No, Claire. I don't think we do.'

Smart man, thought Jameson, breathing an internal sigh of relief. Dan would talk Claire and Jane around, he felt sure.

47

Jameson drove home in the usual manner: never taking the same route and randomly changing course to weave through side roads. It was a habit from his life in MI6 that he had purposefully kept. On average it only took him ten minutes longer to make the journey than it would following the most direct route and he liked to think it kept him sharp.

His phone rang halfway into the trip. He'd spoken to the mobile phone company earlier in the day to report his phone stolen and arranged for them to divert calls and messages to his temporary Pay As You Go number until they could get a replacement SIM to him.

'Hi, Marcus, sorry I haven't called sooner.' Bloom sounded tired and the line was not great.

'You've got an echo. Shall I call you back?'

'The signal's bad here. I don't think it will make any difference.' She paused before saying, 'I'm in Rome.'

'The signal's usually OK at your house. I'll try calling you.'

'Not home, Marcus. I'm in Rome, Italy.'

'Where are you? Tell me exactly.' He'd been so distracted thinking about the conversation with Claire he'd not considered Augusta might be calling for help.

'It's fine. I'm fine. I'm here for work, kind of.'

'Matchbox Murder work? I spoke to Mirza and she didn't mention you'd gone away?' He began to steer to the side of the road so he could park.

Bloom said something indecipherable. The line broke up, making her sound like an eighties comedian performing the broken microphone act.

'I didn't get any of that.'

She spoke again, the line remained bad and eventually cut off but not before he made out one clear word: *Seraphine.*

He tried calling back without any luck. He knew she would try to find a better signal and call again so he continued his journey, trying to put the pieces together. On Friday, Seraphine had called Superintendent Ned Nesbitt to change her statement about the shooting of Stephen Green. He had done his best to assure the police his motive in the shooting had been defence of life, but they had still taken his passport away. Jameson had wrongly assumed Seraphine was petulantly messing with him for her own entertainment, but now things looked much more concerning. Bloom was abroad, it was something to do with Seraphine and he was not allowed to leave the country.

When Bloom called back, he was ready.

'Listen to me. You need to get on the next flight home. My arrest caused me to lose my passport. Seraphine did that on purpose, which means she wants you out there alone.'

'I only have one more visit. I'll be back tomorrow night.' The line was much clearer.

'Did you not hear me? I can't protect you.'

'But I can protect you.'

'What are you talking about?'

'Seraphine changed her story to Ned Nesbitt on purpose. She needed me to do something for her and you were the bargaining chip. When I'm done, she'll make sure your name is cleared.'

The fury ran hot in Jameson's veins but he spoke calmly. 'You do not need to do anything for that woman on my behalf.' It dawned on him that if he did what Porter asked his name might never be cleared because Seraphine would not be around to clear it. He might actually go to jail for the shooting of Green.

'Marcus, don't worry. I'm perfectly fine and getting very close to finally uncovering what Seraphine is doing and why.'

'Who cares?'

'We do. Until we really understand why she has gathered so many high-functioning psychopaths within one organization we won't rest, either of us. It's hanging over us like a dark cloud of paranoia. If we know why, we stand a better chance of stopping it.'

'It is not your responsibility to stop her. How many times do I have to tell you that? You did not make her do any of the things she is doing.'

'I lit a fuse, or started a snowball rolling. Whatever the metaphor, I somehow set Seraphine off on a mission. I won't rest easy until I understand my part in it. The consequences are too dire.'

'The consequences? The consequences are on her and

her circle of psychos. You can't do this to yourself. You. Are. Not. Responsible.'

'Is that what you tell yourself about Stephen Green and the others? How about Jodie?'

The fact that Bloom knew Jodie's name came as a shock. 'How do you know about her?' He couldn't bring himself to say her name out loud.

'Gerald Porter told me she was the reason you left MI6. She is the reason you beat yourself up, isn't she, because you feel responsible? I'm sorry to bring it up but I need you to understand how important it is for me to know whether I'm responsible for what Seraphine has done.'

A number of things clicked into place that he had previously found bemusing. Earlier in the year, Porter had asked Bloom to help find his niece, who was associated with the women's rights group Artemis. At the time, Jameson had not understood why she had agreed when she knew Porter was not only a psychopath but one of Seraphine's people. He had asked her to walk away but she wouldn't, and now he knew why. Porter had used Jameson's past with Jodie to manipulate Bloom. She had even told him as much when she quizzed him about why he'd left MI6, saying they really should talk about it some day because she was worried about him. *He* was the reason she had put herself in harm's way. *He* was the reason she had let Porter use her to escape DCI Mirza and Seraphine. *He* was the reason she had nearly died.

'Marcus? Are you still there?'

'I'm here.'

'I need you to trust me and for you to pick things up with the Matchbox Murders. Can you do that?'

'You should have told me.'

'I know. It all happened last minute and you were reeling from Nesbitt taking you in for questioning. I didn't want to add to that.'

'I mean you should have told me Porter briefed you about why I left MI6. You should have trusted me, then maybe you wouldn't have . . .' He didn't want to say *nearly died*. It was too real.

'I'm sorry. I wasn't sure if broaching it would be an issue.'

'There are things you need to know about . . . Jodie's death.' He left off the phrase *and its consequences*, realizing he knew exactly what Bloom was talking about. He felt hugely responsible for what had happened to Jodie and had spent months trying to uncover the truth. He couldn't stand in Bloom's way with this. It would be hypocritical. Stopping her from digging was not an option. His only option was to keep her safe.

'But forget Jodie for now,' he said. 'Tell me everything. What has Seraphine asked you to do and what have you uncovered?'

48

Sandy reached out into the cold darkness. He felt sure voices had awoken him. He had been here for a long time, he knew. He had no energy to get up and move and yet he wasn't hungry. That was probably a bad sign. His body had given up all hope of food so decided to ignore the impending starvation.

He swallowed back the tears that threatened to come. He was not a crier. His mother had praised him for that. She had called him her tough little soldier and he had felt proud. They had not spoken in years. It was like she stopped loving him when he reached adulthood. She simply wasn't interested any more. He would call and suggest coming over but she always had an excuse for why he shouldn't. Eventually he stopped suggesting it, and then he stopped calling altogether. Part of him expected this to spur her on to call him but she never had and the years had rumbled on.

As he drifted off again a single thought comforted him.

If she knew I was alone and in trouble she would come.

49

Nadia Mirza arrived at work to find her DS, Carl Peters, waiting in her office with the force press officer. That couldn't be good.

'All major news outlets received the same email at midnight last night from someone claiming to be the Matchbox Murderer,' said Peters.

'What did it say?'

The press officer handed Mirza a sheet of A4 with the email printed on it.

From: eyesonyou@gmail.com　　　　　　　　00:01
To: editor@dailymail.co.uk
Subject: 11 London men murdered
(and the police haven't said a word)

What if you're next? How can you protect yourself from us if
they keep you in the dark?
Our beady eyes are watching you
So take this as a little clue
We'll strike the match
You'll feel the burn

And finally
YOU WILL LEARN

'Are they printing this?' said Mirza.

'They agreed to hold off on the email content if we confirmed that these murders are all connected,' said the press officer.

'It says eleven murders. That's what Dr Bloom suggested,' Peters said.

'Of course she did.'

'You still think this is Seraphine Walker's doing?'

Mirza saw the scepticism in her DS's face. She knew this changed everything. The investigation was no longer her own. The press would want answers and continual updates on what she and her team were doing to protect the men of London. If this was Seraphine Walker's doing it was a master stroke. And if it wasn't, well . . . God help them all.

50

Jameson switched on BBC News as he prepared a quick breakfast before heading into the office.

Police have confirmed today that the deaths of as many as eleven men in the Greater London area may be linked to the same killer or group of killers. These include the recent murders of Sheikh Nawaf al Saud at the St Pancras Hotel in April and financier George Shulman, who was attacked metres from his Knightsbridge home on 14 May.

Jameson whistled. He expected DCI Mirza would be furious. He hoped to God that whoever tipped off the press wasn't one of her own team.

Bloom had asked him to take a look at the consistencies she'd spotted across the Matchbox Murder scenes. She wanted to know if he thought it was significant. She had not told him specifically what she'd seen, simply asking him to look for examples of overly ordered neatness.

After half an hour of studying the images he had to agree there was a quirkiness to the way things had been tidied up: from the paperwork in the rear of Keith's Range Rover, which had been stacked in a size-ordered pile that Jameson doubted would survive any journey, to the leaves and branches around George's body in the park, which looked to have been brushed aside into neat little piles. It was as if the killer wanted a perfect canvas on which to display his wares. The more he'd looked, the more examples he'd found. Each was easy to overlook on its own, but Bloom was right about it feeling weirdly similar across the crime scenes.

The only photographs where he could not find any examples were those in Philip Berringer's file. Neither the images of the bar area, where Philip had fallen from the balcony, nor those of Philip's apartment displayed any overly ordered items. Jameson made a note to flag this to Bloom. Why hadn't the killer tidied this scene? Had he run out of time?

Sitting back in his chair to look at the whiteboard Bloom had filled with the details of all the deaths, Jameson was struck by the ridiculousness of trying to solve other people's murders when he had been tasked with carrying out the same deed. His sister had called this morning to say she and Dan were going away to a place in Devon with all three girls. He reminded her to pay for everything in cash and to leave their phones and computers at home. He'd bought her a temporary phone so they could keep in touch. 'Enjoy living off the grid for a bit,' he'd said as light-heartedly as he could. She had sworn at him; then she told him she loved him and to stay safe.

He swallowed the bile that climbed up his throat as he realized he was actually contemplating doing this. One life to save five. The irony was not lost on him that this was the exact moral dilemma Seraphine had presented to Augusta as they neared the end of uncovering the Psychopath Game. Bloom had described how researchers had designed a test to determine the basics of human morality. Imagine you have four patients in a hospital all needing life-saving transplants: when a single visitor who is a match for all four of them arrives, would you sacrifice the one to save the four? Most people say of course not, it would be immoral, but a psychopath would simply see the logic of saving four lives.

What did that make him?

Bloom was desperate to uncover what Seraphine was up to and maybe he could help with that. He could coerce it out of her in the final moments. Make her admit everything in exchange for mercy. The idea was preposterous, he knew. Seraphine would smile and mock him and relinquish nothing, no matter how desperate her fate might look.

Bloom said Seraphine had the President of Latvia in her pocket, along with a minister in the French government and a cardinal with direct access to the Pope, but perhaps most frightening of all a major general in charge of British forces in Cyprus. This was the military's gateway to the Middle East, the source of some of the world's most critical threats to peace. He was also a man in charge of armed personnel. Jameson had made it quite clear that Bloom should not keep that particular appointment.

What Seraphine could do with those four people alone didn't bear thinking about.

If he took her out, effectively removing the head of her organization, the body might die with her. But he knew that was unlikely. Removing the head was exactly what Porter wanted him to do, so the man could step in at the helm. Jameson was certain this would only make things worse. For him and Bloom at least. For some reason Seraphine was attached to them like a twisted kind of magnet. Whether this was driven by obsession or a desire to control them like a puppeteer was irrelevant because the result was the same: contact. He and Bloom had more chance of understanding and affecting whatever this circle of psychos were doing if its founder remained in their orbit. Replace her with Porter and their access dropped away.

The memory of laughing with Seraphine amidst sunlit sheets arrived unexpectedly. It was from a time when he'd thought she was a different person entirely. When he'd stupidly thought she might be his soulmate. Discovering the truth had been a levelling jolt. He had been fooled not only personally but professionally. Which was why he hated her so much.

But was that enough to kill her?

In cold blood?

He knew it wasn't. What he was struggling to find was an alternative solution.

51

Bloom listened to the voicemail message as she waited to clear security at Heathrow.

'Dr Bloom, it's Tyler. We've had a development and the DCI wanted me to brief you. The press have got hold of the serial killer story. It's all over the news. We're having a meeting at eleven and the boss wants us all to attend. I'll send you the link.'

She connected to the airport Wi-Fi and checked BBC News. Sure enough, the lead story read: *Met police confirm that a spate of murders in London may be the work of a serial killing gang.*

A gang. That was something of an exaggeration. Did the press really need to say that?

Given the changing state of the Matchbox Murder investigation, she was relieved she had made the decision to come back to the UK instead of travelling on to Cyprus. In her conversation with Jameson yesterday he had emphasized how dangerous the major general could be if he was in Porter's pocket, and so she had cut the trip short. She knew Seraphine would not be happy but that made two of them. Her disgust at having been used and spied on for years increased every time she thought about it.

Bloom focused on the sound of the rain hitting the

roof of her black cab. The rhythmic pitter-patter made her feel calm and grounded in a way she hadn't at all in the past few days. The people she had met and the conversations she'd had felt surreal in hindsight. The implausibility of stepping off a plane and into the company of some of the most powerful people in Europe felt stark. Nothing about Seraphine's world fitted her prior experience. She had no reference points to help her to make sense of it or even accept it. It felt like a movie plot, something straight out of the pages of Dan Brown or John le Carré.

She knew, from previous dealings, that Seraphine's contacts spread far and wide. But Bloom hadn't seen it in person. So it had been easy to push the idea of it aside and carry on with life as normal. But now she was inside the rabbit warren. The world was tilting ever more sharply. She saw how connected people in power across the world could be. How their allegiances bonded them. Allegiances that in an ideal world were based on shared morals and principles but which could be so much darker. Secret societies and organized crime had existed throughout history, but they were by their nature hidden from view. It was easy to pretend they didn't affect any of your own day-to-day experiences but of course they did. They determined who had power and this in turn affected what got done. Seraphine's dark players were placed on the world's stage in all manner of strategic positions. Ready and waiting. And Bloom might be the only outsider capable of seeing them clearly.

The weight of that responsibility felt heavy. She

wanted to hide from it; to simply walk away and go back to pretending she didn't know what she knew. But that was not an option. She had to steel herself to look at what was there, no matter how disturbing the view might be. It reminded her of the first crime-scene photographs she had ever seen: an inconsiderate bully of a police inspector had walked into the office one day when she was a young psychologist and thrown thirty or so pictures across her desk. The images were brutal: bloody scenes of murder and mayhem, the worst of which were industrial accidents showing destroyed body parts tangled up with unforgiving machinery. 'If you're going to be any use to us, you'll have to develop a strong stomach,' the inspector had said. He wasn't wrong, but his shock tactics were just that: shocking. For months afterwards the images had come back to Bloom – in the middle of a meal with friends or tea with her parents – each time taking her breath and her appetite away.

She needed to brace herself for a similar trauma now. Seraphine had cracked open the door but what Bloom needed to do was be brave enough to push it wide and take a good look inside. She only hoped she had the stomach for it.

52

'Where have you been?'

Jameson turned very slowly in his chair.

Seraphine stood in the office doorway, her navy blouse speckled with raindrops and her hair sticking to her face in wet strands. She brushed it away and behind her ears. She had some nerve walking in here.

'You disappeared for three days. Where were you?' she said.

'I got held up.' He leaned back in his chair and wondered whether the universe had brought her here to help him or to mock him.

'Held up where?'

'What's it to you?'

Seraphine held his gaze, her eyes narrowing a touch, and he felt as though she was trying to telepathically drag the answers from his brain.

He said, 'You wanted rid of me, didn't you? So I couldn't stop you sending Augusta off on your wild goose chase.'

She finally looked away and up at the wall behind him. 'The police have some crazy idea I'm behind these murders.'

'What did you expect? You took the piss out of the justice system. In my experience, the police don't like that.'

'So long as they do not dislike it enough to frame me, I couldn't care less.'

'Why would they need to frame you? I imagine there's a truckload of crimes they could convict you of.'

She stepped towards him. 'Do you think I'm behind this?' Her eyes flicked to the whiteboard. 'You can tell the truth. I won't be angry.'

'Like that would stop me.'

'Do you?'

Jameson folded his arms. 'Answer me this first. What game is Porter playing with you?'

'He's not playing any game.' She smiled and for a second he saw the woman she'd pretended to be. The sexy, funny, potential soulmate. 'Well, if you were worried, let me assure you that these murders are nothing to do with me. I don't dabble in death. That's more up your street, isn't it?'

'I beg your pardon?' Jameson felt a chill. Did she know what Porter had tasked him with?

'Poor Mr Green.'

The audacity of the woman riled him. 'You faked your own suicide and did God knows what to the likes of Lana and the others who failed your test. And for the record I saved your life by killing Green so I suggest you keep your judgements to yourself.'

'I know you did. And thank you, Marcus. Have you asked yourself why you did that yet?'

He had but he wasn't about to share any insights with her. 'Why are you here?'

'I told you. I want to know where you've been?'

'And I'm telling you it's none of your business.' He should tell her the truth. Tell her what Porter had tasked him to do. That might solve all his problems as he felt sure Seraphine and her buddies were more than capable of looking after themselves, but he couldn't risk endangering Bloom or his family.

She nodded slowly and then moved to sit down.

'Oh no you don't.' Jameson could not have her here for much longer. This might be his one opportunity to be alone in a room with her and the pressure to take advantage would only continue to build. He hated himself for it, but he'd already scanned the room for weapons he might use. He couldn't risk her staying. He desperately wanted to protect Augusta and his family, but he needed time to find a way of doing it that he could live with.

'What time are you expecting Augusta back?'

'You know she's coming home early?'

'I know everything, Marcus.'

'Except for where I've been. It's driving you mad, that, isn't it? That's why you've come here to eyeball me personally. Well, suck it up, sweetheart. Some of us have skills your tentacles can't circumvent.'

'I'm banking on it.'

The response threw him. Did she know Porter planned to use him against her? Was she hoping she could twist that in her favour? Is that what that smile had been about, reminding him of some distant connection between them? He wouldn't put it past her.

He said, 'I'll ask her to call you, if you like. You guys

must have tons to catch up on now she's been hanging out with your besties.'

'Do you two really tell each other everything?'

'Everything that matters, yes.' This was a lie. He had told Bloom little of the stuff that mattered. And she was a fricking closed book. He didn't even know if she was gay or straight. Other than her history with Seraphine, he knew nothing of her life experiences prior to their meeting.

'I expected you to be more angry about the arrest.'

Jameson realized he had messed up. She was right. If it weren't for Porter's demands playing on his mind, he'd have been throwing her out with a good number of choice words about how she was trying to frame him for Stephen Green's murder.

'I'm choosing to ignore your idiocy,' he said, but it was a weak defence. She already knew there was something wrong. For all Seraphine's failings, she was as streetwise and astute as any covert operative. He had acted out of character and now she would be watchful, so he had lost the advantage of surprise. It would make the whole thing so much harder.

'I can't let you stand in Augusta's way. She needs to do what I've asked of her.'

'*She* doesn't need to do anything. This is all about you, as always. Augusta is only doing what you ask because she's terrified she's responsible for the monster you've become. But she's not. You and I know it, because we both know what you are. You're a sick cancer eating away

216

at our lives, making yourself stronger by leeching off others.'

'You say the sexiest things.'

'I'm not joking, Seraphine. This is not banter. I wish you had never slithered into our lives and if I could find a cage that would hold you, I'd gladly turn the key and leave you to rot.'

'Now you're getting kinky.'

Jameson inhaled deeply and counted to ten. He hated how she so easily goaded him into losing control but it was good to feel the familiar anger and disgust. He needed it.

'Get out of here, Seraphine. You're not welcome. And please don't turn up without an invitation in future.'

'As you wish.'

He despised how in control she always stayed. It only made his outbursts more uncomfortable. Years of training in MI6 had never enabled him to do what she did so naturally. Jodie had said it was a strength that he felt so passionately about things but faced with the likes of Seraphine he wasn't sure. He knew she looked down on him for it. In her eyes, feelings made you weak and, although he hated to admit it, he agreed with her.

She was standing in the doorway with her back to him. But she made no move to leave.

A tingle of adrenaline began to fizz in his veins. If she'd guessed he had been with Porter for the past few days it wouldn't take much for her to work out what her opposition had called on him to do. What then? She would not hesitate. He knew that absolutely. She would act decisively to protect herself and her empire.

There were scissors in his top drawer. They were his closest means of defence.

'I know you don't want to tell me where you were,' she said eventually. 'But at least tell me . . .' She turned slightly to look at him. 'Are you OK?'

Jameson was still wired and he opened his mouth to answer, but then closed it again. Her words were so unexpected, so concerned, that he was unsure what to say. After a moment of silently processing her question he said, 'I am now.'

'OK then,' she said. Her eyes held his gaze and she smiled. The kind of smile that triggered memories.

'OK then,' he repeated and, despite his better judgement, he smiled back.

53

Bloom made it home with ten minutes to spare before she needed to join DCI Mirza's team briefing. The email invite Tyler Rowe had forwarded on included a terse instruction that all invitees were expected to attend in person or virtually unless a strong reason was provided for their absence. It was not an unfamiliar tone given her background within the police environment but it had been many years since she had been included in such a circular.

After a quick freshen-up and brush of her hair, she set up her laptop on the kitchen island and dialled into the meeting. The screen told her she was in a waiting room and would be let in when the meeting began. While she waited Bloom made a few notes on her thoughts about the case so far.

The screen flickered black and then she saw a number of boxes pop up on her screen. One showed the detective chief inspector with Tyler Rowe and half a dozen other people around a large oval table. The other four windows, including her own, contained individuals who had dialled in remotely.

'Thank you for your prompt arrival, everyone,' DCI Mirza began. 'As you know, the press have become aware of the Matchbox Murders and I'm sure you're all wondering how that happened. Let me assure you this was not a leak.' Mirza projected an email on to the screen in the conference room and simultaneously shared her screen with Bloom and the other virtual attendees. 'Press outlets were sent this at midnight last night claiming to be from one of the killers.'

Bloom read the email.

'We suspect the killers are frustrated that they are not getting the attention they deserve or desire. It's a sad fact that many serial killers crave recognition for their work,' Tyler Rowe said.

'If this is really from the killers,' said DC Morgan. 'It could be a hoax, like that Geordie who pretended to be the Yorkshire Ripper.'

'I think the fact that the email mentions eyes, match-boxes and eleven victims suggests whoever sent this is in the know,' said Mirza.

'If we accept the idea there are two killers, the struck matches suggest eight victims for one killer and three for the other. That gives us eleven,' said Rowe.

'Do we have any idea who the other five victims are?' said an officer Bloom did not know.

'We're looking into it,' said Mirza. 'I've asked the digital team to trace the email but we're anticipating the sender will have covered his tracks.'

'So whoever sent this is goading us?' said DS Peters.

Bloom read and reread the email before turning her microphone on.

'I don't think the writer of this email is goading the police. I think he's trying to create panic. Phrases like

What if you're next? How can you protect yourself? and *You'll feel the burn* are not directed at police but at the public, at potential victims.'

'Which is why this email cannot be made public,' said Mirza. 'I can't emphasize this enough. We do not play into their hands whoever they may be. Is that understood? This remains confidential.'

'Ma'am,' the group chorused together.

'Right. Carl, where are we up to with Prestige Wealth Management?'

Bloom was taken aback that the DCI chose to move on from the email so swiftly. If it had been sent by one of the killers, which Bloom suspected it had, it was a gift. It included clues to the perpetrator's motivation and state of mind. It needed to be fully interrogated.

DS Peters began briefing the team. 'We questioned all five staff. They have three female admin staff and two male independent financial advisors, Russell Rigby and Hardeep Singh. Russell is the MD of the company. He contacted us after the attack on George Shulman because both George and Keith Runnesguard were clients of theirs. He was spooked that they had been murdered within a few months of each other. Obviously, both of these attacks were widely reported within the press so he knew about them. But when we questioned him about the other victims it turns out Jeremy Tomlinson was also a client. So that's three of our victims linked to this company. We're thinking that can't be a coincidence. Our techs are going through their computers as we speak.'

'Good work,' said Mirza.

'Are you viewing the fact that Russell came forward as a sign he's not involved?' said Rowe.

Peters shrugged. 'We'll keep an open mind but both he and Hardeep Singh have tight alibis for the murders of at least two of their clients each. Plus these guys seemed genuinely freaked out that their company might have been targeted. They both independently asked for protection in case the killers come after them. Russell became quite stroppy when we couldn't provide any.'

'And the women? We can't rule them out,' said DC Morgan on the opposite side of the table. 'Who are their husbands, brothers and sons?'

Bloom unmuted her microphone and put a virtual hand up.

'Go ahead, Dr Bloom,' Mirza said.

'Do we have any reason to believe the killer or killers are definitely male?'

Mirza sighed a little. 'Do you enjoy throwing in these red herrings?'

Bloom muted herself again and sat back. Mirza definitely had a problem with her.

'To Dr Bloom's point,' said Peters, 'we have no confirmed physical evidence. The attacks don't have any sexual element to them, for instance, but a good number of them call for physical strength. Lifting Philip over the balcony or stabbing Keith with enough force to chip bones would require male strength, we think.' He turned to Fleur Morgan. 'We're looking into the families of all five but as yet nothing's come up.'

*

Twenty minutes later Bloom was speaking directly to DCI Mirza on the phone. Bloom had texted her in the closing minutes of the meeting to say, *I think we need to talk. Please call me.* She wouldn't have been surprised if her request had been ignored but to Mirza's credit it was not.

'Do we have a problem, Nadia? Have I done something to offend you?'

'Have you had any contact with Seraphine Walker since we interviewed her?'

Bloom was thrown for a moment and then she saw it clearly. Seraphine had purposefully met her outside New Scotland Yard last week to undermine Bloom's reputation with the police. She'd known someone would see them and report back to the DCI. She'd probably hoped Bloom would be thrown off the case so she was completely available to work for her. That's why she'd made that snide little comment about DCI Mirza not being so concerned about Bloom's involvement in the case.

'I have spoken to her, yes, but not about this case.'

'So what did you discuss?'

'A personal matter.'

'Which is?'

'Personal.'

There was a long silence before Mirza said, 'I took a gamble letting you advise on this case, Dr Bloom. I don't appreciate being used and manipulated.'

You and I both, Bloom thought. 'You have nothing to worry about. You asked for my input *because* I have a connection to Seraphine. You can't judge me for the very thing you coveted.'

'If you are to remain on the team, I need to know every instance of contact you have with Walker and what is said that might relate to this case. Is that understood?'

Bloom felt her hackles rise. DCI Mirza clearly thought that Bloom was not to be trusted. It was the kind of insult to her professional credibility that stung. But it explained why Mirza's team were not interrogating the email. The woman was paranoid that Seraphine was manipulating things and most likely suspected the email was some form of deflection.

Bloom read the notes she had made on the content of the killers' email after they hung up: 'Our beady eyes are watching you, So take this as a little clue. We'll strike the match, You'll feel the burn, And finally, YOU WILL LEARN.'

These killers had a truth they wanted to teach the world and people they wanted to destroy. They were focused, motivated professionals adept at avoiding capture. And the fact that the senior investigating officer was stuck on an alternative theory was going to play right into their hands.

54

AJ had never heard Lexi so angry. She often told him off for being impulsive or foolish but she never told Zander off. He was the strongest and the cleverest. So you didn't have a go at him.

'After everything I do to keep you all safe, you go and do something so stupid.' Lexi wasn't shouting but her voice sounded shrill. 'Did you know about this, AJ? Why didn't you tell me?'

AJ kept quiet. This was Zander's fight.

'Whatever possessed you to go to the press? We were doing fine. Everything was safe. You're risking everything, obsessing about teaching the world a lesson. They hadn't linked the men until you went and told them. What do we do now? What do we do about Sandy?'

Everything had kicked off this morning when Russell Rigby had left a message for Sandy saying the police wanted to speak to everyone at the firm, including contractors. Sandy had looked after IT at Prestige Wealth since they launched. He rarely went into the office, working mainly from home and sometimes going months without having anything to do for them. All this meant the company hadn't missed him, but now Russell was asking him to call back and that presented a problem.

'Calm down, Lexi. It had to be done,' Zander said,

and AJ knew the big man was taking charge now. 'What is the point of doing what we do if no one hears our warning? We want these parasites to know we are on to them. They need to feel terrified to step into the street because one of us might be waiting in the shadows. If you want to see real power, look no further than the press. They are the most powerful influencers in the world. They will scare people because that's their job and I will continue feeding them with the truth of things. It is such an obvious solution – I'm amazed I didn't think of it before. The rich think they own it all but it is the press who really do. So we will use the press.'

'Don't the rich own the press?' said Lexi, her voice still hard and tense. 'And what about Sandy? The police want to speak to him. What do we do about that?'

AJ felt ill all of a sudden. He had just realized why the police were looking at Prestige Wealth. He had initially used Sandy's login to search their database. It was an easy way to find rich men. He had found Keith, Jeremy and most recently George that way. Zander would be furious about that. He had made it clear the targets had to be independently sourced and random.

'I'll speak to the police,' said AJ. At least if he spoke to them he stood a chance of deflecting it. 'They don't know Sandy so I could pass for him.'

Lexi's laugh was harsh and mocking. 'You? I don't think so. You'd say something stupid and drop us all in it.'

'Well, you can't do it,' AJ said, feeling stung by the constant put-downs from the other two. He was just as

226

good at what they did. They had no right to treat him like the idiot kid.

'We'll send Sandy,' said Zander.

'We can't,' said Lexi.

'He'll tell them we've had him locked away,' said AJ.

'Not if we manage it right,' said Zander. 'Leave it to me.'

55

When Bloom walked into the office on Wednesday morning, Jameson was sitting at his desk with his usual takeaway coffee and an empty yogurt pot by his side. He looked up and smiled but it didn't quite reach his eyes. He was angry about her helping Seraphine.

Bloom dropped the *Daily Express* she had bought on her walk to the office on to his desk. The headline read: 'Serial Killers Name Their Victims'.

'I saw that on the news. Is it accurate?'

'I spoke to Tyler just now. The press received all eleven names in a second email last night. Tyler said Mirza's team are racing to confirm if the new names are legit but at least two of the five were confirmed to have had a matchbox at the scene.'

'These emails are definitely from our killers then.'

'It's looking like a strong possibility. They've been trying to send some kind of message all along with the matchboxes and the eyes. Now they're taking it public.'

'What about the tidying up? Is that part of their message?'

Bloom thought for a moment. 'It could be, if it's done intentionally, or it could be an unconscious tell; something one of the killers is compelled to do without giving it much thought.'

'I found something interesting when looking for more examples of it. There's no sign of it at all at Philip's scene. At first, I thought the killer was maybe disturbed by the barman coming back, but now I'm wondering if this was the start of it all. Could he have been stunned at what he'd done and got out of there quick, but then got a taste for it so skilled up?'

'It's a reasonable hypothesis but how does it tally with him being prepared enough to leave the matchbox and single match?'

Jameson shrugged. 'Maybe he's a smoker.'

'What was the eye image on Philip's matchbox?'

Jameson looked it up. 'Bulls Eye safety matches.' He showed her the image of the retro-style blue, gold and black box.

'That looks too old and specific to have simply been in his pocket. Plus Bulls Eye feels specially selected, don't you think? And now we have that first email with references to beady eyes watching you, we know that this symbol is important to the killer. Did you have any thoughts on the first email?' Bloom had asked Rowe to send her and Jameson a copy so they could analyse it further.

'Not the content so much as the medium. I think we can infer something about the sender's age by the fact that he went to the printed media. Any younger person would use social media instead, or as well.'

'Good shout.'

Jameson's eyes widened. 'Maybe he made a mistake with Philip. Something that worried him enough—'

'—to make him obsess,' finished Bloom. 'That's not a bad call. Send a note to Tyler and copy the DCI in. They may need to relook at that scene. She's unhappy with me at the moment so it would be good to show her we're still thinking.'

'Why, what have you done?'

'Apparently I'm in cahoots with Seraphine.'

Jameson raised his eyebrows and his expression asked, *Well, aren't you?*

'Mirza made it quite clear she doesn't trust me. I suspect she still thinks Seraphine is behind all of this and I'm feeding her information or something.'

Jameson pulled a face to show what he thought of that idea. 'Speaking of the devil woman, she paid me a visit yesterday. Walked in brazen as you like as if she wasn't responsible for having me arrested for murder.'

'What did she want?'

'Who knows with that meddling nutjob.'

'What did she say?' Bloom removed her jacket and hung it on the hook.

'Nothing of relevance.'

'She came here personally to say nothing of relevance?'

'I think she just wanted to see my pretty face.'

Bloom rolled her eyes.

'If I had to guess I'd say she was making sure I wasn't off somewhere trying to interfere with what she'd asked you to do.'

Bloom sat, closed her eyes and rubbed her temples. 'I need to look at Seraphine like a case and interrogate everything we know, everything she's ever said and done so I can work out a strategy.'

'But I thought you were done with all that – that's why you came home early.'

'I came home early because what I found was not . . .' She opened her eyes. 'It was worrying. I needed time to regroup.'

'Worrying how? And why the hell would you be prepared to carry on?'

'Because I realized I'm the only person who might ever get this close to uncovering the truth. If I'm right, if *we* are right that she is planning some global manoeuvre, I have a responsibility to find out as much as I can.'

Jameson sat back, his jaw tense and his anger bubbling. 'And she's made damn sure I can't help you.' Without a passport he was trapped in the UK.

Bloom smiled at him for the first time. 'Maybe she doesn't want you to see. Have you ever considered that?'

'Do we know the timeline of these new Matchbox Murders?' Jameson said, changing the subject.

Bloom turned to page four of the paper where a graphic had been used with the dates spread across the top of the double page and small round photos of each victim plotted underneath.

'Philip is still the first chronologically,' said Jameson, pointing to the start of the chart. The new victims filled in some of the larger gaps between the murders they already knew about. There was a Charles Sodenburgh and a Francis Green who both fell from internal balconies within their office blocks in between Philip and Simon's murders, William Forrester who had OD'd in his West End apartment two months after Simon died in the same manner, Mickey Glover who died of a single stab wound on his own doorstep a month before Jeremy drowned, and then Stefan Sloan who had been strangled just a few months before Nawaf suffered the same fate.

'Where were the other matches found then?'

'One was found in Mickey Glover's porch. They thought nothing of it as he was a smoker, but the crime-scene photographs clearly showed it next to his body on top of a London Eye matchbox. And five were found in William Forrester's kitchen.'

Bloom made a space on the whiteboard and wrote up the new list in chronological order separating victims by their killers and noting down the number of matches found.

Sept '16	Philip – 1 match	
Dec '16	Charles – ?	
Jan '17	Francis – ?	
Mar '17	Simon – 4 matches	
June '17	William – 5 matches	
Sept '17		Mickey – 1 match
Oct '17	Jeremy – 6 matches	
Nov '17		Keith – 2 matches
Jan '18	Stefan – ?	
Apr '18	Nawaf – 8 matches	
May '18		George – 3 matches

'So that's the full set for killer two and chances are Charles, Francis and Stefan will be found to have had two, three and seven matches left with them respectively,' she said. 'And the fact that we've seen the same neatness across all the scenes we've reviewed except for Philip's implies the OCD sufferer is attending his colleague's kills.'

'You're thinking OCD guy is killer one?' said Jameson. 'And killer two is what – some kind of trainee or apprentice?'

'It looks that way from how much later killer two started, yes. The neatness in the earlier scenes implies killer one is our neat freak. Add to that the fact the first set of murders involves three falls, two overdoses, a drowning and two strangulations all taking place inside the homes, offices or cars of the victims, while the second set has two stabbings and a beating all taking place outdoors, and you have a clear suggestion of different MOs. Clearly killer number one is the more brazen and skilful.'

'How does strangulation fit with your distant killer profile?' Jameson said. 'Didn't you say killer one wasn't interested in seeing the death, so why strangle them? That's pretty personal don't you think?'

'It depends if the killer is facing them or not. Strangle them from behind and that's still a fairly cold kill. Plus I wonder . . .' She looked at the list of victims again. 'Killer one doesn't strangle anyone until after killer two joins in.'

'So the second guy is egging him on?'

'Could be. Couple that with the emails to the press and this smacks of some pretty pacey escalation.'

'Thank goodness our police are totally focused on the task then, and not distracted by another tinpot theory.'

Indeed, thought Bloom.

56

Bloom arrived home early having been unable to shake her headache all day. She turned on Radio 4 for company as she warmed up vegetable soup bought from the deli down the road. Once the soup was hot, she poured it into a large mug and carried it upstairs to her makeshift office in the spare room. She had placed sheets of static whiteboard on the wall the night before and on top of these she'd stuck Post-it notes grouped into loose categories – all related to Seraphine.

She sipped the soup as she read them all again. The hot liquid felt good as it warmed her insides and soothed her head.

As she'd said to Marcus, she needed to treat Seraphine as a case and interrogate everything she knew. The night before she'd opened up her original hard-copy file from fourteen-year-old Seraphine's counselling sessions and spread it across her desk. If she had any chance of working out what Seraphine was up to, she needed to start with what happened first: the stabbing of a school caretaker with a pencil.

Bloom had written up phrases from her original notes on a whole batch of Post-its around the first incident. 'The young girl is intelligent', 'Unemotional about the attack', 'Displays anger at the caretaker being seen as a victim', 'Views her friends as weaker people'. Bloom had then written about Seraphine's apparent suicide as a teenager and how she had lured a young woman to the remote bridge over the railway line, convincing her to swap clothes and personal effects. The Post-its around this incident read, 'Where did she go?', 'How did she live?', 'Who helped her?', 'How long before she was settled?' and 'When did she start watching me?'

The next cluster related to Bloom and Jameson's contact with Seraphine over the past year. Bloom had entitled this section 'Mind Games' because that's what it had felt like. Seraphine had acted like a scorpion playing with its prey before delivering the killer sting. Bloom had notes recording how Seraphine had used the Dare to Play cards to grab Bloom's attention, how she had targeted Jameson's sister's friend Lana to ensure Marcus had a personal need for them to investigate and how she had seduced Marcus and used him to watch their progress. Her last two notes in this section read, 'Why has she recruited high-functioning psychopaths?' and 'Why did she attempt to recruit me?'

They had been in a dank, cold room under the railway arches of Leeds train station when Seraphine had told Bloom she wanted her to join her, believing Bloom was also a high-functioning psychopath. One who had hidden what she was even more successfully than Seraphine. When Bloom had denied it, Seraphine asked if Bloom was lying to herself, a question that had caused a good number of restless nights in the months that followed. Not least because Jameson appeared to buy the theory so readily. She was in no doubt now that the assertion was wrong. She had run through the Hare Psychopathy Checklist numerous times answering the questions as honestly as she could and she always came out with a score of no more than two. Psychopaths score thirty or more. Not that she had needed the test to know in her heart that it wasn't true. Her job required an incredible amount of empathy; if she couldn't apply this, she would never achieve the objectivity and insight needed to figure out why people do the things they do.

Bloom placed the mug down and grabbed the pad of Post-its. On the top one she wrote what Cardinal Sousa had told her, 'S values you for your lack of judgement about people'. She stuck this note up under the others. If this was true Seraphine must have known Bloom was not a psychopath all along. So why had she made such a claim? Was it simply to create the angst that it had? Was it to sow division between Bloom and Marcus? Or was it wishful thinking: did Seraphine simply like the idea of having one person from her past still in her life? Bloom had no idea.

She resumed drinking the soup as she looked at her final set of notes. This group looked like an organizational structure chart with Seraphine at the top and the names and jobs of the originators Bloom had been asked to meet lined up underneath. Below those, but a little separated, she had written Porter's name above a separate Post-it that read '20% of original psychopaths poached'. Finally, under all of that she had written the names of five other people she knew were active in the organization from her investigations of the Psychopath Game. Bloom knew this group was the tip of the iceberg – a small sample of Seraphine's membership that she had crossed paths with. She could almost imagine the many other players continuing to populate her chart in a spiderweb of cascading connections – not to mention the unsuspecting employees of any organizations these people operated within.

Why on earth would Seraphine be prepared to let Bloom see the scale of this now? Perhaps she had always intended to. She had tried to recruit her after all. But then Bloom had stood in her way; she'd sat in the courtroom hoping to see the woman convicted and effectively rejected her at every turn. Why would Seraphine continue to court her?

It couldn't be an emotional thing. It wasn't simply that Seraphine liked Bloom or loved Jameson – although Bloom suspected both of these things might be true to the extent that Seraphine was capable of such feelings. It had to be an intelligent, rational motivation. It had to be born out of logic.

Bloom took another Post-it note and wrote 'LOGICIANS' in capital letters – the description of the group Cardinal Sousa had used. She placed this above Seraphine's name on the wall. She then wrote the question Sousa had posed on the bottom of the whiteboard sheet itself: 'SHOULD YOU TRY TO STAND IN OUR WAY?'

The cardinal had implied she was wrong to be attempting to stop them. Not because any harm might come to her but because it was not the right thing to do. This meant what they were doing might be something she wouldn't wish to stop. Could that really be true, given the chaos represented on this wall?

The sound of her phone ringing downstairs interrupted her ponderings and she carried her now empty mug to the kitchen to answer. As she reached the room the phone on the side stopped ringing and there was a single loud knock on her door. Her phone beeped to indicate a message and Bloom grabbed it as she moved to the hallway. She didn't glance at the message until it was too late, until she had already turned the key and released the deadlock.

Seraphine   16:45
DO NOT OPEN THAT DOOR!

239

57

Jameson enjoyed cycling through the city. He knew it was more risky, especially in a busy city like London, but that simply added to the thrill. He had good skills and bright clothing and it was only a quick ten-mile spin from the office in Russell Square back to his flat in Wembley. The roads were busy, it was commuter hour so he had to keep his wits about him, but the effort was a welcome distraction from the circling thoughts about Porter's request.

He had sent Bloom home early. She looked pale and kept rubbing her forehead. She would never admit to feeling unwell or run-down. She had too much Yorkshire grit for that. So he'd had to force her out. Told her to go home, eat and sleep. She hadn't told him what she'd learned from her visits to Seraphine's people yet, but he knew better than to badger her. She would tell him when she had it straight in her own head. Years of working with her had taught him that. She was a thinker. She didn't like to share an insight or an opinion until she was sure of it herself. This was the opposite of how he liked to work. He operated best when he had someone to bounce thoughts around with. Jodie had been great at that. She was a chatterer like him and they had spent many an hour theorizing about who might be doing what and why. He missed that hugely. He loved Augusta and couldn't deny that his work with her had been challenging and fascinating, but Jodie had been easier company, and more fun.

A memory of sitting in a Leeds cafe talking to Seraphine came to mind. Every time he thought of Jodie these days the memories of Seraphine were quick to follow; his mind appeared determined to lay out some uncomfortable truth.

When the traffic became stationary, he stopped to drink some water and check his phone. He'd had a WhatsApp message from Claire's temporary phone simply saying *All well*. He sensed his sister might be secretly enjoying stepping into the world of espionage. Her messages were short and without detail. He half expected to receive something along the lines of *The swallows fly south for the winter* in true covert comms fashion soon.

He scanned an email from Tyler Rowe thanking Jameson for the message earlier about checking out Philip's murder scene for any mistakes the killer might have made. Rowe also said the new victims had all now been confirmed. He had signed off with the comment, *I really do appreciate all the help you and Dr Bloom can give me on this*. From what Augusta had said Tyler Rowe was as convinced as she was that the Matchbox Murders were the work of serial killers. Jameson could only imagine how frustrated the analyst must be if the police were still working alternate theories.

Jameson's unexpected arrest and subsequent abduction had interrupted the research he had been doing on the first few victims. He had yet to rebook his visit to Keith Runnesguard's country club where he'd been due to interview the manager for an article on the most exclusive clubs in the city. Now Keith's stabbing was part of a series of attacks he wondered if they would still be so keen to court publicity. He'd also intended to sound out Jeremy Tomlinson's colleagues at his tech firm. There had been no call back from Simon Middleton-Moore's family after he left 'Jasper's' number enquiring about his lost watch but that had been a long shot.

Continuing on his ride he pondered on how the first killer was gaining access to the homes and workplaces of these wealthy people without being seen. The second killer's victims, Keith, George and the newly identified Mickey, had been attacked outside so that was easily done. But the rest all took place inside residences or offices that were security protected or had manned receptions. So how had killer one managed that?

Jameson knew the Airbnb angle on Philip's apartment block was a strong contender for explaining this, especially given the killer's behaviour in the St Pancras Hotel where he had brazenly spent two nights living in his victim's room. This killer infiltrated his victim's worlds, waited for the right moment and then attacked. It brought a whole new meaning to the phrase: 'Our beady eyes are watching you.'

58

Gerald Porter stepped over the threshold into Bloom's hallway without invitation. Bloom moved back, wondering if she could somehow reply to Seraphine without looking at the phone in her hand. She felt sure your average teenager would do this without a problem but she had no idea what to press without the help of those little symbols.

'It is polite in British society to offer your guests tea,' said Porter, slowly moving her backwards along the hall to the kitchen.

'What do you want?'

'Milk no sugar would be marvellous, thank you.'

Without replying Bloom turned and walked to the kettle, setting it to boil. With the likes of Porter, she knew it made more sense to play along rather than make a fuss. The latter could bring out the worst in a person.

'And so we meet again, Augusta, in slightly better surroundings than before.'

Describing her home as only slightly better than the tired-looking underground room below MOD Main Building where he had been held by DCI Mirza was hoping for a rise. She was not about to give him the satisfaction. She sensed him take a seat at her kitchen island as she placed a teabag in the Royal Doulton teapot she had acquired from her mother's house. Her mother always refused to use the thing, claiming it was for display only, but Bloom had made it her day-to-day choice. It might be expensive bone china but also it was designed to be used.

She placed a single mug on the island and fetched milk from the fridge, all the time conscious that her notes about Seraphine were on the wall of the room upstairs. She needed to make sure he didn't see that. It wasn't that she thought he would learn anything new from her reflections, it was more that she didn't want him knowing how interested she was in what they were doing. That could prove highly dangerous.

'Why are you here?' she said as she placed the teapot next to his mug.

'I was amused to hear that I had employed you to speak to some important people on my behalf. Despite your reputation as a tinpot detective, I'm not sure you and your sidekick have the skills to identify such people so I can only assume a certain someone sent you.'

'Those tinpot detective skills found your niece, didn't they?'

'And then put her in prison.' He referred to the fact that his niece Scarlett had been incarcerated for her part in the Artemis cult.

'But you and your sister now know where she is for the foreseeable future and, if I remember correctly, that was what you requested of me.'

Porter sat perfectly still, watching her pour the milk and tea into his mug. His red hair was slicked back from his forehead and his skin was as pale as a movie vampire's. 'Did you find out what you hoped to from your trip away?'

'Yes, thank you.' She had placed her phone on the island next to her. She knew Porter would not let her use it without intervening but she willed it to ring so she could click one button to answer and ask for help. Did Seraphine know she had answered the door? If she knew Porter was here, she must have someone watching. The idea would normally infuriate her, but tonight she found it something of a relief.

'What she is planning is inherently wrong. You know that, don't you?' Porter said.

'She?'

'Don't play dumb, Dr Bloom. It doesn't suit you.' His continued stillness made Bloom worry he was reserving his energy for something. 'She cannot see the error of her ways, what she will destroy in her wake and the kinds of people she will upset.'

'Whereas you'd be bringing about world peace, would you?'

'My intentions are irrelevant. It is *she* you need to be concerned with. Don't let yourself be fooled, Augusta; she will present to you whatever mirage she thinks will bring you onside.'

'What makes you think she wants me onside?'

'I read your witness statement for her court case. You said she was a highly manipulative, self-serving personality who would stop at nothing to get what she wants, even if that meant destroying other people's lives along the way. Those are powerful words, especially when you consider your profession. You are not expressing an opinion there, you are making an assessment.'

'I wonder what my assessment would say about you.'

Porter's red eyebrows flickered upwards briefly. 'That I have charm, intelligence and bags of potential.'

'I didn't say you'd get to write it yourself.'

'Oh come on, doctor, we all know you psychologists let your subjects write their own assessments. It's not like you can look inside their minds and see the truth. You are entirely reliant on what they tell you.'

'And show me. Actions speak louder than words is a cliché for a reason.' *And your actions tell me you are desperate for me to see that Seraphine is up to no good.* The realization raised the question of why he was trying so hard to convince her of something she already knew. Perhaps it was time to turn the tables on this little chat.

'Why are you so desperate to bad-mouth her to me? Is it because you know I have friends in the police who might be able to take her out of the picture for you?'

'Oh, Augusta, I have much better friends in the police than you, not to mention barristers, judges and the Home Secretary.'

'And how about Seraphine? Are her friends bigger than your friends? Or are you having to steal them too because you can't find your own?'

'Your defence of her is sweet. Motherly, almost. But do be careful of the friends you keep.'

'Why did you come here, Gerald?' She used his first name on purpose. She wanted him to know he didn't intimidate her, even though her heart was beating just a touch too fast.

'To ensure that you, and your friends, know that I can step into your life whenever I like.' Porter spoke slowly, emphasizing every word.

Bloom felt the knot of fear tighten in her stomach. He was using her to send a message to Seraphine.

'Using my name to gain access to people was foolish, Dr Bloom.'

'It worked though, didn't it? I fooled them.' Bloom kept her breathing steady. She needed to milk this opportunity the best she could.

'How naive. I received a call immediately after you left to check out your story.'

'Well, that is disappointing. And I have no doubt you'll enjoy telling me exactly where I went wrong.'

The smirk on Porter's lips was what she had hoped for. Men like him were a sucker for having their egos stroked. 'Something about your grandiose claim of being solely responsible for securing my freedom.' Porter rolled his eyes in an elaborately overplayed display of disdain.

So Miriam Chevalier *was* the turncoat. Bloom had only made the comment about helping Porter to escape custody to her.

'I understand Seraphine forced your hand by having her pet Marcus arrested.' Porter did not phrase this as a question. 'But do be aware she's not the only one who can find leverage. I'll thank you to not cross me again, Dr Bloom. I won't be as . . . patient next time.'

Porter rose from the chair and downed the mug of

tea in one go. Somehow this made him even more distasteful.

'Will you answer me one question?' she said. He made no response so she continued. 'You're trying to create a psychopath-friendly world. One where you no longer have to hide in the shadows. Am I right?'

'It is only Seraphine who favours hiding in the shadows. I am happy to be out in the open.'

'I'm not sure that would have assisted your political career much. The public don't vote for psychopaths.'

Porter's laugh was deep and heartfelt. 'They always have and they always will. The world works just fine for us as it is.'

'So why do you want Seraphine's empire? Why did you describe her plans as sublime in that letter you wrote?'

'She ran to Mummy with that, did she? Bless.' He turned and loomed over her in the narrow space. It was the second time he had made the mother reference. This was not dissimilar to what Koen Laukums had said about Bloom being Seraphine's liberator, enabling a rebirth into her authentic self. It brought to mind something Miriam Chevalier had said too, about it being the ultimate cruelty for Porter to use Bloom against Seraphine.

'Why do you want it if the world already works fine for you?'

Porter licked his lips. 'You said *one* question.'

'You're scared of her, aren't you? That's why you're here – to send her a message that you can get to me?'

Porter let out a long slow breath. 'It would be wise to

keep your irrelevant opinions to yourself. But rest assured Seraphine's time is up, as will yours be if you interfere again.'

Bloom made sure Porter was safely outside before she said, 'I'm not sure you should include "charming" in your character description.' She closed the door and quickly engaged the lock, including the two deadbolts at the top and bottom. Then she leaned against her doorway and tried to calm her shaking hands.

Unnerving as the whole visit had been, she needed to focus on what she had learned. Miriam Chevalier was Seraphine's mole. That was obvious. In fact, when she reflected on it, too obvious. Koen Laukums had immediately dismissed the idea that Bloom was visiting at Porter's request, plus both he and Cardinal Sousa spoke about the man with a degree of distaste. Only Miriam had sat firmly on the fence. And that was something Seraphine would have seen for herself.

Which of course she had. The cardinal had pretty much told Bloom this in his closing remark: *Do you really think Seraphine sent you to me because of Porter, or because she wants you to discover something of greater importance?*

As always with Seraphine, nothing was ever as it seemed. Bloom now had no doubt that Seraphine knew Miriam was the mole all along and had used Bloom's visit to send a message to the woman. But why send her to Laukums and Sousa too?

Laukums had said Bloom had liberated Seraphine by teaching her that her psychopathy didn't need to be a hindrance; that she could use it to her advantage. The cardinal had appealed to her to think carefully about whether she should try to stand in Seraphine's way. Sousa also revealed that Seraphine had used Bloom as an exemplar to educate her psychopathic colleagues. What did it mean?

She spoke out loud, paraphrasing the words of Cardinal Sousa, 'You view others without judgement,' followed by those of Latvia's president, 'The answer is in your own astute question: who benefits?'

She had been sent to see them so they could educate her.

Be open-minded and think about who benefits.

That was what Seraphine wanted her to hear.

Suddenly she knew exactly how to work out what Seraphine was up to.

59

Bloom took the stairs two at a time. She began removing Post-its from the wall and moving them to one side.

'Stabbed her caretaker with a pencil', 'Kidnapped Jane', 'Killed the nephew of a prominent African warlord', 'Live-streamed events at the Artemis cult's retreat', 'Conned Marcus into shooting Green'.

She had told Porter actions speak louder than words but what she had failed to add was that this was only really true when you knew the motivation behind said actions.

Who benefits?

'Why did she stab the caretaker?' she said out loud to the silent room. 'Because he had raped her friend.' This was the calmly expressed reason Seraphine had given to Bloom all those years ago.

'Why did she kidnap Jane?' Bloom thought for a moment. She had always assumed this was about coercing her and Marcus, but there was another way of looking at it. Seraphine had not returned Jane to Marcus's sister Claire with whom she'd been staying, she'd sent her to the home of the father Jane thought had deserted her. The father who had in fact spent years searching for his daughter.

Bloom scanned down the list of Post-its. 'Why did

you kill the warlord's nephew? Was it because you knew he was abusing under-age girls?' This information had come out in the news following the death of the prominent warlord's nephew. According to reports, he had kidnapped girls as young as fourteen and made them his sex slaves.

'And why did you live-stream the Artemis events? Was it so no one could deny what was being done to all those women?'

Bloom had missed the obvious for so long.

She suspected that if she took a closer look at Stephen Green, the man Jameson had shot, she might find some dastardly deeds in his past. Seraphine's tactics might be manipulative and meddling but her motive in every case had been the same.

'You were righting wrongs.'

She scanned the rest of the wall and the organization chart she had begun. What had Seraphine said when she was sitting on the wall of the Thames across from New Scotland Yard? That Bloom's efforts at saving lives were a drop in the ocean that could never quell the waves. Her eyes rested on Cardinal Sousa's description of the group: 'LOGICIANS'.

'How did it take me so long to see this?'

The ringing phone took her back to the kitchen. She felt conflicted. She couldn't argue with Seraphine's motivations but vigilante justice was illegal for a reason. The idea that a group of psychopaths might be out there punishing the guilty without a chance of defence or a fair trial was almost as frightening as the idea they might be starting wars or manipulating politics to their benefit.

'Dr Bloom, I need you to come to Charing Cross police station as soon as possible to advise on an interview.' Tyler Rowe sounded excited.

'For the Matchbox Murders?'

'Yes.'

Bloom grabbed her coat and work bag. Her headache was gone, which was a bonus. That was the advantage of a good dose of adrenaline.

When she unlocked the door and opened it, she found Jameson on her doorstep.

'What are you doing here?' she said.

'Seraphine said I should keep an eye on you because Porter might be hanging about.'

'Hanging about? He was in my house and I'm pretty sure she knew that.' *What was Seraphine's motivation for this little stunt?* Bloom wondered.

'Are you OK?'

'I need to go to Charing Cross police station. Can you drive me? It'll be quicker than the tube.'

60

Sandy Roper was what you might call a weedy-looking fellow. He wore a *Star Trek* hoody with the kind of straight-leg jeans you buy cheap from a supermarket. He had mousy hair that looked unbrushed and that droopy-eyed expression Bloom associated with the hard-done-by of the world.

'Is this really the guy?' she asked Rowe, who sat alongside her in the observation room. DCI Mirza was yet to join them.

'Someone at Prestige Wealth accessed Jeremy Tomlinson's home address details a week before his attack. The login was Hardeep Singh's but the guy was on honeymoon in Barbados that week, so the team quizzed Russell and he said the only other person who could access Singh's files was their IT guy.'

'That doesn't mean the IT guy killed him. He might have a legitimate reason to look.'

'And that's what we intend to find out,' said Mirza as she entered with DC Fleur Morgan.

The interview-room door opened and DS Peters entered along with another officer.

Mirza said to Bloom and Rowe, 'I've asked them to do a short briefing interview first so you can get a feel for the guy. Then we'll take a break and you two can give us your thoughts on the interview schedule.'

DS Peters began the recording and made the necessary introductions. Sandy Roper looked like a small boy waiting to be shouted at. His whole body sank back into the chair and he was picking at the skin around his fingernails.

'Is this about my using Mrs Brigg's Wi-Fi? It was only a couple of times, I swear.'

'No Sandy. This is about your job with Prestige Wealth Management. How long have you worked for them?'

'A few years.'

'Russell Rigby tells us it's been five years since they set up. Is that correct?' said Peters.

Sandy frowned and nodded.

'Can you speak for the recording please?'

'Yes.'

'Yes you've worked there since the beginning?'

'Yes, sir.'

'And what do you do for them?'

'I set up their website and I do software updates and security checks. The usual IT stuff. Am I in trouble? Did I do something wrong?'

'Security checks – what do they entail?'

'Making sure the data is secure. They have a lot of personal information.'

'Information that you can access?'

'I can access everything IT-wise. I have to be able to.'

'How do you access the data? Do you have to use the login of one of the permanent employees for that?'

'No, I have my own. Mine has all the permissions.'

'So am I understanding you right: are you saying you

can access any files within Prestige Wealth Management without needing approval from Mr Rigby or Mr Singh first?'

'Yes, if they need me to.'

'So they trust you with access to all their company data.'

'What's going on? Have I done something wrong?' He looked at the duty solicitor he'd been assigned.

'I don't know, Sandy. Have you?' said Peters.

After a further twenty minutes of interviewing Sandy Roper about his job, DS Peters suggested a break and joined Bloom, Rowe and DCI Mirza.

'If he doesn't need to use Hardeep's login why did he do so to look at Jeremy and George's files?' said Rowe.

'He looked at George's information too?' said Bloom.

'Yeah. At midnight five nights before he was attacked, Hardeep Singh's login was used to open that file and that file alone,' said DS Peters. 'And I expect he used Singh's login to cover his tracks.'

'Did he not know Hardeep Singh was on holiday the first time?'

'He works remotely. Russell said he hasn't seen Roper in the office for a couple of years now,' said Peters.

'He looks kind of weak,' said DCI Mirza. 'Are we sure he has the physical strength to carry out these crimes?'

'Maybe he gets a burst of strength when he gets riled up,' said Rowe.

'Jeremy was killer one's sixth victim, if my memory serves me correctly?' Bloom said. 'Whereas Keith and

George are killer two's second and third victims if the matches are to be believed and they are also clients of this firm?'

DS Peters confirmed that with a nod.

'So are you thinking this young man is killer one or killer two?'

'Hard to tell,' said Peters. 'None of the other victims are clients though.'

'Is that how they met, maybe? Did killer one use Roper to find Jeremy's address and then recruit him?' said Rowe.

Bloom nodded; that would fit with her and Jameson's hypothesis that killer two was some kind of apprentice.

'Right, what's the plan? Interview strategy,' said Mirza. 'We need to establish his whereabouts on the dates Jeremy, Keith and George were killed and I'd also like to know what he was up to when Mickey Glover and the others died.'

DS Peters outlined their other areas of inquiry, including prior knowledge of any of the victims or contact with them virtually.

'We need intel on who he is working with or for,' said Mirza.

Bloom saw a look pass between the DCI and her DS. Mirza meant Seraphine.

'Have you found any indiscretions on the part of any of our victims? Anything that might have riled our killers?' said Bloom, thinking of Seraphine's previous efforts in imposing justice.

'Not so far,' said Peters. 'No previous arrests, no signs of debt or dubious extra-curricular activities.'

Bloom felt relieved.

Rowe said, 'If we think Roper might be killer two, that would make him the emotional, angry one. I suggest trying to get a rise from him by showing him some of the post-mortem images and talking about the killer being insignificant. Anything to add, Dr Bloom?'

'I think you need to find out if he has a problem with wealthy men. I expect your killer has had a bad experience with someone which has triggered his hatred. An abusive boss, for example.' A memory of something came to her and she flicked through the case notes on her lap. 'Actually,' she said, finding the information in question, 'Mickey, Keith and George are all family men. That might be significant. Our emotional killer attacks with anger but this might not be directed at the victims themselves. The victims might represent someone who requires punishment in the eyes of our killer. It might be worth finding out if he has any issue with his father or another family member.'

'Good,' said Mirza. 'I think we know how to proceed. Remember we also want to find out who his accomplice is once we've got him nailed down.'

'Boss,' said DS Peters.

Bloom looked back at the screen showing Sandy Roper still picking at the skin around his nails. He didn't look like a violent killer capable of stabbings and ruthless beatings. Also, from the untied shoelaces on his dirty Nike trainers and the ketchup on his top, he didn't look like the kind of meticulous person who plans his attacks carefully enough to leave behind no trace of himself. If this was their guy, or one of them, she was genuinely intrigued to see how all the factors were going to stack up.

61

'Sandy, I'm going to show you some photographs and I want you to tell me if you know this person.' Carl Peters placed the image of George Shulman's body in the park on the table. Sandy physically recoiled from the bloody scene and for a moment Bloom thought he was going to throw up.

'Who is that? Why are you showing me that?'

'This is George Shulman. He is a client of Prestige Wealth Management and five nights before he was murdered his personal details were accessed through Hardeep Singh's login.'

Sandy's eyes widened.

'Do you know this man?' Peters said, touching the photograph again. 'Let me show you what he looked like before someone bludgeoned him to death.'

Sandy looked at the second photo, showing a smiling George Shulman from his company brochure. He shook his head. 'I don't know him.'

'How about this man?' The second image showed Jeremy face up in his swimming pool.

Sandy was shaking now. His lips were pressed in a thin line and his eyes looked everywhere but the table. 'Why are you showing me these? I don't understand.'

'This is Jeremy Tomlinson, another Prestige Wealth

client whose files were accessed while Hardeep Singh was out of the country. Can you explain that?'

'No.'

'Was it you, Sandy? Did you look at Jeremy's file before he was attacked in his home? Did you then find out where George lived and attack him in the park opposite his house?'

'No! No! I promise. I don't know these people. I've never hurt anyone. I wouldn't.'

In the small room down the hall, DCI Mirza said, 'What do you think?'

Bloom looked up from her notes. They had agreed that Rowe would watch Sandy's body language and Bloom would focus on his words. Research showed interviewers could often read too much into a glance to the left or a tapping foot, when in fact the evidence of any lies was often more apparent in what was said.

'If he did it, he's a good actor,' said Rowe.

'That's what I'm thinking,' Mirza replied.

There was nothing in what Sandy had said to warrant Bloom making a comment so she stayed quiet.

DS Peters began to quiz Sandy on his whereabouts on the nights Jeremy and George were attacked.

'I was at home.'

'You don't want to check your diary or anything?' said DS Peters.

'I'm always at home. I don't go out. I don't like it. It makes me . . . I don't like it.'

'How do you get food?'

'Online shopping. I do everything online.'

'So if we checked your phone and your computer, we would find evidence that you stay in and order in, is that what you're telling me, Sandy?'

'Yes. Absolutely. Do that. I never go out. I'm always inside, in the dark.'

'Sorry, did you say you are always inside in the dark?'

Bloom glanced up again when there was a pause. Sandy had his head down and for a second she thought he was crying but then he looked up and appeared to have composed himself.

'I'm not a fan of bright lights like these.' He glanced up at the strip lights. 'They bring on my migraines.'

'Sandy, can you understand my concern here? You are the one person capable of accessing Hardeep's client files while he is away and the two files looked at are those of two murdered men. Now you're telling me you were home on your own on both occasions, meaning you have no alibi. How do I know you're not spinning me a line here, Sandy?'

'I wouldn't spin you a line, sir. I assure you I was not there when these men died.'

Bloom circled the words 'I was not there' in her notes, as DS Peters picked up on it too.

'OK, so you weren't there but do you know who was? Did you give Jeremy and George's addresses to someone else?'

'Pardon? What did you say?'

'I asked if you passed Jeremy and George's details to someone else? If you didn't do this, do you know who did?'

'Mr Rigby says it's illegal to share people's personal information. He'd sack me. I never used Hardeep's login. I don't need to.'

'Because you can use your own – yes, you said. But wouldn't you use someone else's if you were trying to cover your tracks?'

'I didn't open those files. I promise.'

DCI Mirza twisted in her chair next to Bloom. 'He likes to make promises.'

Peters went on to question Sandy about where he was on the dates of the other murders, firstly those of Mickey and Keith, who they were assuming had been killed by the same person as George, and then the rest. His answer was always the same. 'I was home. I don't like to go out.' Bloom wrote 'Agoraphobic?' on her notepad.

Peters then showed Sandy pictures of the other victims and asked him if he knew them. Sandy said he did not. Any attempt Peters made to get an emotional rise out of Sandy served to do exactly the opposite. Sandy apologized for not being able to help, promised he wasn't involved and pleaded with them to see that he didn't know these men and he'd never hurt anyone.

Towards the end of the interview DS Peters tried Bloom's suggested line of questioning about motive.

'Do you have a problem with successful men, Sandy?' he said.

'No.'

'How about people with money? Does it make you angry that some people have so much more than you? Do you think it's unfair?'

'It's just life, I suppose. Some people are lucky.'

'And you are not lucky?'

'I'm . . . I'm just normal.'

'"Normal". What does "normal" mean?'

Bloom was impressed with DS Peters. His interviewing skills were effective. He looked to clarify meaning in everything that was said.

'That I'm like most people, I s'pose.'

'Do you consider the clients of Prestige Wealth normal?'

'I don't know.'

'Are they like most people?'

'I've never met them. I only do IT.'

'But you must know about all that money they invest with you? You're able to see that, aren't you?'

'They're just numbers. I don't really think about it.'

'Is that right.' DS Peters left a long silence before asking. 'Anyone in your family well off?'

'I don't have any family.'

'No rich uncles in the background? No wealthy grandparents back in the day?'

Sandy shook his head.

'So your mum and dad were normal like you?'

Sandy shrugged.

'Are your parents deceased, Sandy?'

'My dad left when I was a kid but Mum lives in Cambridge.'

'I thought you said you didn't have any family?'

'I don't . . . I don't see her.'

'Why not, Sandy? Why don't you see your mum?'

'I . . . I don't know.'

'Did you have a falling-out?'

'No.'

'Did she disapprove of your lifestyle?'

'No.'

'Do you disapprove of hers?'

'No!'

'OK. You seem upset by this. Were you close before?'

'Yeah, when I was a kid it was just me and her.'

'And then what happened?'

'I don't know.'

'Did she get a boyfriend you didn't like?'

'Why are you asking about Mother?' The spike of anger in Sandy's voice made Bloom look up. 'What has she got to do with anything? Lots of people don't see their parents when they grow up. It's not a crime.'

'I'm trying to understand, that's all.'

'I think you're desperate to find some evidence that I did these awful things because you have nothing to prove that I did.'

'He's not far wrong,' said Mirza with a sigh.

Sandy looked at the duty solicitor, who had silently taken notes throughout. 'Can I go now? Can you make them let me go?'

'Well, that was entirely unsatisfying,' said DCI Mirza as DS Peters escorted Sandy out of the interview room. The solicitor had requested his release if the police had no intention of charging him. Mirza revealed that they had no basis on which to hold him – not only had he said nothing incriminating, his fingerprints had proven to be an inconclusive match for the partial one found in Nawaf's room at the St Pancras Hotel.

'I didn't see anything to show his reactive side, apart from that bit about his mother. He didn't come over as angry or bitter, which is what we might expect from our emotional killer,' said Rowe.

'More importantly, he said nothing to help us,' said DCI Mirza. 'He looked scared and appalled most of the way through. I don't think he's our guy.'

DS Peters joined them. He looked disappointed. 'We'll check out his home-alone story. We should be able to confirm the location of his phone if he made any calls and we seized his computer as part of the company warrant so we can check for online shopping and the like.'

Mirza sighed heavily. 'I don't believe it's a coincidence three of our victims are clients of this firm. Someone there is involved. I want the whole bunch of them looked at with a microscope. I'm sorry we've wasted your time, Augusta. If there's nothing you'd like to add, please feel free to take off.'

'Did anything ever come of the matchboxes? You said you were looking into a common source.'

'Not so far,' said Mirza. 'There are no manufacturing links but that doesn't mean we can't find a website or shop they're getting them from. We're still looking.'

'OK, I'll take another look through these notes in case anything jumps out before I go.'

DCI Mirza and Rowe left her reading. She always liked to look back and read the words used without the distraction of what a suspect looked or sounded like. Sandy had come over as weak and frightened, as Mirza said, but that didn't mean he was. Sometimes people gave themselves away in the opinions they expressed.

Fifteen minutes later she packed up and headed out, stopping briefly to ask DS Peters, who was in the custody suite, to let his boss know she had found nothing of use in her notes. Sandy's words had matched his demeanour pretty much throughout. It didn't come as an entire shock to Bloom. The guy had looked scruffy and disorganized, which their killers most certainly were not.

62

'You didn't have to wait,' Bloom said, climbing into Jameson's car. 'I'd have jumped on the tube.'

'I was told to keep an eye on you and that's what I'm doing.'

'About that. I think I've worked out what Seraphine is doing and I'm not sure you're going to believe it.'

'Wait, before we get on to that, tell me about catching this guy. How did they do it?'

'It wasn't him so it's back to the drawing board. They're going to look again at this finance company—'

'But . . . are we talking about the chap who came out with officers twenty minutes or so back?'

'Yes. They offered him a lift home. He had a little panic attack when they said he could make his own way. I think he's probably agoraphobic.'

'But I know him.'

'You know Sandy Roper?' Bloom twisted in her seat to look at her partner.

'I don't know his name, just his face. I've been sitting here racking my brains about where I've seen him before. I figured it must have been when I was out researching the scenes and then I remembered, he was in the residents' lounge at Philip Berringer's building.'

'The IT geek in dirty trainers and an unwashed jumper was in a members-only bar? I'm not surprised you remember him.'

'No, you misunderstand. He didn't look like that when I met him. He looked like he belonged. That's why I thought you'd got him. Didn't you say your killer was most likely a master of disguise? Isn't that how he's conning his way into people's lives and homes?'

'Are you sure? He didn't come over as anything other than a scared IT geek in there.'

'So he's a very *good* master of disguise. You know me and faces, Augusta. It's my superpower.'

She knew he was right. He had been identified as a super-recognizer during his time with MI6, making him one of the small percentage of people who could recognize faces they had seen only once before, even when the individual in question had changed their appearance.

'Come with me.' Bloom exited the car and led the way back into the custody suite. DS Peters was no longer around; only the custody sergeant remained. She looked up with a 'what do you want' expression.

'Can you get DCI Mirza for me. Fast.'

The custody sergeant looked at Jameson as she slowly picked up the phone and dialled. This was a woman used to checking people out.

'Ma'am, can you come down. I have . . .'

'Dr Bloom,' Bloom said when the sergeant glanced her way and raised her eyebrows.

'Dr Bloom. She says she needs to speak to you.'

'Can I take that?' Bloom said, holding out her hand.

'I'll put her on,' said the sergeant.

'Nadia, we need to get hold of the officers who've taken Sandy Roper home. I think he may be our man after all.'

63

'Roper asked to be dropped off around the corner,' said Mirza as she entered the custody suite.

'The guy who had a panic attack about making his own way home asked to be dropped off around the corner and you let him go?' said Jameson.

'How exactly do you *know* Sandy Roper is our man?'

Bloom answered, 'First you need to know that Marcus is confirmed to have a heightened ability to recognize faces he's seen before. He is certain he saw Sandy Roper in the residents' lounge from where Philip Berringer fell.'

'What were you doing in that lounge?' Mirza eyeballed Jameson.

'Looking at an apartment to buy. They give you a full tour of all amenities.'

'I thought I made it clear you two were on desk research alone.'

'Lucky for you we're rule-breakers,' said Jameson, flashing her a grin.

Mirza bristled. 'Don't I know it. When was it that you saw him?'

'Last week. Thursday.'

'That was just a few days after George Shulman's murder. What was he doing when you saw him?'

'Having a cup of coffee and reading *The Times*. He looked different, as if he belonged.'

'And yet you're certain it's him?'

'I was quizzing the estate agent about Philip's suicide and this chap chipped in to add the details.'

'And you're only just thinking to mention this now?'

'There was no way of knowing he was connected at that point. The details he gave were what you might expect from a fellow resident, the kind of gossip that might be going around. He said Philip had stood on a chair, which for the record I don't buy. I think it was placed there afterwards.'

'Did he say anything else?'

Jameson started to say no and then remembered something. 'There was one odd thing now I think back: the barman challenged his membership. The agent said it was because a couple of the apartments were rented out as Airbnbs and those guests did not qualify to be in the lounge. I recall this chap lost his rag saying he paid handsomely not to be challenged in such a way.'

'This does not sound like the person we just interviewed, does it?' Mirza said to Bloom. 'He was a jumpy little mouse of a man.'

'He could be a good actor,' said Bloom, echoing Jameson's words from the car. 'This would fit with him gaining access to homes without drawing attention.'

'How accurate is this facial recognition? I mean, could they be related? Could Roper have a brother, for instance? Can you be certain it's the same person? If I bring him in again, I have to have something more concrete than "some witness saw someone who looked like you in Philip Berringer's building".'

'It's possible if they look very alike. Identical twins are tough to distinguish between. If you let me look at the interview tape, I might be able to tell you.' When Mirza hesitated, Jameson said, 'Like I said when I called you, I think the Airbnb is how your guy got in and out of Philip's building. I reckon he lurked there until the time was right.'

'And the fact that he was brazen enough to go back to the residents' lounge fits with him staying in the St Pancras Hotel after killing Nawaf,' said Bloom.

Their words convinced Mirza, who nodded to the custody sergeant.

Once the recording of Roper's interview had been set up on the screen in the small office Bloom had only recently left, she and Jameson sat to watch it. Jameson pulled his chair close to the table and rested his hands under his chin directly in front of the screen. Bloom pressed play and watched for the second time as Roper waited for his interviewers to arrive. He made no effort to speak to the duty solicitor who sat alongside him, angled towards Roper but with eyes down on his paperwork. The solicitor was a middle-aged man who by the look of his hunched shoulders and bored expression was somewhat weary of his role.

Jameson stayed perfectly still throughout the opening minutes of the interview. He watched Roper answer questions about his job at Prestige Wealth Management and the access that gave him to the personal information of clients.

Bloom studied the man too. In the moment she had been taking notes so had not seen much of Roper's body language. Now she looked for signs of 'leakage', where the body gives away signs that a person is lying. But she saw none. If he was faking, he was very good at it.

After ten minutes Jameson lifted his head and sat back in his chair. 'That is not the same guy I saw.'

'Are you sure? You told me you were certain outside.' Bloom did not relish the idea of telling Mirza they'd made a mistake – again.

'His features are very similar but the way he speaks, the way he moves is entirely different.'

'How long were you speaking to the man in the bar?'

'Long enough. He was tall, composed and he had a London accent.'

Sandy Roper's accent had the sort of sing-song intonation common to people from the West Midlands.

'Actors change their demeanour and their accents all the time,' said Bloom.

'I know but the facial expressions are too different. Even with actors you still get their natural look seeping in.'

Bloom nodded. 'So a twin then?'

'That would be my best guess. An identical twin or a family member with a very strong resemblance.'

64

It was after nine by the time Jameson drove Bloom home. DCI Mirza had not been as annoyed with him as Bloom feared. She was a decent copper and she knew a strong lead when she got one. The fact that Sandy strongly resembled the person Jameson met gave them a whole new angle to investigate.

'You're quiet,' he said.

Bloom was staring out of the passenger window and into the darkness.

'Are you OK?'

'I'm fighting a headache. It went away earlier but now it's back.'

'Do you think it's wise going home after Porter's visit? You can come and stay at mine. I'll sleep on the sofa.'

'I'll be fine. His visit was a warning. He wanted to send a message to Seraphine that he can get to her people. I'll bolt the door and set the alarm.'

Jameson knew he would be spending the night in the car outside. Porter's visit was not a warning for Seraphine. It was a *why isn't she dead yet?* message for him.

When Seraphine had called earlier, she'd told him she had Bloom's house watched remotely via the CCTV camera on her street. She had facial-recognition technology set to alert her to visits from specific people. She'd told him Bloom had most likely let Porter in as he was no longer outside. Jameson had raced over immediately, prepared for a showdown with Porter, but when he got there the creep was already gone.

'What did Porter say?' *Would he have told her what Jameson was supposed to be doing?* He didn't like the idea of handling Bloom's opinion on that right now.

Bloom leaned back against the headrest with her eyes closed. 'He wanted me to know that Seraphine is up to no good and not to be trusted.'

'He doesn't think we already know that?'

She didn't answer and he wondered if she'd fallen asleep. She'd said something about Seraphine in the police station car park but he'd been too distracted to listen to her. He decided not to pursue it now. She needed to sleep and he needed to keep her safe.

Once Bloom was inside the house and the lights were off, Jameson put on the hat he kept in the boot and reclined his seat. He listened to Radio 5 Live for half an hour, but when he couldn't relax he sat up and reached for his phone.

First, he texted their tech consultant Lucas George and asked him to check out Sandy Roper. Lucas was an IT wizard who helped them with any digital investigations they needed to do on cases. Jameson asked him to look at whether Roper had a twin or a brother and if either of them had ever booked an Airbnb in Philip Berringer's apartment building. He knew the police would be checking this out, but he also knew Lucas George had a particular knack for uncovering things people wanted to keep hidden. He had no idea how Lucas found out some of the information he came up with and he didn't care. The kid was a genius, and the information he had found for them had saved their asses on many occasions.

His next text was to Seraphine to say Bloom was fine and he was keeping an eye on her.

A few seconds later his phone rang.

'Is that a thank you, Marcus?'

'I suppose.'

'That must have hurt?'

'Not at all. This is one occasion where I think you genuinely did something right. I expect that hurt you more than it did me.'

Her laugh was giggly and once again he was reminded of the alter ego she had presented when they had dated.

'I hear our detective chief inspector friend lucked out this evening.'

'How do you know these things?'

'I have ears everywhere.'

'Do you have any intel on the man they interviewed today, Sandy Roper?'

'I don't waste my time on the riff-raff, Marcus.'

'Well, maybe you should if Mirza still has you in their sights for this. I think Roper's involved or related to someone who is.'

'Are you telling tales out of school?'

He was and he knew Mirza, and most likely Bloom, would be furious. 'What can I say, I'm a gut-feel kinda guy and I have the feeling you're more motivated than most to uncover who these serial killers are and get the police off your back.'

'And what's motivating you to help me, I wonder?'

At this stage in their conversations Jameson usually lost patience with her taunts but right now he had more important things on his mind. So he chose to do something he'd never done since finding out the truth about Seraphine. He chose to be honest.

'I don't fully understand this thing you have with Augusta but I do know that in your own way you care about her, and she also cares about you. I'm worried about her. The last year has taken its toll. She's exhausted and traumatized and I need it all to stop. Outside my family she is the most important person in the world to me. I don't want her hurt any more.'

'Are you in love with her?'

Jameson closed his eyes. He knew how the rest of this conversation would go. She would tease him and goad him and eventually he'd tell her where to go and most likely hang up. He let out a sigh. 'No. I am not. She's my best friend, that's all.'

There was silence and he opened his eyes again.

'Are you still there?' he said.

'I'm here. I'm thinking.'

This was different. *What, no mockery?*

'I wish I could help, Marcus, but I have battles of my own going on.'

'Well, leave Augusta out of them.'

'I can't.'

'Why the hell not? Have you not done enough damage?'

'She's already in the battles. Always has been.'

'What are you talking about? I hope you're not planning to suggest she's a psychopath again because we both know that was more of your bollocks.'

'I'm talking about how Augusta is the nucleus of everything I have done and everything I plan to do.'

'You're never going to let her go, are you? She'll never have any peace while you're in her life.'

'It is what it is, Marcus. I do not have the power to change it now.'

But I might, he thought before saying goodbye and hanging up.

65

'So we're in the clear?' AJ said.

'No thanks to you. I told you to cover your tracks. What about that meant finding three of our targets from the same place? I thought you were some computer genius.'

'No, that's Sandy.' AJ's voice was sulky. 'I covered my tracks by using someone else's login. How was I supposed to know the guy was on his honeymoon for one of those searches? If he'd not been, no one would have suspected a thing because all three targets were the man's clients. I'm not stupid. I figured if anyone looked, they'd conclude Hardeep Singh had looked at the files legitimately.'

'Idiot.'

'Yeah, well, at least I didn't brag to the papers. If you hadn't done that no one would know a thing. I'm not the idiot. You are!'

'We are the biggest news story going on. I have every privileged bastard looking over his shoulder in case *we* are in the shadows. That's not idiocy. That's genius. If you were brighter, you'd know that.'

'Stop doing that. Stop treating me like some stupid kid.'

'Stop behaving like one then.'

AJ stalked off to sulk and Zander stood and rolled his shoulders. He considered clearing the kitchen table but figured Lexi would be happy to do it when she was back. He had more important things to do because it turned out luck was on his side. He knew letting Sandy speak to the police would work. He had kept him in the dark for exactly that reason: plausible deniability. He knew nothing so he could say nothing.

And now Zander could finally – *finally* – focus on his next target.

He had looked at the address AJ had found for Marcus Jameson on Google Street View and found an impressive five-storey building on the corner of a long terrace of offices in Russell Square. The first floor was decorated with a wrought-iron balcony and all the windows had elaborate red stone surrounds. It smacked of the wealth and privilege he hated.

A public relations company operated from the building so he had checked their website for any mention of his target. Marcus Jameson was not named in their list of who's who but it did say the company was owned by a private equity firm. Zander guessed Jameson was either the money behind the business or the landlord. Either way, to own or rent property in that part of town spoke volumes about the kind of money the man must have. And the more money he had, the more power he could wield, which in turn enabled him to make more money. It was a particularly disgusting self-licking lollipop. So far removed from the life Zander had endured as a child, living with nothing and being blown around like litter in the wind, desperately clinging to any branch he could find to make him feel he had a degree of control over his life.

He knew that AJ was angry that the particular branch his mother had chosen to cling to turned out to be an alcoholic and abusive bastard. Zander had never asked AJ what he remembered but he knew that the abuse went on well into the lad's teens; way past the point at which he'd grown big enough to stop it. Zander suspected this was what AJ was so angry about. He was dishing out the punishment he should have done back then, choosing to target absent fathers who fail to protect their kids. Lexi had challenged his chosen target group. 'How do you know they aren't decent fathers working hard for their families?' she'd said. And AJ had countered that his family had looked perfect from the outside so you never knew, and if a father couldn't be bothered to be there who knew what he'd miss or whom the mother might shack up with next. Truth be told, AJ had wanted to go after neglectful mothers, which made sense – his mother had been inside the facade with him and chose to say and do nothing. But Lexi had outright vetoed that. 'Every child needs its mother,' she had said and that had been the end of the discussion. It was testament to how desperate for a mother figure AJ was that he listened so obediently to Lexi.

Zander's motivation was entirely different. He wasn't acting out any anger – what he felt was closer to disgust. He wanted payback on men like his playboy father. Men who took their wealth for granted, flaunted it over those who had less and, worse still, dared to look down on them. The world was nowhere near fair or equitable enough and the masses went along with it like compliant sheep. They needed a shock to waken them to the truth and nothing grabbed people's attention quite like a serial killer. It made them paranoid and willing to question the motivations of those they met, which was exactly what they should be doing.

He was not naive enough to think the police had finished with Sandy. They would continue to look at Prestige Wealth and when everyone else came up clean, they would return to him. It was inevitable. Sandy had done well in the interview but there had been a couple of near misses and it was only because the police did not know what they were looking for that these had gone unnoticed. But that kind of luck could not last. Time was running out. Zander was working against the clock but he was OK with that. Their actions would stand the test of time. They would go down in history and be analysed by generation after generation of fascinated people. The only imperative now was to make as much of a mark as he could in the time they had left. Starting with Marcus Jameson.

66

Bloom had wrapped up warm against the early-morning chill. She wore her black scarf tucked into her grey jacket and her grey hat was pulled down low over her ears. She knew part of the reason she felt so cold was lack of sleep. It had been a restless night playing out the visit from Porter over and over. It could have gone so much worse. In the cold light of day she knew he was too high-profile a person to do her any harm, but in the dead of night that had seemed a weak defence. He was angry. He saw her as the enemy. And he was a psychopath. It was not a combination that sat well together.

When she had finally given up on sleep, she had arranged this morning's meeting by sending a text reminiscent of the many she had received over the past year.

Today   **05:15**
Meet me 8 a.m. The usual place.

She had even chosen to sit in Seraphine's preferred spot, at the table outside the cafe nearest to the hedge. Seraphine had not replied to the message but Bloom waited anyway. Russell Square Gardens bustled with Londoners starting their day. In the coming hours the place would contain tourists from around the world on their way from St Pancras into the city, or making their way to the British Museum nearby. But for now, it was mainly locals walking their dogs, pushing prams or simply passing through to get to work.

Porter's visit hadn't been the only thing playing on her mind overnight. She had also been trying to work out what they were missing with Sandy Roper and the Matchbox Murders. When she'd climbed into Jameson's car outside the police station, she'd been content that Roper had nothing to do with it, but she'd been wrong. She hated feeling duped by someone. It was a silly professional pressure she placed on herself. No psychologist or experienced investigator could spot every liar or fraud. The truth of the matter was that some people were simply too damn good at it. Like Porter had said, it's not as though you can look inside their brain and see the truth.

'You look awful.' Seraphine had appeared without her realizing.

'Nice to see you too.'

'He sat outside all night, you know,' she said as she removed a glove to check her phone.

Bloom knew Seraphine was referring to Jameson. This morning his car had still been parked on her road where he had dropped her the night before. Bloom had stuck a coat over her pyjamas and taken him a flask of coffee before telling him he was overreacting and sending him home to rest.

'He told me you watch my house,' Bloom said.

'Not me personally. That would make me a stalker. It's an algorithm thing.'

'I'm not sure that stops you from being classed as a stalker.' As Seraphine sat down Bloom felt her anger bubble up to the surface. 'Are you not going to apologize for sneaking around in my life for all this time? Did you think I'd be OK with that particular revelation when you sent me off on your fishing expedition?'

'It did you no harm.'

'It . . . no harm . . . Are you kidding me? Seraphine, it's my private life. It's none of your business. I don't have the words for how much this has upset me.'

'Well, before you get too wound up about it, remember the benefits.'

'You mean warning me about Porter's visit a few moments too late?'

'If you had answered your phone . . .' Seraphine let the point hang.

In that moment Bloom realized the obvious. Porter knew Seraphine watched her house which meant the whole thing was part of their cat-and-mouse chase. Bloom took a few deep breaths.

'How many people? How many people have you had injecting themselves into my world without my consent?'

'Nobody consents to the people who enter their world. We meet people, we interact with them, we keep them or we leave them behind.'

'You're describing free will. I have had no free will with your people. They were manipulating me, every single one of them.'

Seraphine pursed her lips for a moment. 'I take your point.'

'Is that an assurance it will stop?'

'Did you really summon me here to tell me off?'

'Yes!' Bloom knew Seraphine would never make a promise to back off out of her life; she suspected the woman saw it as a privilege that someone like her kept a watchful eye. She should ask how Seraphine knew about Greg, whether she had been watching her all this time, but the words wouldn't come out. She didn't want that part of her life infected with all this. Some things were better left alone. Pushing the anger she felt at the intrusiveness of it all down deep, she finally said, 'I wanted to ask you something about people who kill.'

'You mean your matchstick men? I expect they're acting out some emotional angst and bloodlust. But you already know that.'

'Is that why you do it?'

Seraphine looked amused. 'You know that's not my style, Augusta.'

'You stabbed your school caretaker and watched him bleed out on the floor. I recall you said it was fascinating. If that's not bloodlust then what is?'

Seraphine placed her phone on the table and faced Bloom. 'It is true that I found all that blood fascinating, but only because it was the moment I realized I was different. I didn't know I was going to react like that prior to stabbing him.'

'So you're saying the reason why you stabbed him outweighs the enjoyment.' Bloom was testing her theory about Seraphine now, having a conversation within a conversation.

'And why do you think I stabbed him?'

'Because he was raping his stepdaughter Claudia and she was your friend.' Bloom recalled that on hearing this that first time she had thought, *Good for you, Seraphine.*

'He got to live out the rest of his life as a cabbage, hopefully with just enough mental capacity to think about what he had done.'

'Do you think having a good reason makes you different from any other killer? Because the Matchbox Murderers will have their reasons too. Reasons that seem sound to them.'

Seraphine took a moment to study Bloom. 'You know as well as I that people like me have a bias towards self-serving activities. This is an undeniable truth. But you taught me I can be more than that. If I have the right purpose there is nothing to say I can't be a productive member of society. Wasn't that the point of all that "Choose carefully, Seraphine"?'

'You're setting yourself up as some kind of twisted Robin Hood, killing the bad to protect the weak. How is that any different to these Matchbox Murderers attacking those they see as deserving of punishment?'

'Ah yes, but you know as well as I do that such serial killers are only really protecting one weak person and that is themselves, or at least the version of themselves that was mistreated or disrespected.' Seraphine leaned forward a touch. 'Do you know how many children starve every year across the world? How many people are persecuted for ridiculously emotional reasons like which fictitious God they believe in? How about how many girls are subjected to forced marriages or genital mutilation? How many homosexuals are beaten or imprisoned because people are disgusted by them? How many black people are shot for no good reason because white officers feel scared of them? These are illogical, irrational miscarriages of justice. And all the while so-called "normal" people, full of emotional depth and empathy, choose to look away because it suits them to.'

Bloom was lost for words. Seraphine was not trying to manipulate the world for power or even fairness, she was trying to upgrade it. As if humanity were some machine she could make run better.

Seraphine continued, 'I know what it means to be a child locked in the attic for days on end without food because your father believes it will knock some sense into you. I know what it means to have a mother who tells the world you're her perfect girl, but who can't look you in the eye because she's scared of what she sees. I also know what it feels like to know you're different to all your peers, something every minority group can relate to. Your concern has always been my lack of empathy, but what you failed to see is you don't need the ability to put yourself in someone else's shoes when you've worn them yourself.'

Bloom had missed so much in Seraphine's character. She had been so focused on her psychopathy. She had felt sorry for Seraphine's mother, Penny, seeing her as Seraphine's first victim, but she'd never thought to question how Penny and her husband might have handled a child like Seraphine, and how their actions might have contributed to how she was. It was a rookie error. What Porter had said about Bloom being a mother figure made more sense in light of these revelations. The fact that she had looked at Seraphine without judgement had potentially been the first time the young girl had felt accepted. And no matter what your nature might be, feeling valued by others was critical.

Bloom said, 'I'm not disagreeing with the ends, only the means. I'm saying there's a flaw in your plan and that flaw is the people you have trusted. Cardinal Sousa told me Porter serves a different God. He wants the power that your chess players provide, and I can only assume he wants it for personal gain, which means he'll always be able to offer the players more than you can.'

'I am sorry that Porter came to you. I did try to warn you.'

'Miriam Chevalier tipped him off about my visit.'

'How do you know?'

'I told all three of your people different reasons for coming to them. Miriam's version was the one he played back to me.'

Seraphine smiled. 'I knew you were the right person to send.'

'But you already knew she was the mole, didn't you? This whole thing was a PR campaign, a ruse to get me to meet your people.'

'In part, but make no mistake, your visit to Paris ensured I gained the confirmation I needed.'

Bloom realized she might have just signed Miriam Chevalier's death warrant. 'What will you do to her?'

'Don't you be feeling guilty, Augusta. The woman sealed her own fate long ago.'

'You have a mutiny mounting, Seraphine, and that man will not stop until he's taken it all. You know that, don't you?'

'Are you worried about me, Augusta?' The smile was a touch mocking.

'What you have put in place across the world would allow the wrong person to have far, far too much power. That doesn't worry me, Seraphine, it terrifies me.'

67

The reception to Aplomb PR was a crazy combination of pinks and yellows. Zander wondered who in their right mind would employ a company with such awful taste. The young woman behind the desk wore bright red lipstick and a chunky purple sweater. When she looked up her smile was ridiculously wide.

'Good morning, sir, and welcome to Aplomb.' Her accent was plummy and her tone a touch too cheery for the early hour.

'I have a delivery for Mr Jameson.' Zander's uniform had been one of his best acquisitions. People don't suspect postmen and they also don't see past the clothes.

'Do you have a first name?' she said as she checked her screen.

Zander made a point of looking at the parcel he had mocked up. 'Marcus.'

'We don't have anyone here with that name.'

'Well, that's the name I've got.' He stood where he was. He needed her to take the package. He'd placed a tracker inside that he'd bought from a spy shop in East London. It was basic tech but he would be able to see on his phone where the parcel ended up.

'He doesn't work here,' she said as a tall woman

entered the lobby. 'Jacqui, have you heard of a Mr Jameson? Might he be a client?'

'Marcus?' said the tall lady. Zander noted her height was in part due to some very high heels. 'He and Augusta are downstairs. If you take the lift to the basement the office is just there.'

Zander couldn't believe his luck. He mumbled thank you in a manner he assumed the average delivery guy would, and walked back out to the hall to take the lift down one floor. Marcus Jameson had an office on site. Zander wasn't expecting that. Maybe Mr Jameson liked to keep an eye on his investments.

The lift door opened to reveal a basic, utilitarian space. There were no spotlights or funky colours down here, just a corridor with three closed doors. He looked through the window in the first door and was surprised by the room within. It was small with a couple of desks and three chairs. It didn't look like the kind of office a man like Marcus Jameson would inhabit. Maybe the woman upstairs had been wrong.

He walked to the second room. This door had no glass. Zander pushed it wide, ready to play his delivery-man role again, but it was a small, empty kitchen. He walked in and checked the cupboards. There were boxes of green tea and packets of coffee alongside a handful of cups. In the fridge there was a half-drunk carton of milk and two mango yogurts. The yogurt pots faced in opposite directions and one had fallen on to its side. That would drive Lexi crazy. Zander closed the door without touching them.

The final door revealed a small shower room and toilet.

Zander moved back to the office and tried to enter. It was locked.

He was about to return to the reception upstairs and to try and leave the parcel there again when he spotted the whiteboard. It was on the right-hand wall of the office so he had to move to the edge of the door window to see it properly.

Why were the names of all his and AJ's victims written on Marcus Jameson's office wall?

Zander stepped back as he realized the irony that he had been hunting a guy who was in fact hunting him. Marcus Jameson hadn't been in the members' bar because he was buying an apartment, he'd been there to nose around.

Zander knew what Lexi would say. *That's it then. Move on. Find another target.* Zander could see the logic. He shouldn't muddy the water with a kill that didn't fit the profile. But unfortunately for Marcus Jameson, Lexi wasn't here and Zander was hungry.

Halfway along the hall, opposite the kitchen, there was a small half-height door. He opened it and looked inside. It contained a hoover and a mop and a few bottles of cleaning fluid. Zander stuck his head further in and checked out the space. Without the mop in here, it would work nicely. He picked up the mop along with the bucket and carried them into the kitchen, pushing both down the side of the fridge.

And now Zander had what he loved most: a nice little hiding place.

68

'Leave Porter to me.' Seraphine had been looking across the park towards Bloom and Jameson's office for the last few moments. 'I have a little gift for you.' Seraphine took a flash drive from her coat pocket and slid it across the table.

'What's this?'

'The recording of Sandy Roper's interview.'

'How . . . why?'

Seraphine shrugged. 'You should watch it.'

'I was there. I saw it live.'

'Did you? See it?'

Bloom knew Seraphine was avoiding talking about what she needed to. This was more game playing.

'Stop avoiding the issue. You need to stop Porter; you're the only one who can but you have to be prepared to lose too.'

'I never lose.'

'If you're genuine about your purpose, you may need to learn to.'

'It is sweet that you care but you don't need to worry.'

'Oh yes I do because someone has to.' After a few moments of silence, Bloom spoke more quietly. 'I'm sorry, Seraphine.'

'What for?'

'Your cardinal accused me of stereotyping and he was correct. I missed too much for too long. In that sense I failed you.'

'Augusta, you should worry less about failing others and focus more on fulfilling your potential.'

'What does that mean?'

Seraphine stood. 'When you're ready, I'll tell you, but until then' – she pushed the flash drive closer to Bloom – 'watch it. See if you see what I see.'

69

The office felt colder than usual, perhaps because it had been a while since both she and Jameson had been there together. How was she going to explain the truth about Seraphine to her partner? He wouldn't want to hear that they had misjudged her; that all this time she had been driven by a desire to make the world a better place. Bloom saw it clearly now from Seraphine's perspective. The world was broken, unjust and unfair. How could that happen under the watchful eyes of those who had such a capacity for empathy? To Seraphine the answer was simple: to be empathetic required you to be emotional and being emotional interfered with rational thought. So why not leave it to those whose thinking was dominated by reason?

It had a crazy logic to it.

Before settling at the computer, Bloom went to make a hot drink. The lack of sleep followed by sitting outside for an hour meant she couldn't get warm. As she entered the kitchen her phone rang. It was Lucas George.

'I've been calling Marcus but there's no answer.'

'I've sent him home to rest. He had a rough night. What can I do for you?' she said as she filled the kettle and set it to boil. The cleaner had left the mop and bucket stuffed down the side of the fridge and she could smell a musty odour coming from it.

'He asked me to look into Sandy Roper to see if he has any siblings and he doesn't.'

'Are you sure? Might his mum have been married before or put a child up for adoption?'

'I checked all of that and could find no records of Lesley Roper having any other children. She was only seventeen when she had Sandy according to my calculations.'

'That's helpful, thanks, Lucas. Did you find anything else of interest about Sandy or his mother – Lesley, was it?'

'Other than the fact that he's your typical computer geek, no.'

'How do you mean?'

'I found links to a few gaming forums via his Facebook page. He's not live on them now but I sounded out a few of the players, saying I was looking for an old school friend, and they said he used to be a regular but not so much recently.'

'I never go out. I'm always inside, in the dark.'

'How recently?'

'A few years now.'

'This is great, Lucas, as usual. Thank you.'

She hung up and quickly poured hot water over her teabag. What had Seraphine spotted in Sandy Roper's interview? What had she and the police missed?

She glanced at the mop. It needed to go back in the cupboard. She grabbed the bucket handle and wrapped her fingers around the mop so she could lift them together and also carry her tea. In the hall she placed her tea on the small shelf above the radiator in order to open the cupboard door.

'Hey, I was hoping you'd be here.' Jameson's appearance in the hallway made her jump half out of her skin. 'Sorry,' he said on seeing her reaction.

'What are you doing here? I sent you home to rest.'

'I did and now I'm ready to work. I just had an interesting call.'

'From Lucas?'

'No. I need to call him back. My call was for Jasper.'

Bloom followed him into the office and closed the door to keep the heat in.

'It was Simon's sister calling to say she'd searched his apartment and there was no sign of my watch and then we had a little chat. Apparently, the people above Simon were having a new kitchen built the month of Simon's death and the workmen were using the rear entrance to come and go without passing reception.'

'So that could be how the killer got in.'

'Exactly. Like with Philip's building, he could have gone in earlier in the day when workmen were coming and going without raising any questions, then found somewhere to wait.'

The idea reminded Bloom of a film she'd watched years ago where a stalker had made a home for himself in a woman's loft so he could watch her from above. It was one of the creepiest things she'd ever seen.

She filled Jameson in on Lucas's call and the fact that Sandy Roper had no siblings.

299

'Is he absolutely sure?'

'He says from official records Mum had only one child.'

'What about Dad?'

'Would you get that kind of close resemblance from half-siblings?'

'Probably not but what else have we got?'

Bloom lifted up the flash drive.

'What's that?'

'Sandy's police interview.'

'How did you get that?'

'Seraphine gave it to me. She says I missed something.'

A look crossed Jameson's face that Bloom didn't understand. 'Mirza will freak.'

'I'm going to take a look now.'

Jameson nodded. 'I'll give you some peace.'

70

Seraphine remained in the park after her meeting with Augusta. There were very few people who ever caused her to pause for thought but Dr Bloom was one of them. It was not only that she respected the other woman's intelligence, it was something about her motivation too. Seraphine had felt it all those years ago when they first met. Every word the woman spoke, every question she asked was for Seraphine's benefit; all aimed at making her think and challenge herself. It was the same today; Augusta's concerns were focused on ensuring Seraphine saw the risks and considered the alternatives.

The loss of Miriam Chevalier's loyalty was a further blow. She would handle it but that wasn't the real issue. The real problem was that Porter was gaining on her. She couldn't let that continue. The time for sounding people out was over. She needed to take decisive action. Action that would send a clear message to the whole organization.

The sight of Marcus walking across the park towards his and Augusta's office was a pleasant distraction. It had been no hardship seducing him, and she could never have anticipated the fun of their continued interactions. He had said on many occasions how much he hated her and everything she stood for. She was the devil incarnate and he had no time for her games. And yet, despite his obvious anger towards her, he had never once flinched from the reality of what she was. It was a rare thing: being able to drop the mask and simply be herself. The lack of emotional reactiveness usually freaked people out. But Marcus, *her Marcus*, looked right at her and, despite the permanent scowl and irritated tone, he chose to not look away.

71

Jameson went to the kitchen to make a coffee. A full mug of tea was on the radiator shelf and next to it sat the mop and bucket. Bloom must have had a spill.

He reached for his favourite mug in the cupboard and the one-person cafetière. He needed a caffeine hit. After leaving Bloom's house this morning he hadn't slept, choosing instead to take his bike out for a spin. He needed to clear his head. It had spooked him that Porter had made it inside Bloom's house. He'd had more than enough time to hurt her before Jameson had made it over there. Add to that the realization that Seraphine never intended to release Bloom from her web and he had been forced to change his perspective. He saw now that there would be real benefit in removing Seraphine from their lives permanently. They could go back to helping people find out what had happened to their missing loved ones. Plus, Claire and the family could come home as they and Bloom would be safe from Porter.

He'd spent the ride thinking it through tactically. How could he do it? Where would he do it? It had to be in a way that wouldn't point a finger at him and that meant it had to appear to be an accident. He figured he could use the date she said he owed her. He could suggest a walk out in the countryside. They had met for a picnic on their first-ever date back when she had been pretending to be someone else. He could use that as some kind of romantic reason to walk out to a remote location. Once there he would easily be able to overwhelm her. She might be a psychopathic purveyor of all things evil but she was also a slight woman with little muscle mass. The quickest and easiest way would be a blow to the head but he knew that was out of the question. Any good pathologist would be able to tell the difference between someone hitting their head in a fall and being struck by a blunt object. The same went for suffocation or strangulation. He needed something that could pass as an unfortunate accident.

He had used this tactic once before when his cover had been blown by a member of the terrorist group he was tracking. The guy had confronted him in an alley behind a seedy bar and they had fought. Jameson came off worse initially. His cheekbone had been broken as had his right wrist, but then his luck changed. The man stumbled and fell on to a low wall, breaking his back in the process. Jameson had known he couldn't risk calling for help; he had to protect his cover. That also meant he couldn't leave the guy in case someone came along and gave him a chance to talk. And so he sat on the ground next to the man and waited. When the groans of pain became too much to bear, Jameson held his hand over the man's mouth and nose until he passed out. It was a tactic he repeated many times before the guy finally failed to regain consciousness completely.

Jameson had walked away – his cover safe and the job going on to be a success – yet somehow that man had followed Jameson out of the alley, taking up residence in his head and presenting those final moments over and over again. Could he really cope with Seraphine inhabiting his memory that way? Seeing her pleading eyes and hearing her rasping breaths in the middle of the night might be too much to bear.

And he would still have the problem of Porter to handle. It was no good removing the head of the snake only for another to slither into position. He would be forced to remove him from play too. It was a domino effect that would drag him so far back into the person he didn't want to be that there might be no way to escape. Even then, there would still be the others in Seraphine's circle of psychos to consider. How many of them might fancy their chances when the seat at the top became free? Bloom would obsess about finding each one. She would become even more trapped in the game than she was now.

As he cycled, he'd looked at it from every angle. If he could convince MI6 to tackle Seraphine's remaining organization that might work. It was their jurisdiction after all. It wouldn't be easy: the British secret service had its own agenda and priorities; he'd need to make a strong case with evidence. He'd need all the intel Bloom had gathered in her recent trip and he'd need to pump Seraphine for as much extra detail as possible as he walked her to the endgame. He still had a few good contacts. It wouldn't be impossible if he did it right.

It was a plan he knew would destroy everything. It would instigate the destruction of whatever despicable acts Seraphine was planning. But it would also destroy his friendship with Bloom for good. She would never forgive him. And he didn't dare think about the impact on his mental health.

But at least they would all finally be free.

72

When Jameson returned to the office, Bloom pulled up a seat next to her desk.

'Watch this,' she said. She pressed play on the recording of Sandy Roper's police interview. It was the section he had watched the day before. 'This is definitely not the man you met. You're sure of that?'

Jameson watched for a few minutes. 'Yep, this is a different person. I'd place a decent bet on that.'

Bloom forwarded the recording on. 'Roper said something odd during the interview so I wanted to check that out. Watch this section.'

On the screen DS Peters said, 'So if we checked your phone and your computer, we would find evidence that you stay in and order in, is that what you're telling me, Sandy?'

'Yes. Absolutely. Do that. I never go out. I'm always inside, in the dark.'

Bloom paused the video. '"I'm always inside, in the dark." That's an odd turn of phrase, don't you think?'

Jameson nodded.

'Now watch this.' She pressed play again.

DS Peters said, 'Sorry, did you say you are always inside in the dark?'

Sandy dropped his head for a few seconds before

answering. When he lifted his head he said, 'I'm not a fan of bright lights like these.' He glanced up at the strip lights. 'They bring on my migraines.'

'Whoa,' Jameson said. 'What was that?'

'What did you see?' Bloom paused the playback.

'Play it again.'

Bloom played the section again, this time letting it continue on as DS Peters said, 'Sandy, can you understand my concern here? You are the one person capable of accessing Hardeep's client files while he is away and the two files looked at are those of two murdered men. Now you're telling me you were home on your own on both occasions, meaning you have no alibi. How do I know you're not spinning me a line here, Sandy?'

'I wouldn't spin you a line, sir. I assure you I was not there when these men died.'

Bloom paused again and looked at Jameson. 'See it?'

'His accent is different, his body language changes and even his facial expressions shift. So he is a bloody good actor after all.'

'I'm not so sure. Look at this next bit.' She pressed play.

DS Peters said, 'OK, so you weren't there but do you know who was? Did you give Jeremy and George's addresses to someone else?'

'Pardon. What did you say?'

Bloom paused again. 'He looks confused here, yes?'

'He missed the question,' said Jameson.

Bloom pressed play again and the DS said, 'I asked if you passed Jeremy and George's details to someone else? If you didn't do this, do you know who did?'

'Mr Rigby says it's illegal to share people's personal information. He'd sack me. I never used Hardeep's login. I don't need to.'

'Because you can use your own – yes, you said. But wouldn't you use someone else's if you were trying to cover your tracks?' Peters said.

'I didn't open those files. I promise.'

Bloom stopped the playback.

'He goes back into the act,' said Jameson.

'If it is an act.'

'How could it not be?'

'When we spot people lying it is typically via inconsistencies in what they say or how they behave. If we watch and listen carefully, we can spot these, the little slips and cracks in the cover-up. But that all relies on the person knowing that what they are saying is untrue. If the person believes their version of things so deeply there is no such dissonance. There are no cracks to show.'

'OK.'

Bloom forwarded the interview on again. 'This is at the end when the DS asks Roper about his mother. It's the only bit where he gets a bit testy. Ready?'

When Jameson nodded, she let the playback roll.

On screen DS Peters said, 'Did she get a boyfriend you didn't like?'

'Why are you asking about Mother? What has she got to do with anything? Lots of people don't see their parents when they grow up. It's not a crime.'

'No way,' said Jameson as he watched Sandy Roper's body language, accent and tone shift once more. This time Roper somehow made himself seem bigger. He squared his shoulders and lifted his head high and it was possible to make out a pretty muscular frame under the baggy *Star Trek* sweatshirt.

Bloom let the video play on.

'I'm trying to understand, that's all,' said DS Peters.

'I think you're desperate to find some evidence that I did these awful things because you have nothing to prove that I did.' Sandy looked at the duty solicitor. 'Can I go now? Can you make them let me go?'

The recording came to an end and Bloom turned her chair to face Jameson. 'Is that the man you met?'

'Absolutely. That was weird. He clearly can't keep up his act when he gets riled. He leaks his true self.'

'Yes and no. People usually unconsciously leak their true self as they go. When they lie they might fidget or blush but what we are seeing here is compartmentalized. There are no leaks apart from in those two short interactions. Everything about what Roper says and how he behaves in between that comes over as genuine.'

'Like I say, he's a bloody good actor. He must totally convince himself and commit to whatever he's trying to portray.'

'And yet, when he slips, did you notice that he's different?'

'Yeah, like you said, his voice and demeanour all change.'

'No, I mean the difference between the two slips. Watch.' Bloom played the first section again when Sandy talked about the blinding lights giving him a migraine;

then she moved on to the second section when he got angry. 'He looks and sounds different in each of the slips. The first time he's precise in articulating each word and there's something almost feminine about how he crosses his legs and places his hands neatly on his knee. The second time he looks more manly, like a fellow who can handle himself.'

'Because he's angry that second time.'

'Have you ever heard of D.I.D. or dissociative identity disorder?'

'What's that?'

'It's what used to be called a split personality. It would explain a lot of what we've seen not only in the interview but in the murders themselves. We think we have one killer who is cold and calculating and another who is angry and violent and yet tying them together is this obsessive neatness in how the scenes are left. It's like a thread of a trait linking each killer, too consistent to be something coached in or copied. It's a compulsion that both killers share. And it is identically manifested across all the scenes.'

'Because the two killers are really the same person?'

'Different identities within the person, yes. And it would also explain why Roper comes over so genuinely in his interview. There's a chance he really knows nothing.'

'Honestly? How does that work?'

'Different people with D.I.D. experience it differently. Some hear conversations between their various identities as if multiple people are present; others have no such interactions. But what does tend to be common is that each identity takes its turn front of house with many primary identities reporting to have no memory of what their counterparts have done or said in their absence.'

'So when Roper says he stays home in the dark you think that's him being pushed out by the others and these others are the killers?'

'It would be a clever cover-up, wouldn't it? To have an identity who can honestly say they know nothing? At the start of the interview he tells Carl Peters he's worked for Prestige Wealth for a couple of years and when Carl clarifies that Roper's boss said he'd been there since they launched five years ago Sandy looks confused. I think that's because he's lost a few years of time. I think his alters may have taken over.'

'It's like science fiction. How do people end up that way?'

'Typically it's triggered by some trauma in childhood, an event so distressing that the mind creates alternative versions to protect itself from the reality. It may be that the primary identity has little to no recollection of the trauma, for instance. And often one of the identities is locked at the age of the trauma, manifesting as grown adults who behave like a child.'

'You need to show DCI Mirza this,' said Jameson.

'I'm going now. I need to do it in person so she sees what she needs to. Are you coming?'

'No, this is your catch. Go take the glory.'

'This wasn't my catch, it was Seraphine's.'

'At last she does something of value.'

As Bloom packed her laptop and the flash drive into her bag she said, 'Maybe it's time you gave her the benefit of the doubt. There's something I need to tell you later. It's the reason my gut told me she had nothing to do with these murders.'

'For God's sake, Augusta, can't we focus on one nutter at a time? You were right. This wasn't her. Take the win and leave it alone.' His head was full of what he needed to do to Seraphine and its consequences. He couldn't cope with hearing Augusta's latest theories. He watched her recoil and then take a moment to process the jolt.

'You didn't sleep, did you?'

'Whatever gave you that idea?' Jameson closed his eyes for a few seconds; then he let out a long sigh. 'I don't want to hear about Seraphine right now, OK? The woman infuriates me and I'm too tired.'

'Later then.'

'Later,' said Jameson, raising a hand to wave goodbye.

73

On the way to New Scotland Yard, Bloom called DCI Mirza's mobile. It went to voicemail so she left a message to say she was on her way with evidence that Sandy Roper was the man they were looking for. Her next call was to Tyler Rowe.

'Hi, Tyler. I'm heading over to see the DCI about Sandy Roper and I wanted to give you the heads-up. Do you know much about dissociative identity disorder?'

'Not much, why?'

'Do a bit of research. Find all you can about how it manifests and what the best strategies for handling someone with it might be. I'll come and see you when I get there and explain more.'

Bloom had never worked with someone who had D.I.D. but she had read a fair bit about it over the years. It was one of the most fascinating disorders related to how the mind copes with trauma, which is why it had always captured so much public attention. The idea that someone might have multiple personalities was intriguing and frightening. She had often wondered what it must feel like to have different aspects of your identity in play. There was often a main identity, known as a 'host', which those with D.I.D. described as feeling most like them, alongside a number of other identities

314

known as 'alters'. These could be of different ages and genders and often the host had no control of when different alters took over. It was no longer called multiple personality disorder because the current thinking was that each identity was in fact a different part of the same personality. Every individual was capable of being mature at times and silly at others, of thinking calmly and rationally about certain life experiences but then reacting badly to others. Personality was by its nature multi-faceted. It just so happened that with D.I.D. those facets had become distinct and gained their own separate identity within the person's consciousness. As she had told Jameson, this was a natural way the mind had for coping with some sustained childhood trauma like abuse or neglect.

It was only a half-hour walk from Russell Square to the Metropolitan Police's headquarters. She liked to take a route which passed through Covent Garden and Trafalgar Square. Having grown up in Yorkshire and never having visited the capital city as a child, she never tired of seeing the famous landmarks as she moved around her adopted home. She walked past the Ministry of Defence's building where she had first met DCI Mirza and Gerald Porter what felt like an age ago, then she turned left opposite Downing Street and approached the River Thames, her gaze naturally drawn to the London Eye looming large on the opposite side.

When she arrived at New Scotland Yard DCI Mirza was unavailable so she asked for Detective Sergeant Peters, who took her up to their incident room.

'Sandy Roper has no siblings,' DS Peters said as they walked. 'We spoke to his mother, Lesley Roper.'

'Did she say why they were estranged?' Bloom asked as they entered the room where DC Morgan sat at a computer near the wall on which the team had pinned up details of all the Matchbox Murders. A photograph of Roper had been pinned to one side with a red question mark next to it. Underneath had been written 'Alexander John Roper "Sandy"' and 'Find his brother'.

'She said Sandy had always been a bit of a loner and preferred to have his head in a computer.'

'Did she ask you what Sandy had done?'

'We didn't tell her anything, we played it down, said we were looking at Prestige Wealth about an issue.'

Bloom nodded as he spoke, then repeated, 'So she did ask you what he had done? She used those words, or similar?'

DS Peters frowned and then nodded.

'I saw you arrive,' said Tyler Rowe as he joined them. 'I did some research on D.I.D. What's this about?'

'I think we need the DCI.'

'She's in with the super,' said DS Peters. 'They don't like to be disturbed. They're usually done by ten.'

'She'll want to hear this.'

There was a moment of silence as DS Peters decided.

To help him along Bloom said, 'You're right when you say Sandy Roper has no siblings, but what he does have is alternative identities which have separate thoughts and behaviours. That's why Lesley Roper asked you what he had done. My guess is she doesn't see her son any more because she doesn't like one or more of the characters likely to turn up.'

'You are kidding?' said DC Morgan.

'I am deadly serious. Now, please, will you go and get the DCI?'

74

Jameson waited five minutes after Bloom left before starting to plot out his plan to kill Seraphine. He didn't want to risk Bloom walking back in and seeing what he was doing. If this was ever going to work, he needed to be the only person who ever knew anything about it.

He had identified three possible areas where a walk into the countryside might be suitable. Two were areas that he knew well: the South Downs National Park situated south of London, and Dartmoor in Devon. The third was the Yorkshire Dales. Although the latter was the farthest away, he liked the symmetry of taking Seraphine back to where she came from, the place where she'd met Bloom and all this craziness started. There was also a pleasing narrative in the idea that she might have chosen to visit home then headed out for an unfortunate solo walk. The challenge would be convincing her to travel there, but that was not beyond his powers of persuasion.

He printed a map of the Yorkshire Dales National Park and laid it flat on his desk. He circled the town of Ilkley where Seraphine had hidden Jane. From there, he had the option of heading into the national park or alternatively walking across Ilkley Moor. He remembered a song about the place: something about a walker being eaten by worms who are then eaten by ducks who are then eaten by people.

A sound alerted some instinctive part of his brain – the scrape of the door or a footstep too soft and careful to be a legitimate visitor – but there was no time to react. All he saw was something flash in front of his face before a cord tightened around his neck. Jameson's hands moved instantly up to find some weakness where he could squeeze a finger through. Pain seared down his throat and into his chest as he tried to suck the smallest pocket of air through the restricted space. He pushed his chair backwards, using his weight to try and unbalance his attacker; there was a momentary movement as the legs of his chair grated across the floor, but then the body behind strengthened their stance and tightened the cord. Jameson reached out to the desk to find a weapon. The map and papers skidded off the side and he knocked over his coffee. There was a pencil and a few pens just beyond his reach. He stretched his fingers as far as he could. He knew Seraphine could do real damage with a pencil. The light in the room dimmed and a wave of dizziness rocked his whole body. He was fit, strong and trained in self-defence. He had survived so many life-threatening experiences. It couldn't end here, in his own office. He wouldn't let it. He tried to focus, to dampen the panic and take control but his brain was deprived of oxygen and it refused to play. In a final desperate attempt at defence he began rocking side to side on the chair, trying to tip himself over. His feet slid about unable to find purchase so he used his hands against the desk. If he could get a moment of release around his neck he could fight back.

Finally, after what felt like forever, the chair toppled to the left. But his attacker was ready. The man dropped to his knee and pulled even harder on the cord so it felt like hot wire cutting into Jameson's skin. There was nothing more to do.

Jameson's last image was that of a sneering Sandy Roper dressed as a postman.

75

'What's this about?' said DCI Mirza as she entered the incident room. 'Carl says you've got a crazy idea to tell me.'

'It's not an idea.' In the time it had taken the DS to fetch his boss, Rowe had helped Bloom copy Sandy Roper's interview on to two more laptops that now sat alongside hers on the central table. Bloom had written down the time stamps for the switches she had found in Roper's identity and Rowe was setting each video to these separate points. 'If you want to take a seat so you can see all the screens, I'll show you.'

Mirza, Peters and Morgan all moved chairs and sat facing the laptops.

'I think there is a very good reason why Sandy Roper gave no indication of his involvement in the Matchbox Murders,' said Bloom. 'It's because he has had nothing to do with them.'

'What? I thought you told Carl you could prove it was him.'

'Marcus has a skill for facial recognition. When he saw Roper leaving the station, he was certain he'd seen him before in the private members' bar of Philip Berringer's apartment block, but when I showed him the opening ten minutes of your interview, he admitted that although there was a definite resemblance, Roper was not the same man he had met. The reason for this was that everything about his demeanour, his accent and his body language was different. Something which Jameson's years in the secret service has taught him is nigh on impossible to achieve without some leaks. As he told me, even the best actors in the world bring something of themselves to a role. They can't completely remove their unconscious micro-expressions or physical tics. He concluded that Sandy must have a twin. That's how strong he felt the facial similarity was.'

'But Roper doesn't have any siblings,' said Rowe. The young behavioural investigative advisor looked excited about what was coming.

'I need you to watch these three segments of your interview very closely. Look at Roper's body language and what happens to his face and his accent.'

She pressed play on the first laptop. This showed them the same section she had played for Jameson from the point Roper said he stayed home in the dark. The group watched carefully and other than DCI Mirza raising an eyebrow they showed no reaction.

'Did you see anything change in how Roper behaved?'

'His accent became posher,' said Fleur Morgan.

'His posture changed too, he sat upright for the first time. I remember picking up on that at the time,' said Carl Peters. 'It made me think we were on to something.'

'But then Roper reverted back to his former posture and accent,' said Bloom. She pressed play and they watched Roper experience a momentary confusion, before asking DS Peters to repeat the question. 'I think what you have just seen is a switch between alters, which are the different identities that can become dominant within a person who has dissociative identity disorder.'

'We deal with fakes and frauds day in day out,' said Mirza. 'I don't see anything different here.'

Bloom nodded to Rowe who sat nearest to the other laptop. He pressed play and the final part of the interview played out, where Roper was quizzed about his mother.

'He's different again here,' said Morgan. 'I saw the change that time. He looks broader somehow.'

'You can see that he's muscular under his sweatshirt now, can't you?' said Bloom. 'Because he's changed how he's sitting. I think what we're seeing here is a man capable of overpowering another person. When Marcus saw this clip, he said the person you see now is the man he met in Philip's apartment block. He looks and sounds the same.'

'So he's good at faking,' said DS Peters.

'Really, really good,' said Bloom. 'Can you set the clip again please, Tyler?' While Rowe did that, Bloom set the laptop nearest her to the early stages of the interview before either switch and the middle one back to the comment about being in the dark. 'I'm going to play all three identities together so you can see how different they are, then if you're still in doubt we can just listen to the voices one after another.'

'You're really certain of this, aren't you?' said Mirza.

'I know it's hard to believe but it would shed light on things about these murders that are otherwise hard to explain.' She played the clips and the three officers and Rowe watched the screens. DS Peters frowned a little, DC Morgan slowly nodded as she looked from screen to screen and DCI Mirza viewed the whole thing without expression.

As the clips came to an end and Bloom paused the playbacks, another officer came in.

'You wanted to see me, boss?' he said looking at DS Peters.

'When you visited Lesley Roper, did she ask you what Sandy had done or something similar, can you remember?'

The officer was nodding before his sergeant had finished. 'She seemed very agitated that he had got himself into trouble; it took a while to get her to calm down and answer our questions.'

Bloom said, 'I suspect this is because Lesley Roper knows her son is different and that difference scares her.'

'Whether he has this identity thing or not, I think what we've seen here shows he's faking or lying on some level,' said DS Peters.

Nadia Mirza looked at Bloom for a long moment. The woman had a lot resting on this. She had already lost one privileged role due to Porter escaping custody and that had in large part been down to Bloom. She would not want to make a fool of herself again, and certainly not with the same psychologist in tow. In Mirza's eyes Bloom was likely either to steal the glory or make the team a laughing stock.

Bloom said, 'If you bring him in again, Tyler and I can

put together some questions to help you determine if I'm right or not.'

'He's not likely to admit it, though, is he?' said DS Peters.

'That all depends on whether Sandy is in on it.'

'How do you mean?'

'In D.I.D. the different identities can have barriers in between them. It's part of the process for protecting the host; at some point when the person was facing trauma the mind chose to compartmentalize the experiences, making it so some parts of the person can forget what has happened to them. The mind is not creating separate personalities, rather it is segmenting the person into smaller parts. These parts can then go on to have experiences which the others do not recall at all.'

'So you're saying the first Sandy we saw in the interview is innocent?'

'I'm not sure innocent is the right description; like I say, these are different parts of the same whole person, but certainly Sandy could be entirely oblivious. I think that's why the first alter stepped in. When Sandy said he stayed home all the time in the dark, that grabbed your attention,' she said to DS Peters, 'and suddenly we see Sandy's whole posture change. He shakes his head slightly and crosses his legs in an almost feminine manner, resting his hands delicately on his knee. Then he speaks with a raspy tone talking about bright lights giving him migraines and calling you "sir" as he flirtatiously says he would never spin you a line.'

'You think the alter came in to cover up the slip?'

'I do, yes.'

'Is that what happens later as well?' said Rowe. 'Does he say something important and that's why the alter comes back?'

'It's not the same alter,' said DC Morgan. 'I agree with Dr Bloom; the first one is quite feminine but the last one is almost butch.'

Bloom nodded. 'I don't think Sandy messed up at the end, I think the second alter stepped in because you were on to something. The whole origin of this will be in childhood and you started asking questions about the parents, in particular the mother. I think that riled one of the identities, who then stepped in to bring the whole thing to a close.'

'It's a stretch,' said DCI Mirza.

'If I'm right, I think there is a good chance the alters responsible have kept their host in the dark so he can be their innocent front man.'

'"I'm always inside, in the dark,"' said Rowe.

Bloom continued, 'But this could be good news as it means Sandy may well be coaxed into telling you about his D.I.D. without realizing he will be incriminating himself.'

All eyes in the room moved to the detective chief inspector who, after a pause, nodded and said, 'OK. Bring Roper in.'

76

The first sensation Jameson became aware of was a searing hot pain in his throat when he took a breath. His head pounded and his whole body ached. He blinked into the bright light, making out blurry images of his and Bloom's office. He could smell coffee and saw a large pool of it on the floor to his left. He tried to get up out of the chair but he couldn't. A thick rope had been tied around his middle, pinning his arms to his sides. His ankles were tied too, with thick cable ties that were cutting into his skin.

Sandy Roper stood leaning against Bloom's desk across the room. He had removed the postman's jacket and now wore a black T-shirt. He was not as tall as Jameson remembered but he had that stocky, naturally muscular build that gives a person a low centre of gravity. That's why he was so strong.

'What do you want?' Jameson's words sounded gravelly and it hurt to say them.

'Who are you? Why do you have this on your wall?' Roper pointed to the whiteboard where Bloom had written the details of all the Matchbox Murders.

'Let me go.'

'You weren't there to buy an apartment, were you?'

When Jameson said nothing, Roper went on, 'You were poking your nose in. Are you police?'

Jameson remained silent. He knew what to do in an interrogation.

'Have you been following me? And who was the woman?'

Jameson eyeballed the guy. Had he been in the building when Augusta was here? He couldn't have been. There was nowhere to hide.

And then he remembered the mop and bucket. They had been in the hall outside of the cupboard where they were usually kept.

How much had Roper heard? Did he know they had worked it out? Jameson was pretty sure the office door had been shut when Bloom had showed him the video of Roper's interview. This was an old Georgian building with solid stone walls and oak doors. Sound did not travel well.

'I said, who was the woman?'

Jameson moved his eyes to a spot on the wall.

Roper stepped towards him. 'You are not in any position to keep quiet. Do you think I won't finish the job? I'm more than capable.'

The slight smile that touched Jameson's lips had an astonishing effect. The man literally metamorphosed in front of his eyes. His muscular frame seemed to lose all its rigour as it dropped into a curled-up version of itself. The hands tightened into fists and the eyes lost their look of intelligence, taking on a far more animal-like quality.

Jameson tensed. This one looked like a killer – no doubt about it.

'Zander might have tied you up but I'm going to rip you apart.'

Zander? Was that who he'd just been talking to?

'I'll smash your face in and have you bleeding and begging for your life. How do you like the sound of that, you meddling piece of shit? You won't be smiling then, will you?' Roper wiped his arm across Bloom's desk, sending all her notepads and pens flying off on to the floor. Then he kicked over her chair before rounding on Jameson again. 'Scared yet?' The manic look in the man's eyes was entirely terrifying. It was the look of a person losing control and Jameson knew that was the most dangerous kind.

'What do you want?' said Jameson in a calm voice which he hoped might defuse things. 'Tell me what you want?'

'I want a fucking knife, that's what I want. A fucking knife to slice your face with.'

Roper yanked open the office door and walked into the hall towards the kitchen.

Crap. This was bad, Jameson knew. He wriggled within the ropes but they were too tight and too thick to budge. He tried to jump his chair closer to the desk where his phone was. If he could dial 999 and leave the line open the police might come – if he was lucky. The chair moved once, twice, but he could not move close enough, quick enough. Jameson heard Roper's footsteps coming back. He scanned the room for something, anything he could use to defend himself. There was nothing. All he had was his own body and that was tied to a chair and pretty much immobilized.

Roper stood in the door with the wooden-handled knife from the kitchen. It was one Jameson had brought in for slicing cheese. He enjoyed a cheese sandwich or cheese on toast of a lunchtime and the knife was good and sharp. Roper held it in the fist of his right hand with the blade facing forward. He was a man who knew how to wield a sharp weapon.

If Jameson was lucky, he could duck and dive enough to avoid a killer blow. It was either that or hope for something quick and decisive.

Whatever happened, it was going to hurt.

77

'There's no sign of Roper at his house, ma'am,' DS Peters said as DCI Mirza and Bloom left the superintendent's office. 'I told a team to stay there. He has to come home some time, right?'

'So much for staying in all the time,' Mirza said to Bloom.

'It's Sandy who stays in; if they're out one of the others is probably in control.'

'Are you sure about this?'

Their briefing to Mirza's boss had not been the most comfortable experience. The superintendent was young for the rank, most probably on the graduate scheme and obviously ambitious. Like Mirza he looked uncomfortable with the idea of such an unusual scenario. He wanted to know how they planned to prove it. Mirza had talked about the partial print in the St Pancras Hotel that they had checked against Roper. It was inconclusive but that wasn't an out-and-out reject. She also mentioned the Airbnb apartment at Philip Berringer's block, saying that her team was looking into who rented it over the time of Philip's death. After that it was down to some good old-fashioned interrogation. The superintendent said he needed to check with ACC Steve Barker on the best strategy, but that they should proceed with bringing Roper in again.

'Thankfully he didn't enquire as to how you were in possession of a recording of Roper's interview,' said Mirza as they walked.

'Thankfully,' said Bloom, choosing not to elaborate on where she had acquired it. 'I expect Steve will support us though. He's an open-minded copper, in my experience.'

Mirza flashed a look of irritation Bloom's way. It had been obvious that the DCI was trying to impress ACC Barker throughout this investigation and hearing such a familiar insight into his character from Bloom clearly grated.

Bloom changed the subject. 'I'll work with Tyler to get you some good questions. Sandy may not know that he has D.I.D. Often it isn't diagnosed because the individuals think everyone has voices in their head. If that's the case, we may be able to play to it. It'll be trickier if he's aware that he's different and actively tries to hide it.'

DS Peters said, 'I spoke to Russell Rigby earlier. He said Sandy used to work in the office at least once a week until a few years back when he became reluctant to come in. Russell figured the guy had a bit of depression or something so didn't push it.'

'That fits with some insight I heard that Sandy used to be a big player on a few gaming forums until a couple of years ago.'

'I'm not going to ask how you discovered that,' said DCI Mirza. 'So two years ago is not long before Philip is killed and around that time Sandy Roper becomes a hermit. That's not a coincidence, I expect.'

'One of the alters became dominant perhaps,' said Bloom. 'It can happen sometimes, I believe.'

'Like a body snatcher,' said DS Peters with a fake shudder.

'It's still the same person, remember. The alters aren't parasites, they're protectors.'

'Are you thinking these murders could be part of protecting Sandy in some way?' asked DCI Mirza as they entered the incident room.

Rowe was nodding as he heard Mirza's words. 'I've been reading some of the case studies on the MIND website. People with D.I.D. talk about feeling numb and separate from everyone else. They can have short tempers and become irritable quickly and many contemplate suicide because they feel so lost and alone. Add to this the fact that some identities can be stuck at the age that the abuse took place while others can take on the role of a protective parent who was absent in reality, and you have a powerful combination for wanting to seek revenge.'

'We should pursue that, Tyler,' said Bloom. 'Let's put together some questions to explore Sandy's relationship with his parents, particularly his father and any other men in his life: uncles, Mum's boyfriends and the like. He has an issue with rich men. We need to find out who the source of that anger was.'

'Before he finds another target. If he hasn't already,' said Rowe.

78

Roper stood in the doorway as if waiting for something. It was only when he swivelled the knife handle, so that instead of holding it inside an angry fist it hung loosely between his fingertips, that Jameson noticed the man had straightened to his full height. He stepped into the room as if a string were pulling his head up from above; his shoulders were back but not squared and his chest was pushed forward. As he walked, he stepped carefully and almost delicately over the debris on the floor.

'Marcus? Do you mind if I call you Marcus?'

Jameson could not help his raised eyebrows. Roper's voice had become husky and feminine. He watched as this new version of the man placed the knife on Bloom's desk and began to pick up the pens and pencils from the floor.

'I do apologize for AJ; he's temperamental, like all teenagers. He doesn't understand that sometimes the word is more powerful than the sword.' Roper was placing the pens in size order on the desk, each with the nib pointing to the front and the clips facing to the left. 'Now, you asked what we want.' Roper turned to Jameson. 'We want you to call the woman and bring her back here.'

Fat chance of that, thought Jameson. 'Why? She's nothing to do with this.'

'Oh, I beg to differ, Marcus. The young lady upstairs said you shared this office with Augusta, and Zander heard her talking about Sandy and our mother on the phone.'

'If the first guy was Zander and the nutter was AJ, who are you? You're not Sandy, I'm pretty sure of that.'

'Oh, how rude of me. I'm so sorry. Lexi.' Roper gave a little curtsey.

Zander, AJ, Lexi and Sandy. All derivatives of Alexander. Neat, thought Jameson.

'Bring her back,' Lexi said, picking up Jameson's phone. 'Pretty please?'

'She doesn't know anything,' he said, hoping his hunch was right about this room being soundproof.

'I think I will be the judge of that, Marcus.'

Jameson shook his head.

The switch was quick this time. Zander's cool intelligence and muscular stance returned as he said, 'If you refuse, I will do away with you and then leave AJ waiting for her. She has to come back here sometime and, like you, she'll have no idea he's waiting.'

Jameson knew Roper could do this. He couldn't let Bloom walk into a trap like that. He could imagine her coming in and seeing those pens lined up in order. She would instantly know Roper was here but it would be too late. The lift back up was slow and the stairs were past the broom cupboard.

Jameson realized he had no choice. He looked at the phone in Zander's hand. It was the Pay As You Go one he'd been using since Gerald Porter's people had taken his. He had not bothered programming in any names, knowing a replacement for his stolen phone would be arriving soon.

'Scroll through my recent calls,' he said finally. 'You need the number ending in 0931.' At least if he brought her here there would be two of them against one. All he had to do was stay alive until she got here.

He watched Roper do as he suggested, the smirk on his face self-satisfied.

Please don't let this be a mistake, thought Jameson.

Before activating the loudspeaker Zander said, 'Careful what you say. She needs to come alone or I'll let AJ rip your face apart.'

'Hello?'

Part of Jameson had hoped she wouldn't answer; that she'd have no signal or see it was him and decide to call back later. What he was about to do made him a weaker man than he ever wanted to be, but he saw no other option. If he didn't get her here, AJ would lie in wait and Bloom's days would be done.

'I need you to come back to the office straight away.'

'I'm—'

'It's important; I'm not playing games,' he said, interrupting her. 'I'm asking you, please, come to the office as quick as you can. I need to show you something and it can't wait.'

The line was quiet and he hoped she'd heard the meaning behind his words.

'I'll be there in half an hour,' she said.

79

Zander was struggling to keep control. AJ's anger made him strong and persistent. Lexi was helping and that was good. She knew as well as Zander that if they let AJ loose too soon, they would lose control of the whole thing. Marcus Jameson and this Augusta woman were obviously connected to the police somehow. He knew that killing them would dilute their message but as soon as he'd heard the woman mention Sandy and Lesley, he knew it was game over. Lesley would give them up. She had never protected them before, so why would she start now?

Marcus Jameson had put up a decent fight, better than any of the others ever had, but the element of surprise had ultimately given Zander the advantage. The ligature was tight before Jameson began his fight, by which time he was already losing. It would have been easy to end it then, especially when the guy passed out, but then Zander remembered what he'd overheard. He hadn't been able to make out their conversation from his hiding place once they'd moved into the office, but he did hear Sandy's voice. They had been playing a recording of the police interview. It kept stopping and starting and despite the low sound quality he could tell they were watching some sections again and again. His gut told him that somehow this woman had worked it out or was very close to doing so.

He had known that their time was running out but this was too soon. He wasn't finished and he didn't want his last kill to be a nobody working in a basement office. He needed time for one last real target. A swan song.

And so Marcus and his friend needed dealing with.

Marcus Jameson was sitting very still in the chair and staring at Zander. This man was a different beast to the others. Even when he'd been fighting for breath there had been no sense of fear or stench of urine as there had been in the Lamborghini with Nawaf or in Stefan's swish apartment. Even now as the guy waited for the inevitable to happen, he looked calm. But Zander expected that would all change when the woman arrived. When Zander finally let AJ through and Marcus was made to watch.

80

Jameson watched the clock on the wall. Fourteen minutes had passed. She had said she'd be here in thirty.

Roper looked agitated, as if he was in pain. His expression shifted from concentration to irritation in waves and Jameson wondered at the internal turmoil going on. There must be some tactical advantage to be gained from Roper's unstable mental state. If only he knew more about it. Should he mention the murders? Try to find out why they were committing them? Or would that bring AJ out swinging again? He didn't fancy his chances against AJ, he was unhinged, and Jameson wasn't sure about this current guy, Zander, either, but Lexi was a flirt. He could work with that.

'You certainly know how to clean a scene,' he said finally, hoping this might draw out Lexi again. It was clear that she was the neat freak.

Zander glared at him.

'Not many people do. You'd be amazed how many criminals forget they are leaving traces of themselves all over the place.'

'We're not criminals.'

Jameson balked: 'Are you not?'

'We're activists. Setting right the wrongs.'

'Like vigilantes.'

'No, like activists.'

Because you're not punishing the guilty, you're simply killing those who represent them, Jameson thought but did not say. Riling the guy would not be smart.

'Alexander means defender of man, did you know that? We were born to take up arms.'

The guy's a fruit loop, thought Jameson, but asked, 'What are you defending against?' with a tone of curiosity.

'People need to open their eyes and see. They are blind to the truth. Marx said religion was the opiate of the people but these days it's consumerism. Give people enough tat to buy and they won't notice that you're getting richer while they're getting poorer.'

Jameson was genuinely surprised. This did not sound as batty a motive as he'd been expecting. He recalled the first time he'd heard Bloom speak at the conference where they'd met. She'd been talking about the main motivations behind all crimes: some were emotionally driven, such as crimes of passion; some were financially driven for personal gain; some came from a delusion or faulty state of mind, such as schizophrenia; and some were based on a principle. The latter was much rarer, she had said, where perpetrators want to right a wrong or see themselves as fighting for a cause. Jameson had found the whole thing fascinating. He could see the clear links between some of the terrorist organizations he had come across in MI6 and the idea that sometimes people do bad things for good reasons, or at least that's the way it seems to them.

And Roper saw himself as one of these. Or Zander did.

Jameson heard the lift begin to move. She'd got here in under sixteen minutes. Saying she would be thirty had been smart. He hoped this meant she'd picked up on his comment that he wasn't playing games. It was all he could think of to say without raising suspicion. If he was lucky she would assume this was something to do with Porter and bring help.

'It can't go on much longer now, can it? Now you're all over the press and beginning to attack random members of the investigation team,' he said, hoping to keep Roper's attention away from the lift.

'I thought you were one of those over-privileged pricks. How was I to know you were bluffing?'

'They say it takes one to know one,' Jameson said, risking a cheeky response because behind Zander the lift door had opened.

81

Roper looked momentarily startled, having missed the lift arriving, but he recovered quickly, retrieving the knife from the desk behind him.

'Augusta. Surprise!' he said with all the menace of a practised killer.

A confused expression crossed her face as she looked between the two men. 'Sandy Roper. What are you doing here?'

Jameson watched Roper's body loosen and curl like before, the animal look returning to his eyes. He swivelled the knife skilfully in his hand and moved between Jameson and the door. Jameson had no time to react, not that he could do much from his position. Roper lunged forwards, the hand with the knife rising in slow motion and then dropping forcefully towards her.

'Not Sandy, AJ, which is unlucky for you.'

Jameson thought there would be more time: more opportunity to get the better of Roper and find a way to outsmart him. That was a lie. He'd actually hoped she would bring back-up to instantly overpower the guy. When she'd arrived earlier than she'd said he'd assumed this was the plan and he felt smug about successfully tipping her off. But now he was faced with watching this and that was *not* what he'd wanted. The knife was too sharp and AJ too confident with it.

At least he wouldn't be haunted by this death and his role in it as he'd been with Jodie. Because within the hour he would be dead too. It was an odd reality to be faced with. Life-threatening situations had been something he'd experienced more than anyone should but there had always been an angle to work, a negotiation to be made or a trade that had bought him the time to escape or overpower. But that was because he'd never met a serial killer before.

Jameson couldn't take his eyes off Roper's body. It jumped and jolted as he stabbed her over and over. She never screamed. In fact, she made no sound whatsoever. All he could hear was a distinctive electrical buzz. It took a second for his mind to catch up. Roper's body wasn't jumping and jolting as a result of him delivering a frenzied attack. He was being tasered.

And then he dropped like a dead weight to the floor.

'Not Augusta,' Seraphine said as she stepped over the writhing man to look him in the eye. 'Which is unlucky for you.'

82

Bloom watched DCI Mirza and DS Peters untie Sandy Roper from her office chair and handcuff him. The guy was spaced out and confused, as if he'd been drugged.

'So, he tried to attack you and you managed to over-power him and tie him to the chair,' Bloom said to Jameson, who was having his neck looked at by a para-medic. There was an angry red line running around it and bruising was starting to show.

'Ah-ha,' he said, opening his mouth so the medic could check his throat.

'All by yourself?' she said. He could tell the police whatever story he wanted but Bloom could smell Seraphine's perfume in the room.

The paramedic was explaining to Jameson that he needed to be taken to hospital to see a doctor as more swelling might occur which could occlude his airway. When the paramedic had moved away, Jameson said to Bloom, 'He'd been hiding in the cupboard; that's why the mop and bucket were out.'

'I nearly put them away,' she said.

'When?'

'When you arrived this morning. I'd carried them out of the kitchen to put them back. If you hadn't turned up ...' They were both silent for a moment, realizing how close she had come to danger herself. 'What did he want? Why was he here?'

'I think he believed that I was who I pretended to be when I went to Philip Berringer's apartment block. He must have picked me as his next wealthy target.'

'But how did he find you?'

Jameson shrugged. 'He could have followed me that day. I came back here after.'

'Or maybe he saw you outside the police station when you saw him?'

'Could be, yeah.'

DCI Mirza came to join them as DS Peters led Roper away. 'You've been very lucky, Marcus,' she said, looking at his neck. 'We'll need you to come to the station to give us a statement. Did Sandy say anything about the murders?'

'Sandy didn't but Zander did, and AJ and Lexi for that matter.'

'Who?' said DCI Mirza.

'Are they the alters?' said Bloom.

Jameson nodded. 'I'd guess that Zander is your cold killer, he was controlled and said they were killing these men to make the world open its eyes to the truth about the rich oppressing the poor. AJ was definitely your angry one and Lexi referred to him as a teenager. She was your neat freak. She tidied up the pens.' He pointed at the line of neatly ordered pens on Bloom's desk.

'So you were right,' DCI Mirza said to Bloom. 'Part of me didn't think it was possible.'

'The mind is a mysterious thing,' Bloom said.

Mirza hovered for a moment before saying, 'I suppose

I owe you an apology, Augusta. You and Tyler were right and I was mistaken.'

'I'd say you remained open-minded, which is no bad thing. And it was your team who found Sandy Roper, remember. You had him. It was just a matter of time, so take the credit.'

'You're very kind. I'm not sure I deserve that.' Nadia Mirza held out her hand to shake Bloom's. 'Thank you.'

When the DCI had moved away to talk to the scenes-of-crime officers, Bloom said to Jameson, 'You got all that insight while he was strangling you and you were overpowering him, did you?'

Jameson winked. 'I got skills.'

'Or help,' she said.

'My lips are sealed.'

'How many dates do you owe now?'

The strange look she'd seen earlier crossed his eyes again before he smiled and said, 'Still just the one. I'm a good negotiator.'

Bloom knew she had to drop the subject for now. If DCI Mirza and team found out Seraphine had been in their crime scene, they would have a field day. Plus it was probably best not to know the ins and outs of Jameson's negotiations with the woman. There was definitely something he wasn't telling her and she felt quite sure she didn't want to know what it was.

83

'That's us done then,' said Zander.

'I hope you're happy with yourself,' said Lexi. 'You know you ruined everything for all of us.'

'Not for all of us, Lexi, only for Sandy.'

'We can't leave him. It's our job to look after him.'

'No it's not. Our job was making our mark and we've done that.'

'I tried to protect you all. I thought AJ was the reckless one but it was you all along.'

'Lexi, what is the point of existing if no one knows you're there? We will not be forgotten now.'

'And Sandy spends the rest of his life in jail.'

'I for one have no interest in sticking around for that, and AJ is out already.'

'You can't opt out.'

'You know we can, Lexi. Remember little Alexander? None of us have heard from him in years. It's better this way. We pushed Sandy out for too long – we need to let him take back the reins.'

Sandy Roper opened his eyes. It was dark and cold and he had no idea where he was. A familiar dread began to rise and then he made out the cell door and remembered he was in prison on remand, charged with murdering eleven men. They had found his fingerprints all over an Airbnb in the apartment block of one of the victims and they also had CCTV footage of him dressed as a workman which was relevant somehow. He didn't understand everything that they had said. He had no recollection of any of it, but the police said there was no doubt whatsoever that he had killed all of them. Or rather, *they* had: Zander, Lexi and AJ.

It had all been so nice before. They had been his friends and constant companions. For years he'd thought everyone had friends like these in their heads, chatting away, but then the weirdness started. He began to experience feelings of disorientation, as though his body wasn't his own. He would say and do things but feel like he was watching himself in a movie rather than living. He had felt numb, as if he was lost, and then the periods of darkness came. They were fleeting at first but then the people he worked with at Prestige would mention things he'd done or said that he had no memory of, and he began to feel more distressed. He couldn't understand what was happening. And then Zander and the others stopped talking to him. They were still talking to each other, he could hear them, and he became paranoid that they were talking about him. He tried to block them out and ignore them but that only made things worse. The periods of darkness became longer. He lost track of time; days, weeks and even months would pass that he had no recollection of. Now he knew why. They had taken over and were out there doing awful things to these poor people.

It was too quiet and he knew they'd left him in the dark again.

He would be alone in this place for ever.

And he hadn't done any of it.

'Sandy?' Lexi's voice was soft and distant. 'I'm going to stay with you. Don't worry, I'm here.'

Sandy Roper closed his eyes as a single tear trickled down his cheek.

84

Bloom headed into the office on Sunday to clean up after the previous week's activities. She had spent the rest of Thursday working with Tyler on an interview strategy for Sandy Roper but it turned out it wasn't needed. Sandy had talked openly about his alters and how he felt they had pushed him out. After that it was simply down to Mirza's team to lay out the case against him, and with the attack on Marcus, they had plenty of evidence to charge him. He had looked genuinely distraught and Bloom couldn't help but feel a little sorry for him.

She had slept for the majority of Friday and then spent Saturday reading and making some of her favourite soups to freeze. It was therapeutic and rejuvenating. She had received a text from Jameson on Thursday night to say the hospital had given him the all-clear and he had given a statement to the police about Roper's attack so he was going away for a few days to visit Claire and her family at their holiday home. She understood he needed a break. They had experienced so much together over recent years. It sometimes felt as if they brought each other bad luck. If she were a more superstitious person, she might have put some store in the idea but she knew it was nonsense. They both went looking for it. They couldn't leave a mystery or unanswered question alone. It was their combined strength but also their weakness, because of what it brought with it: psychopaths, serial killers, warlords and cults. The world was a crazier place than she could ever have imagined.

She had to admire Seraphine for trying to do something about it at least. For trying to right some wrongs. The idea was ridiculous and unsustainable but she admired the ambition and the audacity to go out in the world and try to effect change. She desperately wanted to explain it all to Jameson. She felt sure it would make him feel better about everything they had been through. It was certainly that way for her.

There was still a strong smell of coffee in the office and she went to the broom cupboard, pausing only slightly before opening the door to retrieve the mop. She filled the bucket with warm water and a good glug of pine-scented disinfectant and then she cleaned the floor. Some papers had fallen down the side of Jameson's desk and she retrieved them and placed them in a pile. One was a printed map of Yorkshire.

He had been so lucky. It didn't bear thinking about. She would never have been able to come back here if Roper had been successful. She might not even have been able to continue doing what she did. The memories of him would have been too awful to bear.

In spite of all the drama of recent years, she had to acknowledge that they had also been incredibly lucky.

Jameson's iPad screen came to life on his desk and

beeped an alert. Ordinarily she wouldn't look at his messages. They were his private business. But she was standing too close not to see it. And what she read sent a chill through her.

> **Porter**   8:16
> Is it done yet? Time is ticking if you want
> to save your girls. It's her or them.

Bloom read it a few times to make sure she understood it. Porter was asking Jameson to do something for him. How had they become entangled together? Jameson hadn't said a word. And who was the 'her' it referred to?

Bloom's eyes moved to the map of Yorkshire and the town of Ilkley circled in red. The town Seraphine had grown up in.

'Oh God.'

She'd not had the chance to tell him that they had been wrong about Seraphine's plans. That Seraphine wasn't planning some ghastly attack or grasp for power. Yes, she was placing her own unemotional, intelligent and logical people into positions of influence across the globe. But they were people who would work with the facts and stay focused on a single core philosophy: that no one should be disadvantaged or suffer without a good – rational – reason.

That same infrastructure in Porter's hands was an unthinkable alternative.

Bloom dialled Jameson's house number. There was no answer. She tried his mobile. It was switched off. Next she called Seraphine. There was no answer and no option to leave a voicemail.

What was Porter making him do?

She should have told him last week even when he said he didn't want to hear it. She should have forced him to listen. Maybe then he wouldn't be poised to make the worst mistake of his life.

85

The view from the picturesque town of Ilkley was quite stunning. The hills above underlined the bright blue sky with a lush streak of green and purple. Summer was in the air and as they walked he spotted little clusters of flowers ready to bloom.

'So this is where you grew up?' Jameson said.

Seraphine wore hiking boots and walking gear. On her back was a small rucksack containing her share of the picnic they had agreed to bring along. She turned and looked back down the hill briefly.

'Yes, this is the location of my own little sadistic household. Mummy, Daddy and scary little Seraphine locked in a Victorian terrace together. Happy days.'

'I'll bet.'

He looked up at the Cow and Calf Rocks: an imposing crag and its smaller counterpart, which had been marked by visitors carving names and symbols into the stone since the Bronze Age. He had plotted a route to a section of moorland distant from the town and hopefully on a less-trodden path. Ilkley Moor was a popular place to hike and he could see a good number of people already milling around the rocks. For the time being he let Seraphine lead the way. This was her home turf and there was something fascinating about watching her weave through the rural gates and pick her way up the rocky pathway.

'I expect you never imagined you'd go through with this date,' she said as she smiled and nodded at some hikers coming the other way. It was unnerving how normal she looked out here.

'True. I figured I'd be able to dodge it for a few more years yet.'

'There was bound to come a time when you needed me to save you, Marcus.' She glanced back at him and the look in her eyes was smugly satisfied.

She was enjoying this fact just a little too much. He had no room to complain though; not only had she overpowered Roper, she had also set things straight with Superintendent Nesbitt about the shooting of Stephen Green. It turned out she'd recorded the whole thing on the voice recorder of her phone and she could clearly be heard begging for her life in the seconds before a shot rang out. 'It pays to be prepared,' she had told Jameson. When he'd quizzed her on the consequences of wasting police time, she told him she'd apologized profusely to the superintendent and even cried a little as she blamed PTSD for her confusion. Apparently Nesbitt had given her a stern talking-to and a caution, no doubt because Seraphine's people within the CPS were pulling strings. Her ability to think ahead so many moves scared Jameson. Nothing the woman ever did was spontaneous or without purpose. And that made her a very dangerous foe.

'I used to come up here a lot,' she said, looking up the hill. 'When you get to the top it feels vast and free like you could go anywhere and do anything.'

'Is this where you came up with the idea of meddling in everything then?'

'I suspect it may have been. The start of it at least.'

'So are you going to tell me why you've had Augusta running around Europe for you?'

'I needed a spy and I thought you'd refuse.'

'Damn right I would. Why send her though?'

'I trust her.'

'You know she is continually trying to find out what you're up to so she can stop it.'

'I know. It's part of her charm.'

'You don't think she *can* stop you, do you?'

'Marcus, don't be silly.' She turned at the top of a steep climb and held her hand out to help him. When he shook his head and deftly stepped up and around her, she said, 'I *know* she can't.'

'What about me?'

She caught up with him and they walked side by side on the wider stretch of path. When she didn't respond he wondered if she had any idea what thoughts had been going through his mind over the previous week. What would she think of him if she knew? Part of him expected she might be pleased. She was always trying to point out how similar they were. This would seal the deal in her eyes.

'You must be worried that Porter could stop you, otherwise you wouldn't need Augusta to spy for you.'

'He doesn't want to stop it; he wants to steal it. That's different.'

'How?'

'He's blinded by his desire. He's become emotional about it.'

'And that makes him a lesser person, does it?'

'Not a lesser person, no. I do see that you normals can have your moments. But it certainly makes him a lesser threat. My power lies in my lack of emotion. I don't worry, or get scared, or want to run. I also don't get over-excited and lose my focus.'

'You're basically a cold-hearted machine.'

She laughed. '"Why won't it die?"' she said in a pretty good impression of Sarah Connor from the *Terminator* movies where Arnold Schwarzenegger's robot from the future proves impossible to stop.

'I don't buy that. I think your whole ambition is wrapped up in emotion. You want to be the queen of the world and will go about it in whatever warped way you can find.'

'You're sexy when you flirt.' She reached out and took his hand.

Jameson glanced down at their hands but didn't pull away. There was still a long way to go and so much he needed to learn. Better to keep things friendly.

'And you're wrong. I don't want to be queen of the world. I'm happy to stay in the shadows.' She walked them to a flat stone that overlooked a deep valley that dropped away from them. The moor on the other side looked rugged and desolate and he couldn't see any other hikers walking across it. 'You are right, though, there is some emotion to it. I'm doing it for her.'

'Augusta?'

Their eyes met and she leaned in close as if to kiss him before pointing across the valley and saying, 'Is that where you plan to do it?'

86

Jameson walked back through Ilkley town centre alone. The hike had not gone entirely as planned but the outcome was the same. He'd be able to get confirmation from Porter soon that Bloom, his sister and his nieces were off the hook. As for Jameson himself, he knew his life was never going to be the same again. He had stepped through a door and there was no way back.

As he passed Bettys Tea Rooms, a voicemail arrived from Bloom. He listened to her panicked voice asking him to call her back as soon as possible. He returned the call.

'Where are you? I've been calling all morning. Are you with Seraphine?'

'Why would I be with Seraphine?' The lie was easy because the woman no longer walked beside him.

'Where are you? Why has your phone been off?'

'Calm down, Augusta, you sound like a paranoid wife. I've been out on my bike, that's all.'

'You don't usually turn your phone off for that.'

'I wanted a bit of peace. It's been a tough week, in case you hadn't noticed. I told you I'm taking a few days off to recharge the batteries. You should too.'

'You had a message from Porter asking if it was done yet.'

Jameson stopped at the corner. He could see his car parked outside a nice little gift shop. The sort of place that sold mugs and tea towels with funny phrases in Yorkshire slang.

'I didn't look on purpose. It flashed up as I was tidying your desk.' After another beat she said, 'And I found a map of Ilkley Moor.'

Jameson took a deep breath. *Busted*. He had hoped to keep all of this from her but that chance had passed. He would have to come clean and live with the consequences.

'What are you planning, Marcus? What is he making you do? Because we were wrong about Seraphine. She's not doing all of this for any of the reasons we thought. She's trying to improve things. It's a little crazy and I absolutely don't agree with her means but the motive – the motive is sound, Marcus. Marcus, are you still there?'

Jameson watched a toddler giggle as he chased a ball along the pavement. The ball bounced a couple of times before rolling off the kerb and plopping into the drain. The toddler came to a halt staring into the dark hole in the road and then he started to scream.

87

Porter walked through the Roastery and Bake Hall of Harrods, intending to treat himself to something indulgent. The patisserie was second to none and the best place to get a millefeuille outside of Paris. From this point on he would only have the best: one of the perks of the new job. As Foreign Secretary he'd been restricted on accepting gratuities, having to register all gifts received to ensure no bribery was occurring. But now he was free of all that British bureaucracy. Free of everything, in fact. He now existed above and beyond every single seat of power across the globe. The network of people he now commanded infiltrated every government of worth, meaning he had eyes and ears on every move they made. But it was even better than that. They had influence and, in some cases, all-out control. His intelligent, educated and ruthless operatives were everywhere and capable of anything. As he'd said to Seraphine Walker, it was pure genius. She had planned and executed things perfectly, taking her time to select the right people and place them in perfect positions. It was almost a shame she was gone.

Almost.

Without her he was free of the restrictions she was placing on them. The positions afforded to members of the organization were powerful and lucrative; the only thing she required in return was complete focus on the goal. To ensure world affairs were not infected by irrational emotion. They would keep in power those people who brought stability. It was fine to start a war for strategic gain but not out of hatred or prejudice. It was OK for those who did wrong or contributed little to be punished, but no group should be made to suffer simply because they were different or disliked. It was fine to take as much as you could from life, but intentionally harming others to scratch a personal itch was out of the question. These were hard lines. Non-negotiable. It was not going to be easy, she had said. It required intelligence. It required the brightest minds who were capable of seeing through the fog of emotion. People uninhibited by fear or remorse. In the spirit of every secret society which had gone before them, they would silently secure more and more power until no other body could compare.

It was this power without her restrictions that he craved. As Foreign Secretary he had witnessed how influential the British secret service and American CIA could be, and they were small fry compared to what Seraphine aimed for. She was well on her way too. They had people all over the globe now. *He* had people all over the globe. He had already made progress, convincing many to see his ambitions were a better bet than hers. He would make them rich beyond their wildest dreams. He would enable them to wield their power in a liberated manner, and if they wanted to scratch the odd itch, he was cool with that too. It would not take long for the others to fall into line. Especially now she was gone.

He was not at all surprised that Marcus Jameson had come through for him. He had researched the fellow well and found him to be a ruthless bastard when stung. Jodie Sinclair had been his Achilles heel and the way he had hunted down every person associated with her demise had been impressive. Jameson wasn't a natural killer. He clearly disliked the messy work. Most of his activity in interrogation and revenge involved threatening to ruin people's lives rather than take them. But the fact that he had ruined a fair few, exactly as he'd promised, told Porter this was a man who would see things through if given the right motivation.

It had taken a few final pushes but eventually the boy had done good.

Porter had received nothing more than a set of coordinates with the message: *Are we done now?* Jameson was not about to incriminate himself with sending any evidence electronically. So Porter had dispatched two of his best men to the location as he waited in London. He would not put it past Jameson to try to pin the thing on him so he was going nowhere near the site and he told his men to make no contact other than in person. It had taken a whole eight hours until they turned up at his house. She was definitely dead. It looked as though she'd fallen on a walk in a remote area of Yorkshire and hit her head. They had taken Polaroid photographs. Porter had studied them carefully to make sure it really was her and she really was dead. Even then he couldn't be sure.

Visiting the funeral directors in Ilkley to view the body for himself was out of the question. He was a former public figure who was widely known to have escaped custody and successfully evaded capture ever since. So he had done the next best thing and had her autopsy recorded and sent to him. It was amazing what you could get done when you had the right people in your pocket.

He'd watched it over and over. Pausing on the initial images showing her face. She had sustained a large injury from her left cheekbone to above her eye. It looked like her but still he remained sceptical.

Only when the press reported her death did he allow himself to believe it. She had become quite infamous after Jameson and Dr Bloom had exposed what came to be known as her Psychopath Game, even more so when she had evaded justice and claimed it had all been an elaborate lie, so the news of her death was big. There was a lengthy profile on her childhood in Yorkshire and how she had maimed her school caretaker with a sharpened pencil. It went on to describe how she'd reinvented herself as a respectable psychiatrist who insisted she had put her troubled childhood behind her. The comments made by her barrister after her trial collapsed were quoted: *'As a world-renowned psychiatrist, she has a wealth of insight into the minds of those who are different, but this does not make her a manipulative psychopath.'*

He'd had to admire that. She'd certainly had a talent for looking innocent.

What she hadn't had, ironically, was a true wealth of insight into the minds of those who were different. She'd underestimated him at every turn. And she'd underestimated Marcus Jameson. Porter would love to know how she'd reacted when she realized what was coming. He hoped Jameson had left time for that: a moment of realization that her favourite little normal had turned against her.

His PA Joshua met him in the lobby of their Knightsbridge headquarters.

'Is everyone here?' Porter asked as they stepped into the lift and Joshua selected the top floor.

'As you requested, sir, everyone of importance is here,' Joshua said.

Porter allowed himself a smile before settling his face into a hard mask. There would be no weakness in his leadership. No strings to pull to win his favour. He would be his true self for the first time. No more pretence. He no longer needed to fit in and look respectable. He was free. And powerful.

So, so powerful.

'A big day for you, sir. You must be looking forward to this,' said Joshua.

Porter didn't respond. He hadn't decided whether to keep Joshua around yet. The man had been Seraphine's recruit. The lift opened and Porter pushed past Joshua to reach the security door. He placed his hand flat on the biometric scanner and faced the screen. Once his identity was confirmed he pushed the door firmly open.

It was quiet. Only the hum of their many computers could be heard. There was no conversation. Porter looked at Joshua, who gestured to the closed boardroom door.

They awaited him in silence. This was a good start. Excellent in fact.

He placed his Harrods bag on a nearby desk, straightened his tie and ruffled his hair. At the double doors to the boardroom, he paused before placing both hands on the handles, taking a deep breath and pulling them wide.

The chairs around the table were empty. There were no silently waiting generals ready to take his orders, no fawning minions to push around, only a white card propped against a glass in the middle of the table. Porter stared at the three words printed on it.

Dare to Play?

He turned on Joshua. 'What is the meaning of this? Where is everyone?'

'As I said, everyone of importance is here.'

'No one is here, you imbecile,' Porter said, losing his temper.

'Technically that's not true,' said a voice. 'Thank you, Joshua, you can go home now.'

The sound of her voice filled him with rage and then he began to laugh. How typical of Seraphine to pull such a stunt. All she needed was a recording and a willing servant to deliver her epitaph. After participating in this little ruse Porter decided Joshua would have to go. Maybe he'd offer him up as bait for something. Set a little test for the generals. Porter was about to dispatch the man when he realized something critical: she had replied to what he'd said. It couldn't be a recording.

He watched in disbelief as Seraphine emerged from the small annexe at the end of the room and walked to the edge of the table in front of him before sliding up to sit on it.

'Faking my death is kind of a thing of mine. You know that, right?'

'I saw your body,' he said through gritted teeth.

'You saw what I wanted you to see.' She picked up the card and held it out in front of her. 'Sorry, Gerald,' she said as she slowly tore it in half. 'Game over.'

88

'You didn't really believe I'd hurt her, did you?'

'I didn't know what to believe, Marcus, because you never tell me anything. I know nothing of who you were or what you did before I met you. You call me a closed book; well, I say it takes one to know one.'

'Oh, come on, you know me better than to think I'd put someone out of their misery just because a bully told me to.'

'Do I? You shot Stephen Green in Scotland.'

'That was different. There was a threat to life.'

'Don't be naive, Marcus. There was no such thing. She engineered the whole scene to prove to me that you two are more similar than I wanted to believe.'

For a split second, Jameson looked horrified and then an expression of resignation settled on his face. 'And now you believe I'm a cold-blooded killer like Sandy Roper, do you?'

'Of course not. But I don't think you're beyond being manipulated. I don't think either of us are. Seraphine and Porter have only managed to pitch us against each other because we let them by keeping secrets.'

'Augusta, you know me better than anyone. Better than Jodie ever did and certainly better than Seraphine Walker does. You have nothing to worry about, bestie.'

'Don't make fun of me. That won't get us anywhere.'

'What do you suggest then, some in-depth counselling session where I bare my soul? What would you like to know?' he said in a wistful voice as he placed a hand under his chin and stared up at the sky. 'Let me see, I'm a Gemini, I like long walks on the beach and . . . what?' he said looking at Bloom's expression.

'For such an intelligent man, you really can be an idiot.'

'Wow, thanks. Don't hold back.'

Bloom looked out across Russell Square Gardens. The cafe terrace seemed as good a place as any to debrief their latest run-in with Seraphine.

'Tell me how you came up with this little plot against Porter then. I know you're dying to,' she said.

'Well . . . after she came to my aid with Roper, she said I needed to return the favour.' Jameson twisted in his seat and Bloom met his gaze. 'She was furious when I told her Porter had tasked me with getting rid of her, and even more so when I explained that he'd threatened to kill you and my family if I didn't. Ironically, when I told her how I'd been thinking about doing it, that didn't faze her. That's odd, don't you think?'

'By the point you were telling her, she knew you'd decided not to do it. There was nothing for her to be angry about.' Bloom smiled at Jameson's frowning eyes. 'That's psychopaths for you. Ever logical.'

'Well, whatever. We then decided we could use this to fool Porter and make him think she was out of the picture so he'd drop his guard.'

'And you even made the papers.'

'Hey, the details were nothing to do with me. I simply walked her to where I'd thought might be a good spot and then she told me to leave. She said she could sort it from there. I only needed to wait a couple of hours and then text Porter with an agreed message.'

'I hope she didn't use some poor innocent like before.' Bloom referred to the young drug addict whom fourteen-year-old Seraphine had lured to her death on the railway tracks.

'I didn't ask any details.'

Bloom reached out and squeezed his hand. 'I understand why you did it, but you know you've crossed a line now. She'll never let you go.'

Jameson shrugged. 'It's clear she had no intention of ever letting us go. Like you once said, she possesses the people she cares about. So I may as well stay for the ride.'

'Did she come clean about what she was really doing?'

'Oh yeah. That was part of the deal. She had to fess up about everything if I was going to willingly slide down the rabbit hole.'

'And?'

'Surprising.'

'Did you believe her?'

He tilted his head from side to side.

'Even if she means it – even if she *is* trying to make things better, she's created a monster. There'll be more Porters, you know that, and the next one might well get the better of her. Then what?'

'You think we have to stop her anyway.'

'Either that or make her stop. I don't think we have a choice.'

Jameson squeezed her hand back and then let go. 'She is not going to like that.'

A silence descended as they both contemplated that. After a while Bloom looked at her partner. There were things she needed to know, things she needed him to open up about so she could check he was OK.

'Can I ask about Jodie?'

'What do you want to know?'

'What happened?'

'I let her down. She lost her life and the life of her unborn child. Our child maybe.' He smiled fleetingly.

'I'm so sorry.'

'I'd resigned myself to never finding out why she died or who'd ordered it, you know, but Porter said he knew the answers to all my questions.'

Bloom thought about how people were often left most broken by the unanswered questions: *Why did they die? How did they die? What were their last moments like?* It was the kind of angst that ate away at your soul. The fact that he'd had the chance to have that taken away but had chosen to reject it showed the measure of the man sitting alongside her.

'He might have been lying,' she said, 'but if not, someone else out there will know.'

Jameson nodded slowly and Bloom looked up at the cumulus clouds above with their round, puffy tops and flat bottoms. If there was one thing she had learned in life it was that no one is really what they seem. There were no easy-to-spot good guys and bad guys. Life was messy and people were damaged. You couldn't see that from looking at them. In her line of work it was easy to think there were more broken people than not, but this was only because she saw a skewed population. It was the same for police officers, prosecutors and the like. The brain becomes accustomed to what it sees. So if all it sees are bad people doing bad things, that's all it expects to see.

So what would they do now, she and Jameson? How could they move forward? How did they avoid seeing ever more bad?

Bloom smelled Seraphine's perfume and closed her eyes. *Here we go.*

'Everything go OK?' Jameson said.

'As if there was ever any doubt,' said Seraphine.

Bloom opened her eyes and moved them from the clouds and back to reality. Seraphine stood on the far side of Jameson. She looked happy and relaxed, like a woman without a care in the world. As she pulled up a chair from a nearby table she looked from Jameson to Bloom.

'Is it OK if I join you?' she said with a smile.

Acknowledgements

When I started writing novels and aspired to being published, I never dreamed I would be lucky enough to write the acknowledgements for my fourth book. Even more humbling is the fact that so many people I do not know have read my stories. I think this is the thing most writers wish for and I can't thank my readers enough. To those of you who have followed the whole Dr Bloom series so far, thank you for joining me on this incredible journey. To those who have taken the time to write a review, I am indebted to you. Your feedback and observations about the things you've enjoyed, and the things you have not, have helped me to learn and – hopefully – improve a bit. To those who have discovered Dr Bloom here for the first time, I hope you enjoyed it enough to stay with us a little longer.

Writing *The Imposter* was a bit of a roller coaster. Weaving two storylines together in a believable way was a challenge and I'm indebted to my wonderful editors, Lizzy Goudsmit, Natasha Barsby and Imogen Nelson, for helping me to make sense of it all. Their calls to make it more pacy made sense, but I struggled. That was until I called on the help of two lifelong crime-thriller fans, my sister Elizabeth Ensor and her best friend Amra Akhtar. They read the opening chapters of my book, then – in the nicest possible way – ripped them to shreds and told me how to do it better. The result was a totally rejigged first hundred pages. Thank you, ladies. Your insights into what thrills a reader were awesome, if not a little unnerving at times!

Thank you to pathologist Dr Daniel Scott, who taught me how incredibly difficult it is for a killer to leave no trace of themselves. You gladly talked about different causes of death with me and your patience and advice were much appreciated. Thanks also to prosecutors Joanne and Paul Brown, for talking all things legal and helping me to understand how the police would build a case. Our discussion around the nature of 'strikingly similar evidence' inspired a lot of ideas in the book. I hope I didn't make any glaring mistakes, and if I did, they are entirely my fault.

To my best friend and partner in crime, Jamie. Thank you for every idea we discuss when walking the dog, going for a run or drinking wine. You constantly inspire me to write the best story I can and I couldn't do it without you. Also thanks for not losing your temper when I ask you to read sections then hover around you with an impatient 'Well?' As always, a massive thanks to everyone at Transworld who has worked with me over the years. In particular, thank you to Kate Samano and Richenda Todd for your copy-editing expertise, Josh Benn, Lorraine Jerram and Joanne Hill for performing your proofreading magic, Hayley Barnes, Sophie Bruce, Holly Minter, and all the team who market and promote the books so well. Thanks also to Frankie Gray, for reassuring me when I needed it, and my new editor Finn Cotton, for your support and enthusiasm in the final stages of producing the book.

Thank you to my lovely, loud, laughter-filled family: Jamie, Erica, Ella and Henry, Mum and Mike, Dad and Gwynne, Liz, Dave, Harris and Mai, Jo, Tom and Amelie, Aunty Barb and Uncle Malc, Cath, Paul, Jools and Drew, favourite cousin called Dave, Martyn, Clare, Emily, Lucy, Tom and Jess, Vicky, Ash and 'little' Jess.

Finally, there are a whole raft of family, friends and colleagues who continue to support me and to promote my books. I am eternally grateful for every kind word, piece of advice and recommendation you give. If I had the space to thank you all, I would, but you know who you are and you know I love you.

Four strangers are missing. Left at their last-known
locations are birthday cards that read:

YOUR GIFT IS THE GAME.
DARE TO PLAY?

The police aren't worried – it's just a game.
But the families are frantic, and psychologist and
private detective Dr Augusta Bloom is persuaded to
investigate. As she delves into the lives of the missing
people, she finds something that binds them all.

And that something makes them very
dangerous indeed.

As more disappearances are reported and new
birthday cards uncovered, Dr Bloom races to
unravel the mystery and find the puppeteer.
But is she playing into their hands?